BECOMING
BARKER

C.A. FRANCIS

Edited by Alicia Woods
Momsreadingcorner.com
Cover Design by Caitlan Cecere and JadebyDesign
Blurb written by Karissa Whitlow

"She believed she could, so she did."

~ R.S. Grey

CHAPTER 1

"I Sabine Montgomery, will have an amazing and productive day today. I am strong. I am healthy. I am ready for what today has in store for me," I repeat my affirmation in the mirror a few more times. I pull my medium long, straightened, black hair up into a high ponytail with a toothbrush hanging from my mouth, while looking at my options of scrubs. Only fifteen minutes 'til I leave for my morning shift at the hospital. My choice is obvious, the nightmare before Christmas scrubs is perfect to celebrate the spooky season of October. I throw on my top with Jack the Skeleton printed over a purple and orange tie dye theme. My black pants cover and tuck in my loose skin well, not to mention it complements the shape of my butt I work so hard for. My boyfriend Joseph walks in and stands behind me while I glance at myself in the full-length mirror hanging on the wall. He grabs my hips and pulls me closer to him, hugs me from behind and kisses my cheek.

"Good morning, babe," he says into the crook of my neck.

"Good morning! Do you want to catch a movie and dinner tonight after my shift," I say softly with excitement.

"That sounds great, but what's even better is staying in to watch a movie and cuddle," he tries to switch plans with the usual compromise of staying in.

"Oh, come on, it will be fun. We never go out anymore. We work so hard; I think we deserve to spoil ourselves every once in a while." I don't hold my breath while trying to put on a convincing smile.

"Any time I get to spend in your presence is more than good enough for me. I will see you later, I love you babe," he ends the conversation without an invitation for further discussion. He kisses my forehead before walking away.

The beautifully, cold morning air has to be one of my all-time favorite weatherly things here in Oregon. I take a moment or two of appreciation and then heading to work at Cedar Hills hospital. Normally, the route to work takes roughly six minutes, the long way takes seventeen. The seventeen-minute drive to work is filled with feelings of frustration about how my boyfriend never wants to do anything. It was electric between us in the beginning, but we both grew into different people over the years. I am a stranger compared to the person I was three years ago. Am I a stranger to Joseph? My body used to be rather large, and my mind was soaked with fear and anxiety. My life changed forever when I decided to lose weight and get healthy. I didn't just lose weight and get healthy; I gained a life that I never thought was possible. Why would he go out with the old me and stay in with present me? Is it him? Is it me? Is it us?

My scattered thoughts become boxed up when I pull into the hospital parking lot in my grandpa's old Classic 1960 Convertible Pontiac Bonneville. My grandpa, Eugene, passed right before I got my driver's license, and he left me this yellow beauty in his will. The man practically raised me since my parents have always been in and out exploring the world separately. Bugsby is the last material object I have to remember him by, the good times brush my mind. My newish tradition is to park in the farthest space in the lot to get my daily steps in. The good thing is no one ever wants to park far from the hospital, which leaves the spots vacant. Killing two birds with one stone seems to be my mantra these days. The designated cup holder for my sparkly pumpkin travel mug is empty, I forgot my coffee. It must be sitting on the kitchen counter waiting to be picked up and taken to work. I have to go back and get it; coffee is a must. An unexpected horn goes off as a car abruptly pulls into the spot next to me. I look at the driver as an automatic response from being startled. Joseph holds up my favorite coffee filled mug with the sweetest smile painted on his face. All the love in the world automatically rushes into my heart, flushing out any irritation towards my man. Joseph puts his car in park and gets out while leaving the engine running.

"I thought you might like this." He kisses my lips when I roll my window.

"You are a life saver! The sweetest man of mine. Not to mention, you smell delicious baby," I blush.

"I'm going out with some of the guys and thought I would bring the love of my life, the love of hers." He says his line and all I heard was he was going out.

"Thank you again, I will see you tonight," I smile. "Yes, you will." He smirks and walks back to his car.

The lobby presents orange and black streamers and miniature pumpkins scattered around the area to help spread the Halloween spirit throughout the neonatal intensive care unit. Everyone who works in this unit is usually cheerful in the mornings to keep the moral of our patients and parents up. The waiting room is semi full with a few small families either waiting for a surgery to finish or they are visiting their little loved ones. A pile of papers waits in the back for all my time and attention.

"Good morning, Sabine! Guess what? Anushka was discharged last night," Ophelia smiles sweetly.

"That is amazing news! Oh, bless her sweet little heart. The poor girl was in here for a few months. Whoever is up in the sky is good. I love your scrubs. Do you have any Halloween Disney ones?" I ask.

"Girl, I have a million pairs of scrubs. I will go through them and see what I can find. There's probably something in my closet I can rep for scary season!" she responds with her best ghost impression.

"It's spooky season!" My eyes grow wide as I laugh.

"I know," Ophelia jokingly sighs as she walks out of the room. Ophelia is one of the best things to come out of working here, this place wouldn't be the same without her. She's about a decade older than me, with two kids and a fiery presence. I don't know what can get fierier than her bright, beautiful red hair grazing her shoulders. There is no living without her big warm smile every time we work together, which is often. I stroll into the sizably, sanitized room occupied with a dozen babies fighting for their lives in large plastic containers. The room smells like sweet milk and fresh clean hospital sheets, it doesn't last long most of the time. The constant beeping of the monitors always seems to be louder than the adorable coos and noises of the precious bundles of joy.

My favorite part of being a nurse in the NICU is sitting down with a healing baby in my arms and rocking them to sleep when they feel uneasy. So beautiful, so soft and so tiny. There are only a few patients in my section who need extra care, which should make my shift fly by. I linger around and check their vitals while another patient is being moved into their new temporary plastic home. The first baby I check on is Elie, her vitals are normal. She has the cutest little button nose. The second baby I check on is Chandan and he's already got a full head of red hair. My third patient is Sebastian, he's one of my favorites. When he gets fussy and starts crying, I love to rock him in the rocking chair. He's calm and peaceful while sleeping in my arms. Time starts to move slowly as everyone has been taken care of. Sebastian starts cooing, which leads me straight to him. He is far more than precious and delicate with his eyes closed and his tiny fragile body bundled up. I grab a chair and sit right next to his container and put my finger in his little wrinkled hand.

"You better watch out or the other babies are going to know you have a favorite." Ophelia smirks.

"Shhhhh, they can hear you," a quiet laugh escapes my whispering mouth.

"So, did you have the baby conversation with Joseph yet?"

Ophelia raises her perfectly arched eyebrow.

"I did and he said 'oh, you were serious about that kid thing?'" I respond with attitude, mocking him.

"You literally told him in the beginning that it's a dream of yours and a big motivation for your extreme weight loss transformation. The goal was to be healthy enough to grow a healthy baby. No way he thought you weren't serious." Her energy boils in annoyance with a dash of disbelief.

"Yeah, I don't know what is up with him lately. He's been acting different and I don't know what's going on. He just wants to stay in and lounge, I guess." I respond with a shrug.

"You better figure it out soon and make sure you're not wasting your time with a loser that will weigh you down, no pun intended." She winks then chuckles to herself.

"Ophelia! He wouldn't be a loser; we would just want different things. People grow apart. I mean I hope that it is not the case." The wheels in my brain start to turn.

We both turn quite suddenly when Dr. Hu enters the room with a clipboard of documents. He walks in looking for an update on a patient with underdeveloped lungs, which would be Chandan. A minute later the front desk receptionist calls me to the lobby. The parents of Anushka are waiting for me there. Anushka's mom put both of her hands on my shoulder blades and pull me in for a tight squeeze. Her husband thanks me and the staff for all the care we provided for their new and healthy baby girl.

"Here's the blanket Anushka was bundled up in. We washed it for you guys. We appreciate all of you for helping our baby girl!" her eyes filled with tears. Clutched in her hands is the hospital blanket we wrap the babies in when they get discharged.

"The blanket is yours to keep! You are more than welcome, but we are just doing our jobs. We are so happy that your daughter recovered" I smile.

"Yes, tha......"

"I can't believe the hospital hired you with all those tattoos on your arms. That's a very unprofessional look nurse.... Montgomery," a rude old lady mindlessly interrupts.

It takes everything in me to keep my professional composure after the arrogant woman word vomits at me about my permanent ink. If I had a dollar for every time someone has commented negatively about them, I could cover my whole body in ink. Most of the commentary come from older people who come into my workplace. I'm here to help people, not to model. I take a second to pause and take a deep breath.

"Hi, ma'am. If you need help with something, I am sure the kind woman at the front desk can help you with what you need. I hope you have a nice day." I smile while unnoticeably clenching my jaw, she scoffs and goes on her way.

"We should get going. Thank you again nurse Montgomery," Anushka's mom awkwardly interrupts and leaves.

My apple watch vibrates and I look at the time; this shift went by fast, yet felt stalled. I swipe my badge and say my goodbyes before heading to the bathroom for a good hand washing session. Scanning my reflection in the mirror as I wash my hands and can't help but smile when my attention meets my tattoos. I love my tattoos that paint my skin, it's how I choose to love and express my body. No one can ever convince me otherwise, it's strange when people try. There was a time when I didn't like my body like I should have and decorating my body with art helped me celebrate it. My tattoos make me feel sexy. The ink on my body is a part of who I am. I lose my track of thought while checking myself out until a knock on the door startles me. After leaving the bathroom, I make my way out towards the lobby and I notice that it is pouring rain outside. I have to run to my dear old Bugsby. The only time I regret parking so far is when the sky blesses us with rain and snow. Thankfully, I remembered to close the top of my car before I went inside.

When I get home, Joseph is laying on the couch watching tv in his boxers. He's an electrician who refuses work on the weekends. He has let his beard grow out a little and has unaffected, short, brown hair. He mutes his show before getting up to greet me with a smile.

"Hi, baby," he kisses my forehead with his hands on my hips.

"Hi," I smile back.

"How was your day? Was it as long and boring as mine?" he adds.

"Very eventful as always. Sebastian hasn't gotten better or worse. Also, Anushka was discharged," I hug him with glee and we both fall on the couch.

"Well, that's great news. Are you ready to unwind for a movie night with yours truly? Or we can skip the movies and just stay in bed and have sex. Netflix and chill," he grins.

"Not unless you're trying to put a baby in me," I smirk in response.

"Not with this again. I thought we already discussed this," he responds with a tone of strong annoyance.

"No, forget it. It's just a joke. What movie are we watching?" I change the subject to help mask my true feelings.

"Hocus Pocus or Beetlejuice?" he asks.

"Damn, that's tough. Let's start with Hocus Pocus and see if we are up for Beetlejuice after," I cheer after responding.

Joseph puts on the movie while I go to the kitchen and make us a bag of movie theatre popcorn. T minus two minutes for the bag to be done, perfect amount of time to change out of these smelly scrubs and get into comfy pajamas. The smell of popcorn fills the apartment as the kernels pop. I bring the big bowl of popcorn to the couch as Joseph starts the classic film. I lay next to him for some cuddles and he wraps his comforting arms around me. It feels good to relax after a long day of working in an intense environment. I guess I am a little glad we stayed in. It's impossible to get tired of watching this witchy children's movie every year with the man I love. He is a great cuddle bug for spooky movies. well, all movies. "Oh, babe I forgot to ask if you wanted to go to the Halloweentown festival in St. Helens this year. We've been talking about it for years, you know, wouldn't it be fun to be nostalgic and relive our childhood? Plus, I am asking way in advance. It's the middle of September, plenty of time." The biggest smile paints my face.

"That sounds fun, but St. Helens is a far drive for a Halloween night don't you think? We should really be home passing out candy to the neighborhood kids." He shoots down my suggestion, what a shocker.

"You're acting like we pass out candy every year. I've always wanted to go and what perfect time?" Irritation seeps from my voice.

"You can go with your friends and I'll just stay home." His eyes

roll to the back of his head with a dramatic sigh.

"Joey, come on. Why are you being like this? You never want to go out and do anything anymore," I soften my tone to defuse a serious fight.

"Don't do that. You're the one who has changed, not me," his tone growing more aggressive.

"What are you referring to? I have always wanted kids and you know that." My voice grows shaky.

"It has nothing to do with kids. I want kids. It's just....you lost a bunch of weight and now you prioritize different things and you want to do everything. So much to do. Do this, do that. You don't even appreciate the nights in anymore. Everything has changed, we just..... want different things now." His tone becomes softer.

"I'm sorry, none of that sounds like a bad thing. Also, none of this is news to you. I didn't just get like this overnight," my attitude creeping to the surface.

"I don't like the person you've become. You've changed," he huffs and puffs.

"You don't like the person I've become? Hold that thought," I'm interrupted by the sound of my ringing phone.

"No, please answer your phone. This conversation isn't important at all," Joseph sarcastically says under his breath.

"Hey girl. What's going on? Short staffed again? I mean I just got home and changed, but if it's okay with you, I can be there in twenty minutes. Perfect. See you soon," I speak into my phone to Ophelia.

"You're really going to leave? Babe, you always take on shifts. They will survive without you." Joseph pleads with heavy annoyance.

"I have to go back into work for the night shift. Someone called in sick and they need me. I'm sorry, we can finish this later." I avoid eye contact with him to hide my hurt.

"Hey, look at me. I love you. You know that right?" He raises my chin with his finger and looks into my eyes.

"Yes, of course I know that. I love you too." I kiss his lips and head back out the door.

The hospital calls me back in before I can even catch my breath, but there's no way I could leave them hanging with a short staff. Not in my line of work. Parking in the farthest spot for the night shifts isn't the smartest move, especially for us female employees. I pull into the closest spot available. More spots become vacant the later the day gets. My mind won't stop wandering to my conversation with Joseph. Should I have stayed and let someone else take this shift? No matter how bad the argument is, we never leave it without love. He doesn't like the person I have become. He doesn't like that I am happy and healthier. I am dumfounded by that thought. I have changed, that was the whole point. I don't have time for fighting, my patients need me. Another nurse who wasn't on the schedule walks in around the same time as myself. They were only short one person, why did they call in two?

"Hey girl! They call you in too?" Xavier asks.

"Oh! I didn't know someone called you in Sabine." Pam, the receptionist, overwhelmingly states.

"Yeah, Ophelia called me to come in." My tone speaks confusion.

"If you want to go home, I can take this shift. The extra money would be great anyway." Xavier speaks up.

"I am so sorry," Pam says.

"I will gladly pass it off to you Xavier!" Relief hits my soul.

I should be grateful for the mix up for getting me out of an uncomfortably, annoying fight with my boyfriend, but they don't need to know that part.

"Hey Sabine, the nurses are a behind on feeding and changing the patients. Would you mind helping them get back on schedule since you are already here?" Pam asks sweetly.

"How can I ever say no to you Pam!" I give her an enthusiastic response and get to work.

We get the babies fed and cleaned up in no time. The hour of extra work gives me some time to clear my head, a win-win situation. I've never been more ready to get back home to watch a movie on the couch with my man, maybe he's right and I haven't been appreciating our nights in. I stop by the liquor store to get a bottle of our favorite cheap wine as an apology gift. Listening to my hype playlist in the car might have done the trick a little too well.

"Baby, I got something for us!" I open the door with excitement to fix things.

The room starts to spin when as I see a naked woman rushing to get covered with my bed sheets. No, I was never the problem.

CHAPTER 2

The cold morning air hits my face as I race through it. Run and run and run 'til I can't breathe. I feel as if someone punched me in the gut and all the air in the world gets knocked out of me. The look on Joseph's face replays in my head.

How could someone do that to a person they love? Why would they?

Did he ever love me at all?

Who was that woman? Does he love her?

How long has he been doing this behind my back?

What about the two of them does he like so much to lose the love and respect for me?

I can't breathe.

I reach a park bench on the trail and collapse down into it. My mind goes blank as my lungs gasp for the oxygen my mind and body deprived them of. I feel like I can't get enough oxygen in my body and I start to panic. An overwhelming sense of dread spreads through my entire body causing my skin to crawl. My hands are clammy and my stomach has a strong need to barf everything up from breakfast. My elbows immediately fall to my knees and I rock with my face in my hands. Tears fill my eyes as I try to calm down. But, I can't. What is happening to me? What is this? I can't breathe. A curvy middle-aged woman with a glowing dark complexion, and glamourous curly hair that kiss her shoulders walks towards me with her baby stroller. Her head bobs to the beat of the music pouring out of her air pods as her hips sway to the melody of her song. As she gets closer, I hear coos sounding from the tiny human listening to the ABC's song on a kid's tablet. I've never heard this version before; this was a good distraction to collect my mind and allow it to start functioning properly again.

"Are you okay honey?" The woman comes up to me, bends down to meet me at eye level.

"No," I look into her eyes and completely lose it.

"Oh, it's okay sweetheart," she says in a comforting tone.

This mysterious woman gets up, pulls the stroller closer to her, and sits right next to me on the bench. She wraps her arms around my upper body and holds me tightly. We sit here hugging while I sob, and she hums a sweet melody as she holds me tight. I don't know what or how to feel, but all I know is my heart aches. There are no words. I let go and ugly cry all over this comforting stranger generously holding space for me. After a few minutes, it's all out of my system. She takes a silent second before letting go. Her sparkly big brown eyes meet mine as she wipes the evidence of my sadness off my face with the sleeve of her long sleeve, green, tie dye shirt.

"You are okay, I promise you. Whatever it is, you'll get through it," she sweetly states.

"I really hope so." My eyes begin to tear up again, but I am able to hold them in.

"It will, I promise." She rubs her hand on my back.

"Thank you so much. You are a miracle. I'm so sorry I'm disgusting and getting my tears and snot on you, but that felt really good," I nervously laugh.

"Oh sweetie. We all have these moments, and it sucks to be alone during them. No one should be alone. I'm Diane, it's nice to meet you! Oh, and don't worry about the snot, I have a kid. Wait 'til you get one, you're in for a treat." She giggles and hugs me again. "I'm Sabine. You're a blessing, Diane. That kid is going to have one amazing life with you in it." A smile appears on my face.

"Oh, he is spoiled! This is Jackson," she caresses his cute chubby face with her hand.

"Jackson is precious. I noticed the ABC song is different," the thought pops into my head and spews out of my mouth.

"Girl, they changed it!" her energy turns upbeat.

"No way!" I react in disbelief.

"You have no idea. They shouldn't have fixed something that wasn't broken." Diane laughs.

"Want to talk about your situation? You aren't in any danger, are you?" she adds.

"No, I am safe thankfully. I really needed that release and support. Honestly, I don't remember a time someone held me like that. I walked in on my boyfriend with another woman when I got home from work last night. Naked. She was naked, in my bed. I don't understand why, we've been together forever, we are high school sweethearts." My mouth begins to ramble and Diane gently places her hand on my shoulder.

"I am so sorry, honey. You know it's not your fault, right?" Diane engages.

"Yeah, that's what everyone says, but a night of isolation made my brain run wild with all the reasons I could have caused him to stray. I've changed." My head shakes with disbelief and disappointment.

"Nuh uh, girl. If you changed and he doesn't like it, then he needed to man up and choose a new future for you two. There is no excuse or reason to cheat. Especially in your apartment? In your bed! Oh, hell no!" Her voice rises.

The tears start to flow again from my irritated eyes and down my puffy red cheeks. I can't stop crying on and off to save the life of me.

"He cheated on me; what's wrong him? What's so wrong about me?" I ramble on as Diane continues to listen and allows the words to pour from my hurting heart. It's just her and I right now, plus Jackson. The people walking by staring don't phase me. My brain doesn't hear the baby humming to the beat of his silly little kid show. It's just me and Diane. My face lays sobbing in her chest with her arms firmly wrapped around the mess of me. I need this. I need her. The waterworks have finally stopped, deep breathes should normalize my beathing to calm down.

"Don't ever apologize for being yourself. If a man doesn't like a strong badass woman with ambition and goals, he is not the one. Shedding all that weight and gaining your life, people don't realize how much strength and personal discipline it takes. I would set you up with my brother if he was single-single," she laughs which paints a smile on my sad puffy face.

"I had no clue how much I needed this, and you. It's lonely and isolating on the personal journey grind, your words mean the world to me. Thank you for going on a walk and showing up for me," I laugh as the thought of her walking just to hold me randomly.

We hug one last time before she walks off into the future with her son. I feel as if I'm in the twilight zone. What just happened? Do angels exist? I sit here in stillness for a few more minutes and take nice, long, deep breaths. I am okay. I feel numb, but okay. My body feels like jelly when I stand up, then my butt meets the bench again. Go easy, Sabine. You got this. I get up again and slowly walk the rest of the distance back to the apartment.

As I let myself into my apartment, I think that there is a good chance they slept here last night. The smell of her perfume lingers in the thick air of disgusting betrayal. Oddly, this place looks like someone took a vacuum and Mr. Clean to it. I don't want to be in here any longer than I have to be. The kitchen is spotless. The bathroom is spotless. The bedroom is spotless. There it is, the guilt gift. A bouquet of black roses and a fresh bottle of our favorite cheap wine with an envelope taped to it. I don't know what is more triggering, being back in the scene of the crime or the shitty absent apology attempt on the freshly made bed. The coffee pot beeps ready as no one is here, but me. My favorite coffee mug sits next to the maker with the lid next door. Keys jingle and my body freezes, paralyzed at the possibility of running into *them* again. It's just Joseph with a box of my favorite donuts. His face looks just as surprised as mine to be in front of each other again for the first time since the incident.

"What are you doing here?" I manage to say while shaky and frozen.

"I.. uh. I was going to bring you coffee and your favorite donuts at work. I didn't think you were going to come back here and I needed to see you and talk about last night." He avoids eye contact and fumbles a few of his words.

"There is nothing to talk about. Last night was self-explanatory, simple as that. I hope you're exhausted from all that deceitful cheating because you have a full pot of coffee to drink. I want you gone by the time I get back. Leave your key on the table," staying strong feels impossible right now, but I somehow manage.

"Sabine!" Joseph calls my name for the last time before I leave the apartment.

My heart is racing and my adrenaline is pumping. Breathe. It's over. It is over. I'm stuck in disbelief over the events in the past twenty-four hours. A well needed day off from work couldn't have come at a better time. I check the time on my apple watch, two hours until I pick my mom up at her hotel for lunch. Being early never hurt anybody, I drive straight to the hotel and find her room. A knock at door three twenty-six.

"Sabi? What are you doing here so early? Oh my God look at you, you're so skinny. You know you still need those nice round child bearing hips still!" Her eyes are barely open.

"It's great to see you to mom," I laugh as I hug her close not wanting to let go.

She has always given the best hugs in the world, so tight and comforting. Our hug is long, it's been years since she's been here. She bombards my face with sweet kisses then climbs back into bed. It lets me do exactly what I need to do, shower.

"Hey mama, I'm going to jump in the shower, if you don't mind,"

I warn my mother.

"Not at all, go ahead, sweetie." She smiles.

My clothes hit the floor as I quickly tear them off my sweaty, smelly body. The 5'9 woman in the full body mirror is staring back at me. The messy bun on top is filled with greasy strands of hair; my fair loose skin sags without clothes to keep it in place. Colorful tattoos decorate my body. Random moles strategically placed in the making of my existence along with many of the tiger stripe

stretch marks on my belly, thighs, breasts, and shoulders. Those brown eyes staring into my brown eyes through the extravagant hotel mirror. This is me. My breathing begins to get heavier as I feel more and more vulnerable. This body has been through decades of trauma. This body has been through it all with me.

The second the water drowns my hair; the tears come pouring down my cheeks. It hurts like I never expected it to. I feel so stupid, I love him and don't want him out of my life forever. Am I making a huge mistake? The feeling of self-hatred and not being worthy turns all the way up as I sob under water. How could I spend so much time changing my life and escaping these exact feelings for them to just reappear? I did it, I lost the weight and life I didn't want and became the person I wanted to become. I'm healthy. Yet, I am still not good enough. Why am I not good enough? My hand begins to hurt as I repeatedly hit the stone shower wall, with silent screams spilling from my mouth. So, this is what a full-blown mental breakdown looks and feels like.

I begin to choke on my hysteria, then gasp for air. Deep breaths, Sabine, I'm starting to sense a pattern today. I close my tear-filled eyes and inhale and exhale. Inhale. Exhale.

Rinse and repeat.

I squirt shampoo into my hands and scrub it good into my wet, black hair. This is what I need right now, a shower meditation.

I just want to feel something other than pain.

Here goes nothing. I love my hair because it allows me to style it however I please, every day. I rinse my hands and go for the face wash. I love my face because it gives me a sense of physical identity and allows me to see, smell and breathe. I love my beautiful brown eyes. I love my slight medium sized nose. I love my lips and teeth. I love my ears. Breathe. My hands get a good rinse again before I rub the bar of body soap into the wash cloth. Here is where the real work begins. I'm grateful for my hands that allow me to do everything and anything. I'm grateful for my arms for getting me through the work days and doing the work to get healthy. Soapy water drips down the saggy loose skin hanging from my arm, my beautiful saggy skin. I move the soapy wash cloth to my neck. I'm grateful for my neck for holding my head held high through the blessings and tragedies. I graze my slightly lower hanging breasts and my nipples. I am grateful for my breasts for the opportunity to feed my future children. Maybe Joseph was tired of looking at my loose saggy body. I'll never be like those other women, the woman he slept… Sabine! I clear my mind to redirect back to my shower body meditation. I am grateful for my saggy body being with me through it all, gotten me through the worse of the worsts. Another round of rubbing the bar of soap on the washcloth will finish the cleaning job. My eyes and hands meet my belly all at once, a warm sigh leaves my mouth. The relationship with my belly has been the toughest one, but the most beautiful battle. Vowing to love every part of me will always be a physical and mental challenge.

"We have come a long way haven't we," I say out loud and my eyes begin to tear up as I rub the wash cloth over my belly and the rest of my body.

Joseph has been there through the thick and thin, I laugh at myself for the *punny* joke. He fell in love with the large version of me. Of course, I was still me and wasn't ever afraid to be myself, but I was always a work in progress. Why isn't he capable of loving me at my best when he stayed through the worse. There is no telling how long I have been in the shower. I rinse the soap and sadness off my body before I get out, dry off and get dressed.

"Good morning mama. I've missed you." I sit on the bed next to her.

"I've missed you too sweetheart. I'm glad you showed up early because I was going to have to cancel on you. I have a chance to catch an earlier flight to South Africa. Which leaves in an hour and thirty-seven minutes," she states noticing the time.

"You've always been such a travel bug. Well, I'm disappointed you have to go." I'm sad she's leaving me when she just got into town.

"I know honey, I'm sorry. Well, we have a good fifteen minutes to catch up. Tell me about your life these days, baby. How's work? When are you and Joey getting married, huh?" Mom means well.

"Honestly, I don't think marriage is in the cards for us." My face falls to sad to finish my answer.

"Oh, sweetheart. What's wrong?" My mom props herself up and scoots next to me.

"I walked in on him with another woman last night, sorry it's still so raw." I manage to hold the waterworks in, but my eyes are glued to the ground.

"That bastard. God dammit. Men, just like your father. Blind, they are! Don't know when they've got a good thing. I'm sorry, honey!" She hugs me like every mother should hug their daughter in her time of need.

"What should I do? We have built a whole life together. Did you regret leaving dad? How did you get over it?" I ask my mom the uncomfortable questions on a topic we've never discussed.

"I wish I trusted and leaned on my friends more. I became a hermit and isolated myself. Sadness, anger, resentment and all the others were bottled up inside me. I held it all in and the anger was eating me alive. Eventually, I got help when my life got out of control and I got over him, filled my time with my travels and met new people." She answers with transparency.

"But, I love him." I hate to say, but it's true.

"I'm not telling you to stay or leave, but you have to ask yourself important questions. How does this man make me feel? Who am I around this man? Do I trust him after the ultimate betrayal? Relationships don't work just on love. I'm sorry, baby. You deserve someone who treats you like a queen." My mom shares her words of wisdom.

"Yeah, I suppose you're right. I have a lot to think about. Thank you for this chat. It means a lot, mom. You sure you can't stay another night?" I ask with little hope.

"I wish, Sabi. I've got to get going. I promise I will send you a postcard. Would you be a doll and check out for me? I really don't want to miss this flight. The next time I see you, I promise we will have more time to have girl chat. I love you." She kisses my forehead and disappears out the door.

The travel bug bit her when I was seven. That is a better thought then her choosing herself after my father cheated on her, seems to be a pattern in the family. I can't blame her, she's happy. Well, I hope she is. One day I will get the chance to have some real quality time with my mother again. On the plus side, her postcards never fail to make me smile. My phone vibrates.

Joseph: All my stuff is out. The place is all yours.

My eyes catch my reflection in the black phone screen, my eyes are still puffy, and redness fills my fair cheeks. I check out for my mom and head back to the apartment. It feels cold and empty now that all the love is shattered. My brain is scrambling how to comprehend moving on after the first man I ever loved is gone forever. I pace back and forth between the bedroom and front door, contemplating whether to call in sick for the next few days to get my mind right. It feels impossible to care for others when you have nothing to give in this moment. I sit on my bed as my eyes scan the room while my mind is numb. A fortune cookie fortune pinned to the wall reads, "A gambler not only will lose what he has, but also will lose what he doesn't have." My head flips and does a double take on what the fortune says and means. What are the odds? The universe will always bring you hope in a hopeless state of mind. I think I can survive the day or at least I will die trying.

CHAPTER 3

"You look like shit," Ophelia says from across the room.

"What? Really? I spent like seven hours getting ready this morning to impress you and all these new babies who have no idea what is going on." A playfully sarcastic tone hit back.

"No seriously, you don't look like you have slept. Also, being here for hours can do the trick," she says concerned.

"Yeah, I'll be fine. That is what caffeine is for right?" I respond. "Sleep will treat you better. You need your sleep to take care of your patients, they need us to be at our best. Don't tell me Joseph kept you up the past few days with all that baby making. Sex is not a reason to miss three days of work," she jokingly lectures.

"Joseph left a few days ago. I walked in on him cheating. Nope, I will not want to talk about it, but thank you," I stop her in her tracks. Has it really been days of sleeping alone? I miss him. Is he broken like me or is he the happiest he's ever been? Is he in a relationship with the woman he cheated with? The next baby I walk up to is a patient I have not met yet. The name on the hospital tag reads Tamara Lewin. She is fresh, small and pure. Born into this world is the odds against her from the start. She will grow up fighting for her life, getting into trouble, fall in love, getting her heart broken. Maybe she will heal, love the hell out of life, and change the world. There is so much potential in this little miracle laying in the plastic container with machines guiding her to recovery.

Tamara Lewin has no idea what life has in store for her. None of these babies do, uncertainty is the beauty of life. I don't even know if I really believe that myself. I get out of my thoughts and back to work.

I do a full round of checking vitals before it's time to do diaper checks. Being short staffed lately has me doing a lot by myself or with one other nurse. It tends to take us a little longer with less people. My apple watch vibrates to let me know that it's time for my much needed break as I finish up changing Miss Lewin. I close her container and wash my hands then, grab my lunch out of the fridge. "Hey hot stuff. We're going to the cafeteria for lunch and you are eating with us. I won't take no for an answer. Sorry not sorry." Ophelia comes up behind me with a compassionate order. Ophelia There is no energy in me to give an appeal to those orders. The fridge is filled with food and drinks with all sorts of names on them. A bowl of rice, chicken and broccoli sits with a fresh red apple on top of the glass container. It's quite common for doctors and nurses to eat lunch alone for peace and quiet to recuperate for the rest of their shift. Downtime on breaks is important to take time to ourselves.

"Hey babe," Ophelia and Xavier sit down at the table next to me.

"Hey. Hey Xavier." I greet them.

"What did Joseph do to you? We will beat the shit out of him or his car. Maybe we will get less jail time if we just go for his car." Ophelia is at it again with her sassy jokes.

"You only get jail time if you get caught," I chuckle for the first time in seems like forever.

"I can't get caught, I'm too sexy for prison," Xavier comments with his smooth Latino accent.

"You really are too sexy for prison. I love the stubble facial hair you got going on with your cute combover look. Plus, being five foot five makes you an easy target in the yard. Sorry not sorry," I join in on the jokes and somehow it makes me feel better.

"You're the whole package deal. What man in his right mind would ever treat you like that? I can't believe it. Oh, you're probably torn," Ophelia redirects the conversation back to my recent life events, she puts her hand on mine with pity eyes.

"Stop. Please don't make me cry. This aspirin just kicked in to help my head stop pounding. I'm tired of crying over this man," I plead.

"It's not good for you to hold it in Sabine. Let it out so you can heal and move on. No wonder you look like you haven't slept. No, all the nurses are not discussing your personal life and mental state," Xavier pretends.

"I'm fine you guys, really. I've been through harder things. I get the whole bed to myself and I get to do whatever the hell I want without consulting with anyone," I try to convince them, and myself. "You took multiple vacation days to sulk alone in your room?

That is tragically sad," Ophelia says bluntly.

"Hey, you know what. My cousin was cheated on and she was depressed and lost for the longest time. She also looked like a zombie...."

"Hey!" I interrupt him.

"Sorry, too soon? Anyways. She went to like this support group kind of like AA, but it's for people who have infidelity issues or something.

Like cheaters anonymous." Xavier tries to remember the name.

"Yeah, they have support groups for literally anything these days," Ophelia adds.

"I am not going to that." I laugh.

"Why not? Are you too good for it? Don't be so closed-minded Sabi," Xavier calls me out.

"I'm not too good for it, I just don't need it." My tone becomes defensive.

"You're not fine, Ms. Denial." Ophelia rolls her eyes.

"We love you and want you to be happy again. This isn't you. It's almost October and freaky Halloween Sabine hasn't even arrived yet. There is no light in that Halloween town pumpkin of yours," Xavier playfully pinches my cheek while baby talking at me before he gets up and leaves.

"Yes, we love you and need you to take care of yourself. I must get going before my break is over. Go hold baby Sebastian or something. You have been so distant from the poor thing. He probably feels abandoned." Ophelia kisses my cheek and leaves me alone at the table.

Babies can sense energy from a mile away, I don't want Sebastian or any of them feeling my sadness. He already has enough on his plate with growing, healing and being a baby. Being a baby is hard work, there is so much to do for a new dependent tiny human. Holding and cuddling with babies does sound better than going home alone to an empty apartment. The judgment of other nurses and doctors is overwhelming to stay past my work hours, I decide to go to the pediatric wing of the hospital. There are not as many familiar faces in other hospital departments. On the other side of the hospital is a playroom for toddlers and children where volunteers like to come and spend time with the kids. It is a colorful and vibrant play room for such a dark and depressing place for children to live. It's most likely one of the cleanest playrooms anyone will ever come across.

I walk inside and see a little girl sitting at the Disney decorated table, coloring. She is attached to an IV that goes everywhere with her as long as she's admitted here. Her head has few strands of hair left and her gown has the Moana Disney princess on it. She looks around the age when the baby teeth fall out and random teeth can be seen missing at any time.

"Hi there," I speak softly as I sit next to her. "Hi, are you a doctor?" she sweetly asks.

"No, I am a nurse that works with babies on the other side of the hospital." I smile.

"Cool! Would you like to color with me or are you here for me?" She asks.

"I would love to color with you. Seems like you know how to stay in the lines really well." I smile again.

"Yeah, I've been practicing. I'm Alma, I'm six. What's your name?" her inquisitive mind is turning.

"It's nice to meet you Ms. Alma. My name is Sabine." I smile and grab the green crayon.

"You can color that page while I color this one, okay?" She points to the right page of the superhero coloring book.

"Sounds good to me. It's so quiet in here. Are you always in here alone?" I ask.

"I like it because there is no beeping noises, shots or medicine to take. Plus, I like being alone in the quiet. The other kids can be loud sometimes. My mom says I am independent" she says proudly.

"Yes, you are Alma. Independent, brave, smart and very talented with your coloring." I smile.

"I want to be a strong independent woman like my mom…… and you!" Her smile is so big.

"Alma honey, it's time to get back for your treatment," her mom interrupts from the door.

"Hi there, I'm nurse Montgomery. It's nice to meet you. You have one strong independent lady right here. She's great!" I greet her. "Joan. Nice to meet you. Yeah, she's the best, isn't she?" she firmly shakes my hand.

"Thanks for coloring with me. Will you come back?" Alma asks with puppy dog eyes.

"I would be honored." I have a big genuine smile.

Alma excitedly, gets up and wraps her tiny arms around my waist. I never knew how much I needed and loved hugs. There was never a time I wanted to be touched when I was bigger. Alma has an abundance of light in her spirit, I mean she must, just like my babies in the NICU. Seeing Alma wave goodbye as she walks out the door warms my heart. How can a six-year-old be so impressive? I am pretty sure I ate dirt at six years old. Just as I am about to get up, four teenagers walk in the playroom.

"Who are you?" One of the boys' smirks at me.

"Aren't you kids a little old to be in this playroom?" I laugh to myself.

"Not many places to go when you're a sick kid. Plus, these nurses stay up our asses. No way they would let us go anywhere. So, they let us come in here for an hour a day without the little kids, the other boy responds.

"You are kids. You deserve this room too. That's cool they reserve privacy for you guys. So, what do you do in here?" I'm curious.

"Get high. Party it up!! Hi, I'm Raquel! The teenage girl laughs.

"Don't tell her your name! You a patient here too? What's your illness?" The flirty boy speaks again.

"I'm a nurse who works here and old enough to be your mother."

The lie doesn't hurt anything but his ego.

"Want to sample my blood Nurse Montgomery?" Finley moves closer.

"Finley. Do you want to fuck your mother? Cool it, bro." Raquel taunts him.

"That's gross!" Taylor chimes in.

"Hey, we are about to play Game of Thrones Monopoly. Did you want to play?" Raquel asks and the rest encourage the idea.

"I love Game of Thrones! You kids are way too young for that show." I catch myself in an uncool adult moment. "But, I'm not your mother. Plus, hospitals ready age you." I add.

"Don't speak, perv," Taylor tells Finley before he opens his mouth.

"I'm going to kick your butts!" I challenge them competitively.

"Game on!" The fourth kid finally speaks.

Everyone moves to the table and sits in the tiny toddler chairs. Taylor pulls out the game and sets it up while the other kids crack jokes with each other. It's amazing they have one another to connect with, hospitals can be quite lonely. Loving Game of Thrones was a slight exaggeration on my part, but I couldn't break their hearts by declining a seat at their table. The bird piece is my chariot of choice. A few rounds and a couple trips to the jail house, I own only four properties. How naive of me to think these kids will play nice, monopoly seemed self-explanatory. I probably haven't played since I was their age. Eventually, I am the first to go bankrupt. It's been a long day, but these kids were a nice distraction and a good time. But now all I want to do is get in bed.

"You guys are a good time. I would love to stay and hang, but I have to get going and do boring adult responsibilities." I stretch the truth one more time but I am exhausted.

"You're pretty cool, Nurse Montgomery," Finley says.

"Yeah, I wish our nurses were more like you," Taylor adds. "Call me Sabine. Just keep in mind that they have your best interest, okay? Even if they are hard on you." I encourage them before I head out the playroom.

We all exchange goodbyes and smiles. On my way out the hospital doors, I see an empty line to get a flu shot; I take off my jacket and roll my scrub sleeve up before I take a seat. My boss has been reminding us for weeks to fit it in our schedules to get the vaccination. Of course, it's mandatory for the job. The nurse takes my ID and Medical card to make sure I'm not a fraud, although having the same employee ID card as her is a dead giveaway. She giggles as she hands over my cards, her laugh is contagious. First comes the alcohol wipe, then the tiny needle filled with the dead flu virus. My arm never gets sore and my body has not had any side effects yet. Fingers crossed. I thank the nurse and go on my way to Bugsy. It never seems quick and easy until it's over. I can't wait to get in my cozy bed while watching a rom com to sob my way through the night. Tomorrow is my day off, maybe a few movies are in the cards for me tonight.

I get home, throw a flat bag of popcorn kernels in the microwave, and throw on an oversized olive-green nightgown. Watching the kernels pop making the bag grow bigger and bigger is awfully satisfying. I pour the steaming hot popcorn in a big orange plastic bowl and hop in bed. There are too many options to choose from and at the same time there is nothing good to watch. I scroll down and press play on "Ten Things I Hate About You." Health Ledger is truly missed. Thank God I'm alone tonight, no one needs to see me shoving handfuls of popcorn in my mouth. Kat is so uptight yet so relatable. No wonder people are scared to fall in love, they don't want to get hurt or cheated on. At the rate I'm going, I'll be alone with ten cats in a few years. Halfway through the movie my phone lights up at the same time as it vibrates. Who is texting me at ten thirty at night? It's Xavier.

Xavier: Hey girl, got the info on the support group. Here it is. Infidelity Survivors Anonymous. The group is facilitated by a woman named Maliha Patel and her number is (503) 948- 2783. Go get that healing, girl. Love, Xavier.

He can't be serious right now; I am not going to a support group for infidelity. Support groups are for serious things like drug addiction or trauma. No, I can't. I throw my phone at the end of my bed and continue watching Patrick serenade Kat in the bleachers while dodging security. Where are the guys like Patrick Verona? Yes, he hurts Kat in the beginning and middle, but makes up for it in the end. At least the man knows what he wants. My phone must have landed right side up because the phone screen turned on again with a two-minute message reminder. The moment with Alma comes to mind right after kicking my phone off the bed.

"I am a strong independent woman like my mom, and you."

What is she seeing that I can't? What is so strong about a woman who lost the love of her life to another woman? Alma is doing her part to recover and get better. I realize I am refusing to heal. I don't want to go to the meeting. It's filled with suckers. I am a sucker. Suddenly, I remember what my mom told me about holding it all in. Shit. I have to go.

CHAPTER 4

Here I am, in a smelly high school gym with a bunch of suckers. The temperature is satisfyingly warm on this cold Saturday morning. This support group is filled with heartbroken people waking up at seven in the morning to try and feel less shitty. It's been eight years since stepping foot in this gymnasium, I'm going to need a whole other support group for that topic. Arriving early gives me time to give myself a pep-talk before going inside. Three others show up early as well, my guess is one is Maliha Patel. She is a middle-aged Indian woman who seems to be about seven and a half months pregnant, whatever that looks like. She looks radiant, rocking that baby bump. My body starts to get nervous after a few more people pile in for the meeting. Everyone is greeting each other as if they know everyone already, seems I may be the odd one out. The closer the start time gets; I question if I am brave enough to be here. I want to run for the hills. With ten minutes to go, I get some coffee from the small table of refreshments.

"Good morning, I'm Maliha Patel," she smiles and reaches out her hand to shake mine.

"Hi, good morning. I'm Sabine." I shake her hand without trying to be obvious about being nervous.

"Welcome Sabine! I am glad you came. It's nice to see new faces, more people reaching out. I look forward to seeing you here, group is twice a week, but one meeting is just a check in." She gracefully touches my shoulder and walks to greet others.

Twice a week seems a bit proactive, check ins sound nice. This place doesn't look too horrifying. The coffee is strong, no need to worry about being awake enough to be fully present while hearing people pour their hearts out to random strangers. The people in this gym are all different ages, shapes and sizes from different walks of life. They look normal, not heartbroken. It seems I might be the only sucker sitting in the circle. What's with the circle structure anyway? Having the group sit in a circle feels exposing, there is nowhere to hide. Am I ready for this?

"Good morning. I haven't seen you before." A voice speaks on the right of me.

"Holy hell, you're tall," I turn, and shock hits my face when I see this giant of a man.

"I am so sorry, that was rude." I gasp at my own ignorance.

"It's okay. Believe it or not, but being six foot nine means I get that a lot. I'm Alistair Barker," he chuckles and sits down in the chair next to me.

"Nice to meet you. Sabine Montgomery." I awkwardly wave.

Alistair Barker is one tall, dark and handsome man. A black man with a well-groomed mustache and beard. His body is covered in tattoos. There is a gentle sparkle in his dark brown eyes. A woman who is sitting across from me has the most beautiful natural red hair and a face full of freckles, her name tag reads Hannah. An older man with a cane has an old papa look sits two seats left of me. Maliha Patel is the woman with a heart of gold to run a group like this, especially at this time of day. How could any of their partners choose someone else over them?

"Good morning, everyone! My name is Maliha Patel, welcome. I facilitate Infidelity Survivors' Anonymous meetings on Mondays, Wednesdays, and Saturdays. All of you sit here in this room this morning because someone dear in your life broke the sacred trust in your relationship. We are here to share our personal experiences, learn tools and to heal the deep hurt caused by someone we loved or still love. You are not alone, and your partners' infidelity problem is not your fault. In this group, you will share your stories and learn how to heal from the trauma. I will go first. A little over a decade ago, I came here from India on a K1 visa. My ex-husband and I were madly in love, which led my decision to leave everything I knew in India for a new life in America with the love of my life. At first, I was completely dependent on him because I wasn't allowed to work yet, and I didn't know anyone. I went from being a doctor in India to being a stay-at-home woman in America. Of course, I was lost and dependent on my partner. After a while, he took advantage of being in control and started lying about working late and eventually I found out he was having an affair with a woman he worked with. It broke me or I thought it did. I was in a brand-new country for only a year and the one person I trusted with my life left me, alone. It felt impossible to live after. It took me a couple of years to work on myself and find my self-worth again. Long story short, I met my current husband at the farmers market, and we have our first baby girl coming soon. Would anyone else like to go next?" She shares with her hand on her growing belly.

"I will," a woman raised her hand.

"Okay, whenever you're ready." Maliha gives her a comforting nod.

"My name is Hannah.... my boyfriend cheated on me with his ex-girlfriend. The first few times he brought me flowers the next day with apology chocolates, but after a while he denied it and constantly said I was paranoid from his previous mistakes. It's like he doesn't even care about getting caught anymore." Her voice is shaky as she shares.

"Thank you for sharing, Hannah. Sometimes the people who are in the wrong tend to project onto the person they are hurting to help make themselves feel better. You may have been paranoid or not, but it would make sense why you would be. I'm glad you're here and keep showing up for yourself, shows strength. Who is next?" Maliha's voice is calm.

"I think our new friend Sabine would like to share," Alistair taps my knee with a supporting nod.

"Uhmm no, no it's okay." My eyes grow wide after being called out.

"You sure?" he questions my decision.

"Alright, I'll go. Hi, I'm Alistair. I'm 32 and I have been ready to start having kids for a few years now, my husband Lennox has decided to change his mind after all this time. It completely blindsided me when he finally told me. We argued for a while about the topic, eventually he sought for his fulfillment somewhere else. What hurts the most is the cause of his cheating was to escape. To escape me. He didn't fall in love with someone. He just didn't want me or us in fact. I wasn't enough for him. It took me a while to decide to file for divorce and when I did, he pled for forgiveness. He said he wanted to have kids and it would just fix things. I just had to find my strength to say no and choose me. It's a process." Alistair's eyes wondered to the floor a few times during his share.

"Thank you for sharing, Alistair. Taking space after infidelity is a healthy response to figure out what is best for you moving forward. Some people choose to leave right away and others decide the relationship is worth working on. I know this stuff can be very hard and vulnerable to share, you guys are doing great." Maliha speaks to the group and nods at Alistair.

The rest of the group takes their time to share their dark and vulnerable experiences with infidelity, their trauma. Most of everyone shared, some cried and others nodding with compassion. All the stories are entirely different, but the results are the same. Betrayal. Pain. We are all hurting because someone we love rejected us in one way or another. My story isn't any different from theirs.

"Sabine, would you like to share?" Maliha encourages after the rest have gone.

"Ummm, sure okay," my body shifts, and I start to fidget with my jacket zipper.

"When you're ready," she smiles.

"Hi, I'm Sabine, but you all probably know that already," I laugh awkwardly. I feel out of place.

"Joseph was my first boyfriend, my first love. We were completely different people when we met years ago. Time changed everything. I lost over one hundred and fifty pounds and a lot of my priorities changed. He doesn't like the 'new' me. I want more out of life then working and coming home and being a homebody. Nothing wrong with being a home body, I've just done it for so long. I came home from work early and walked right into the middle of whatever they were doing. She was naked in my apartment with my boyfriend. It's sad coming home to an empty apartment when you already feel empty inside, especially where the violation happened. I guess." Tears run down my face.

The woman sitting left of me reaches over and gives me a warm hug. Alistair puts his hand on my shoulder for comfort. For the first time in a week, I don't feel alone.

"Thank you, Sabine for stepping out of your comfort zone, it's brave. I know it's not easy for anyone to share what's vulnerable to them with others." Maliha thanks me for sharing as she did for everyone else. I'm glad I opened up; they relate to me. She goes on about how this new reality can feel impossible, but it will get better with time and healing. Her baby might come out with a PhD in psychology by the time we are all moved on, onto bigger and better things.

Our homework is to write a letter to our significant others and pinpoint what we feel. It's still so fresh for me, I don't know what to feel yet. I feel it all. All I want to do is write down a list of swear words that I want to scream at Joseph, and the rest of idiots that mistreated my new peers. I was wrong, the suckers aren't us, the suckers are the cheaters who didn't love us the way we deserved. After the meeting, a few stay back to put the chairs away and clean up the refreshment's tables. The tiny garbage cans are filled with coffee cups, tissues, and tears. My contribution is taking out the trash and hopefully it will be a metaphor to my current life status. This whole support group for being cheated on is weird but slightly rewarding. It's not what I thought it would feel like, but exactly what I thought it would look like. I appreciate this meeting time being early because now we all have the whole day ahead of us. The clean-up is done and everyone left is walking out and saying their goodbyes. I'm digging for my keys that somehow went missing in the bottomless pit of my purse.

"Hey, wait up!" a deep voice sounds from behind.

"Me?" I turn around and see Alistair.

"How was your first meeting? You coming back or is this meeting going to scare you off? This kind of thing isn't for everyone," he asks as we continue walking.

"It's out of my comfort zone for sure, but unfortunately I think it's where I need to be." I continue to look for my keys.

"You might surprise yourself. Look, I have an empty place to myself too and all the time in the world not being able to sleep at night. You can call me if you ever need to," he hands me a piece of paper with his number on it.

"Are you like a sponsor?" I'm ask and immediately feel embarrassment.

"No. Just like a new friend." He laughs and playfully mocks my question.

"That was a stupid question!" I laugh at myself. "Woah, this is your car?" he impressively asks. "Yes, sir! The name's Bugsby." I smile big.

"Sweet! Nice to meet you, Bugsby," he checks my car out like it's an Abercrombie & Fitch model.

"It was nice to meet you Alistair." I get in my car and start the ignition.

"You too, Ms. Sabine." He checks me out in my old beauty.

The drive home is spent decompressing on what crazy interesting morning I've had. Was Alistair flirting? I roll my eyes at myself and instantly feel shame for that thought considering he has a husband. Ex-husband. They say that being nice is often mistaken for flirting, especially from the attractive ones. He is Godlike, Lennox is plain stupid. No,

Joseph is stupid. I was the perfect girlfriend anyone could ever ask for. Anger starts to overrule my body the more my mind thinks of everything Joseph has put me through. My eyes start to bring on the waterworks, I turn the music up and just let go. I start screaming at the top of my lungs. There are no more tears, just rage. Words come flying out of my mouth. It's becoming too hard to drive during this mental break down, I pull over to calm down. After my messy moment, I turn the radio on and finish driving home. *Best thing I never had* by Beyonce

conveniently comes on the radio as I stare at the road while I drive in autopilot mode. The day is young, but I am ready to be done. I did what I needed to do and I am going to grab a bottle of wine and get back in bed to enjoy my day off. What if I do need a sponsor? It feels impossible to go through this alone. I miss Joseph and his touch.

Me: Hey Alistair, It's Sabine.

CHAPTER 5

It's the next day and still no response from my new friend from my new group. He's probably busy. Why give your number to someone and offer support when you have no plan to follow through? Do I actually need support from him or am I just happy to have a new friend?

"Sabine! Are you even listening to me, woman?" Alma waves her hands, pulling my attention back to her.

"Oh, sorry. I got lost in thought. My turn?" I arrive back into reality and receive the cutest sassy look.

"It's time for you to get married. Dun dun dun! Do you want to marry a boy or a girl?" The progressive six-year-old asks.

"Edward Scissorhands is a man, I say boy." I smirk at her. "Who? You're married to a man with scissors as hands? Does his mom know?" She's clueless in my dating life and I plan to keep it that way.

"We aren't married yet, but a girl can dream." I respond and Joan laughs from the background.

"When I get out of here and have to go back to real school, can we still be friends? I don't think I will make any there." Her face falls sad.

"Of course, we can make plans to do fun things when you're feeling better, that's the most important thing. Why would you think you won't make friends honey?" I scoot closer to comfort the sad girl.

"Do you think they will want to be my friend when I have no hair and I look sick? I might be attached to the air tube thing. I have bruises and scars from like a billion surgeries. They will think I am a freak, I'm ugly." Her thought process overwhelms her as she gets deeper into it.

"Alma, you are the farthest from ugly. You're so beautiful. There is no comparison between you and the other kids. Hair grows back and if people don't want to be your friend because of your hair, then it's their loss. Not to mention, you are the coolest kid I've ever known! Do you want to know a secret that I don't tell many people?" my piss poor attempt to cheer her up.

"Yes," a sparkle shines from her eyes.

"You see this black compression shirt I wear underneath my really cool Halloween scrubs? I always have it on to hold my loose skin in. My body used to be a lot bigger and I have a bunch of saggy skin that hangs in the way when I work. This shirt helps hold it in nice and tight and helps me feel a little better about the way I look." I open up to the six-year-old, while she soaks it up like a sponge.

"I don't understand. Can I see?" Confusion fills her face.

My eyes immediately dart to Joan as I panic for her to intervene, but her eyes radiate with nothing, but love and admiration for this moment I have with her daughter. What did I think would happen? Of course, Alma would ask to see it, I would if I were her. I hesitate, but declining seems counterproductive to the point I'm trying to make. Deep breath, Sabine. I pull my pant trim down to my waist line and then comes down the compression shorts underneath. Pulling my shirts up exposes a vulnerable side to me. Alma gasps with wide eyes, the next thing I know, her hands are touching and squeezing my stretchy, squishy, big pile of skin. She busts out in happy laughter as she jiggles my fat.

"It flaps like a pancake! I want a pancake belly just like you!" Her eyes are just as wide as the smile on her face.

The three of us break into laughter after Alma's surprisingly silly reaction to such a raw moment. The image of a stomach like mine on her tiny body is unimaginable. Pancake belly. Kids are hilarious. Her innocence with one of my biggest imperfections almost brings me to tears. Brings me to think how people don't see you the way you see yourself. The little fat girl inside me feels seen while Alma enjoys herself in the mystery of my pancake belly, whatever that means. A happy tear falls from my eye, she grabs my head with her miniature hands, pulls it closer and kisses my forehead. Where did this child come from? The heart and compassion she has, incredible. A slight chuckle sigh escapes my lips when she wipes my tear away. My intention was to not make this about me, but she seems to understand my point.

"I get it now. We are all ugly somewhere and it's okay," she acts like a lightbulb came on in her head.

"That's another way to put it. For example, a lot of the time I am so scared to show my belly and underneath my arms and legs because it's not what people think is beautiful. I lose track of sight and forget how amazing I am. Who we are on the inside is more important and you, my dear are worthy," I say as I caress her cheek.

"I like jiggling your fat, it's fun. I still want to be your friend." She giggles while she jiggles.

"Likewise, my beautiful, strong and independent young lady. I better get going. Rest easy sweetheart." I get up from her bed.

"I feel better now. You have to be around in case I forget how awesome I am. When will you come back?!?" Slight panic sets in. "You mom is here to remind you when you forget, silly. Don't you worry, you can't get rid of me that easy. I will be back." I wrap my arms around her.

Alma's medicine starts to kick in, which usually makes her drowsy. The game of life is going to have to wait for real life. I wait until she falls asleep to leave her with her mom by her side. I give a tight squeeze to Joan and carry on to my group meeting.

Here I am, sitting in a chair in the circle. The check in. The group is missing a few people this time around, people must skip often. Does that mean they went back to their ex or they have been miraculously cured? Maybe the check in meetings isn't as popular as ones professionally led by Maliha. My eyes scan the circle is people who conveniently have handwritten name tags stuck to their tops. Hannah, Gregory, Luis, Alistair, Suri and I. Some have a piece of paper out and others are scrolling on their phones.

Suddenly it dawns on me that I forgot to do the at homework assignment. My mind has been occupied with work and depression; the task slipped right through my fingers. It's been a while since I have felt such an uncomfortable feeling, forgetting to complete a homework assignment. Is it still acceptable to say our imaginary dog ate our homework? Missing a task could be misconstrued for not caring or taking the program seriously. My posture adjusts in my seat when I remember I am a grown adult who doesn't need excuses. Maliha Patel wobbles in a few minutes late, but she is ready to start.

"Good afternoon, everyone!" she takes a seat.

"Good afternoon" voices stagger through the group.

"So… last meeting I left you guys with an assignment to write a letter to your ex or partner who committed infidelity. Let's check in. How was it to write the letter? What came up for you? Who wants to read their letter? We will just go around the circle, starting with Hannah. I see some of you totally freaking out. If you are rather new here, assignments are more of a mindfulness check for yourself and if you don't have anything to share for check ins, the assignment normally helps you think of something to share. My apologies if I was unclear." She nods at Hannah for the green light. "I debated on coming today because Jude and I got back together. The feelings that came up while I was writing my letter led me to reaching out to him. I just needed to know why he treats me like that. He ended up coming over and apologizing for everything. This time feels different, it's a hopeful feeling. After our reconciliation, I wrote him a letter of the man I want him to be and gave it to him. He was offended and now we are in this weird stage.

I'm not quite sure how to feel about it, so here I am." Hannah confides in her peers.

Hannah goes on and on about how she feels as if she is too old to start all over to find someone new. She loves him too much to let him go and is hopeful he will change for her. The thing is men or people in general, they don't change for anyone but themselves. Actually, it's quite unfair to expect anyone to change and alter who they are for you. The people they love might be motivation but we all have to choose to do it for ourselves. Jude sounds like he misses the comfort of being in a relationship. He is failing to hold himself accountable for his actions, but she takes him back every time and he doesn't have to learn how to treat her properly.

The man sitting next to Hannah wrote his letter blaming himself for not seeing the signs of being cheated on. His letter was hurtful and harsh to himself, poor guy. A takeaway from being in gender mingled meetings is seeing men be vulnerable and share the same experiences as women. One stereotype in society is that men are always the cheaters who break the woman's heart. An evenly mix of gender in this group proves otherwise. It's more a myth than a stereotype because women are just as bad as men in relationships. Who really knows what they are doing anyway?

A few more people read their letters to the group, pouring their hearts out. Alistair is up next.

"It took some wine and time to get ready to sit down and write this letter. Let me tell you, it was an emotional rollercoaster. Here it goes. Lennox, time was not on our side. At first, we were young and in love but over the years our love ran thin. Marriage isn't easy, it's something couples have to constantly work at. I used to think there was no easy way out, love is worth it. Congratulations, you proved me wrong. Instead of being continuously transparent, you chose to escape. I blamed myself for a long time and thought I wasn't enough but the problem was within you. Our time ran out and we weren't meant....." he chokes up then takes a pause. Alistair continues. "We weren't meant to be. I am still angry and heartbroken. To be honest, I still want to take a baseball bat to your car. You don't deserve nice things. After a while, I realized our separation was a long time coming and your actions sped up the process. I know better is coming for me. Thank you for setting me free. Sincerely, Alistair. This letter doesn't do my feelings and pain justice, but it's all I could do." He finishes.

"The letter you wrote is perfect, from your heart. The purpose of this assignment is to allow you guys to recognize what you are feeling and to allow you to feel them. It's to practice self-awareness. As always, last but not least, Sabine" Maliha pointed with her whole hand.

"I didn't do it," I reply as guilt surrounds my heart like it did in school when I missed an assignment.

"It's okay, like I said its more of guide. Would you like to check in?" Maliha asks with compassion.

"This whole situation is still so new and fresh. I don't know how to feel and the same time I am feeling everything. To be completely honest, there are times I hate him and other times I miss him. Deep down, I never want to see him again. The story changes when I'm sobbing in bed at three in the morning watching a romantic movie to torture myself. I guess, I grieve more the life I wanted for us then him." My voice is soft.

"Yeah, that's how I felt every time. I wanted him, but then I didn't. It's mind boggling, for sure. It does get better with time," Hannah adds.

"Just knowing that you are all over the place is a start. These aren't strangers you are dealing with and you wouldn't be here if you didn't love and care for them. It's not normal to be perfectly fine after a breakup, and then you add infidelity? No way, not a chance," Maliha states.

"Millions of people get cheated on, I'm surprised we as a whole we don't talk about it more openly. You just hear people bashing and being self-destructive. No one should go through this alone, let alone anything," Alistair chimes in, fidgeting with his chair.

"Yeah, I agree. It's rough," Gregory adds.

The conversation continues to flow and people continue to share and connect. Alistair brings up a great question. What do we do when we run into our exes? How should we feel? How do we keep our composer? Hannah jokes about reconnecting with Jude every time she sees him. The simple answer is there is no right way. Do whatever feels right to you in that moment because running into people you know, especially people you want to avoid is inevitable. Who would have thought that bonding with these guys would be a great time?

"Great work today, everyone. Next meeting, we will be discussing self-destructive behaviors and forms of self-care. Of course, check ins as well. If you're up for the challenge, I want you to write down five things you do for self-care and five ways you personally do that can be considered self-destructive. Have a wonderful day!" Maliha dismisses the meeting.

Everyone gets up to put the chairs away and clean up as usual. The meeting was intense this morning. Somehow, I feel closer to people I didn't know a week ago. It feels good to have been around people who understand what I am going through. My phone dings with a text from Ophelia as I stack chairs.

Ophelia: Hey Sabine. You can totally say no but something personal came up with Maddy and I can't work on Thursday. I checked the schedule and you're off that day. Can we switch shifts? I will work yours today and you take Thursday's night shift?

My life has freed recently with the events that happened, and I have nothing to do. Why not?

Me: Yes, of course. Please make sure Dr. Hu is informed.

Have a great day, Phee.

"Hey Sabine! A few of us are going to Kkoki Korean BBQ, would you like to join?" Hannah approaches.

"Yes, we would love for you to come!" Luis yells from across the room.

"Looks like my shift was just switched anyways. I would love to.

Thank you for the invite, Hannah." I smile.

The restaurant is on the other side of Cedar Mills. This place is nearly empty, weird considering its seven-thirty in the evening. Hannah walks in with her boyfriend, the cheating boyfriend. Maybe I shouldn't judge because I think about taking Joseph back sometimes. I mean, it's a little weird to go to an infidelity support group and hang out after with your cheating boyfriend. It's just like telling your friends all the terrible things your man does and then you all hang out like everything is dandy. We get a table for six in the back of the restaurant. Hannah, her boyfriend Jude, Luis,

Alistair and I sit around a big circular booth in the back. Maliha is supposed to join, but it looks like she didn't make it.

The energy is different with Alistair considering he never texted me back the other day. I feel stupid for reaching out, maybe he was just trying to be nice when he gave me his number. Hannah is a bubbly and a chipper person with cute hoop piercing wrapped around her nostril. She is talking our ears off about a new fashion line her boss designed while Jude is oblivious on his phone.

Luis is fascinated with her story, or maybe her. The way he looks at her is the *look* you observe from the movies. The *look*. His body language and attention are dead giveaways for signs of admiration. If her and Jude don't work out, she might not be doomed for a lonely life.

Occasionally, my eyes wander and meet Alistair's, I can feel him looking at me. It's unknown how much longer we can avoid speaking to each other. Nothing happened between the time he gave me his number and now, besides my text. Does he judge me? Why do I even care? The food arrives with another round of drinks for everyone. The waiter places two hot plates of Mul Mandu and Topokki in front of us. We take a few more minutes to eat the appetizers and decide on the main course.

"Hey, would you like to share the beef tripe or sausage casserole with me? It's more of a two-person meal." Alistair breaks our silence with a tap to my arm.

"That sounds great. I could grub on some Gopchang Jeongol," I struggle to say the name of the dish.

"Sabine, what do you do for work? I overheard you got your shift switched," Luis breaks the silence after we all order dinner.

"I am a nurse in the Neonatal Intensive Care unit at Cedar Mills Hospital. I work a lot so it's nice to get an unexpected day off," I respond.

"No way! My brother works there. Do you know Rodrigo Del Leon?" he asks with excitement.

"No, I don't know him. I feel like I've read his name before though." Small world.

"I bet you get major baby fever working in the NICU," Hannah jokes.

"Big time! I love to hold them when I have downtime. It's good for the babies to be held and have touch, me too." I smile sweetly at that thought.

"Maybe I should volunteer to come and hold some babies. It's year three with having baby fever and who knows when I'll get the chance," Alistair speaks up.

"I can look into it if you want. They might have a volunteer program for that actually. I believe it's called the cuddler program," I offer.

"Wow, all we needed to do was get cheated on to meet each

other." Hannah giggles and Jude tenses up.

The evening continues to flow with light conversation while we all finish our meals. The check comes split in four ways. I look at my watch. We've been here for a couple of hours, where did the time go? I could get used to this. Learning about these guys on a more personal level is an interesting time. This is my new life now, should be embracing it. Before we all get up and go our separate ways, Alistair invites everyone to go to the Spirit Halloween store with him. He needs to go and look for a Mike Wazoski from Monsters Inc. costume for his nephew. Everyone declines because it's getting later in the day and they have things to do.

"What about you Ms. Spooky?" he turns to me.

"Yeah, okay I'm down." I take the opportunity to bond and maybe dissolve our awkward energy problem.

Alistair begs to drive Bugsby, so we take my car and leave his at the restaurant. This is a great opportunity to look around and get ideas for my costume this year. There are no plans as of yet but who knows, no one wants to be alone on any holiday. He looks extremely happy to be driving my grandpa's old vintage car, his smile is priceless. The Spirit store is packed with all kinds of things like costumes, accessories, decorations, people and anything else you can imagine. Now, I just have to decide on a goofy costume or slutty. Last year, my body was a lot bigger and was more comfortable dressing goofy. I was a gumball machine. My top was covered in colorful pompom balls with a long red skirt. A sign was in the top middle of the skirt with a twenty-five-cent sticker, a turning handle and the part where the gumball comes it. The homemade gumball machine costume was a hit and a great conversation starter. Just as he suspected, the Mike Wazowski costume is in plain side in the children's section. He grabbed one and meets me in the adult women's sections.

"'In Girl World, Halloween is the one day a year when a girl can dress up like a total slut and no other girls can say anything else about it.'" Alistair recited a quote from the movie "Mean Girls," word for word.

"Wow, that's impressive," surprised he knows it.

"Well, it's the most quotable movie I know. Look at all the sexy, slutty costumes. I didn't think you were that kind of costume wearer," he looks me up and down.

"Hey. Hey, don't judge me Mr. Judgy. I'm just browsing anyways. Any costume can be made from home. There is no way I am paying for a Seventy-dollar costume," I scoff at the price tags. "Halloween is serious business for you. I dig it," he smirks. "Oh, it's very serious business," emphasizing on the word serious and smile.

"What do you do on Halloween? Throw a huge house party filled with people in wild costumes?" he's curious.

"No, no, no. I am more of a low-key kind of girl and like to hang with the people I love. I wanted to go to the Halloween Town event in ST. Helens this year. Been wanting to go for years and Joseph refused to go and we got into a stupid argument about it. Look where we are now." My voice comes out sadder than intended.

"You are anything, but low key Sabi. Seems like you can be shy and loud at the same time." His tone comforting.

He called me Sabi. We spend an hour exploring the store and playing with the accessories and displays they put out for advertisement. The killer clowns with blood dripping from their vampire teeth have to be my favorite exhibit. I'm posing for a selfie with the zombie baby with one arm to send to my coworkers. Yes, dark humor cures.

"Boo!" Alistair jumps out and growls in front of me making my heart drop to my stomach.

The grown man child takes the mask off and drops to the floor in a full laughing attack. Just like that, all the awkwardness has vanished. I can't help but laugh at my embarrassing screaming reaction. By the looks on some of the others in the store, they are amused. We continue to model the costumes and disgusting masks to laugh our asses off at each other. I cannot remember the last time I had this much fun, my belly is sore. Alistair purchases the monster costume for his nephew while I buy a few packs of Halloween stickers. Then, he drives Bugsby back to the restaurant to go our separate ways in the end of a good night. The thought of asking him about the unanswered text runs through my mind a few times on the way back, but decide to let it go. He could have just forgotten or maybe he didn't have time to open it. Some people are really bad at texting, but great conversationalists in person. He is incredibly entertaining in person. He parks next to his classy, black, Range Rover, we both get out and he goes in for a hug. A hug from someone this tall feels like a nice comfy cloud. Not to mention his cologne smells like man heaven.

"Hey. I gave you my number last time, but forgot to get yours. I could use a sponsor sometimes too." He smiles and still has his hands on my hips.

"You should have my number, I texted you and you never

responded," my heart races waiting to see what he says.

"I did not get a text from you. Texts are kind of hard to miss, don't you think?" His eyebrow raised.

"No, I really did." I take out my phone and show him.

"Let me see. Do you have the right number?" He takes the phone from my hand.

"The last number is supposed to be a three, not a seven." He fixes it.

"Well, that's embarrassing." I awkwardly look down.

"Don't worry about it. I'll see you next meeting Sabine. Try not

to miss me!" He smiles sarcastically with spirit fingers.

He has no clue of the mental torture I put myself through when there was no text back. Stupid number seven. At least it's a little comforting to know it was all in my head. Alistair comes across put together, it's surprising he would need or want a "*sponsor.*" Wow, looks like we already have our own little inside joke. An alert sound from my phone as I pull in to park.

Alistair: Hey, just saw this. Sorry for the late reply. My bad.

He is quite the character, Alistair Barker. We are going to be great friends.

CHAPTER 6

Sebastian is slowly getting better every day, it's almost time for him to be discharged and take on the world. He's so close, yet so far. His lungs are finally starting to develop into healthy lungs from his treatments. There is a part of any caretaking job when it's sad to see your patients leave, especially the favorites. In this case, it's a miracle when babies get to go home for the first time with their parents. Sebastian has a single mom who doesn't come see him as much as she should. Karen Osgood. She had to go back to work full time to support her and her new baby boy. The hospital bills are going to kill her bank account and future financial goals for a long time. Unfortunately, the American Health Care system needs an abundance of change. She comes when she can and that's all we can hope for. I can't wait to have a little one to call my own and watch them grow up. The loud sound of crying means the babies lungs are strong. Sebastian's lungs are strong and fully developed, he is loud and clear. He needs a diaper change, I'm on it.

"How was support group? Did you go back?" Xavier walks up to me with a new diaper.

"How did you know I went?" His question catches me off guard.

"Oh… uh I just assumed." He backtracks while being completely obvious.

"How did you know I went?" Firmly repeating my question.

"Alistair Barker, you met him I assume. We have mutual friends."

He cautiously responds.

"I see anonymous means nothing," feeling uncomfortable.

"Don't get weird girl, he would never share anything. That is not something he would do. I just told him to look out for a girl of your description. I haven't talked to him since. Just wanted to make sure you didn't feel alone," Xavier explains.

"Yeah, he's my sponsor," a giggle escapes my lips.

"Sponsor for what? I don't think that's a thing for this type of support group. Did you go to the wrong type of meeting?" he chuckles.

"Hey. Have some faith in me. What do you know about Alistair anyway?" My curiosity is peaked.

"I know that he is going to be a recently divorced, sexy, eligible bachelor. I was Lennox's friend before they got together, but Alistair gets me in the divorce. Maybe he needs a new husband," Xavier smirks at me.

"Let him get over the old one first," I laugh.

"Don't tell me what to do." Xavier winks and leaves the room.

What a small world we live in. What are the odds these two men know each other and I happen to know them both? This support group could be a good opportunity for my journey and I don't want any chance of drama or my personal business being spread through my community. I don't think Alistair would do that, but then again, he's a stranger. If I won't be able to stay out my head for long, I will have to find another support group. The big point of it is the anonymous part.

The vibration coming from the apple watch around my wrist put my thought chain to a halt. My shift is over. I pass along a few notes to the nurse taking over my patients. My work mailbox is full, it's been days since I've last checked it. The bundle has a couple of work notices, an October event calendar and a folded paper with my name on it. I unfold the piece of paper and it's a colored wonder woman picture from Alma in room 386. She is the sweetest little girl in the world, so bright. I fold the picture back and put it in my bag, and set a reminder to go visit her again when I get the chance. My apple watch starts to vibrate again, but someone is calling.

"Hey, Alistair!" I answer the phone with a racing heartbeat.

"Hey, I have tickets to a comedy show; I was supposed to go with Lennox, but we both know that story. Would you like to go? It's Bert Kreischer, he's a good time," he firmly asks.

"I appreciate the offer, but I don't need you to pity me. I know Xavier mentioned me to you." I respond letting Xavier get in my head.

"I don't pity you. Would it make you feel better that you were the last person I asked, the last resort?" he responds.

"A little," I smile to myself.

"I'll pick you up around 7. Don't wear pity party attire, we are going to a comedy club. Dress normal, Sabi. Also, text me your address, please." He chuckles.

"Normal? Whatever do you mean?" I laugh with sarcasm and hang up the phone.

Look at me now, making new friends and going out to experience life just as I wanted. Joseph bought us tickets one time for a comedy show, but his brother heard about them and invited himself to my ticket. The comedian was an hour late and a few shots deep in a bottle of hard liquor. Comedians are funny because most of them have tragic history to make content from. Some say stand-up comedy can be therapeutic for the jokers.

I have two hours until Alistair will show up at my place to go to the show. I rush home to shower and get ready for a long overdue night out with a new friend. There's an envelope with my name on the front, under my front door as I walk into the apartment. The clock is ticking and getting ready has to be my top priority. I throw the envelope on the kitchen counter and rush to get butt naked for a quick shower. Time to not look like shit. Things to do before he arrives: pick outfit, shower, shave, hair and makeup. Rummaging through my closet to find the perfect spooky outfit for this occasion, have to represent. Then, I envision the perfect outfit in my head and grab the shirt, skirt, socks and booties. My shower is lukewarm as usual, my legs are as smooth as a baby's bottom, sweet bliss. It's been forever, the razor and my legs needed a reintroduction.

After my shower, Whitney Houston sings *I wanna dance with somebody* to me through the speaker of the phone. My towel drops to the floor and my body starts to move wild and free to the words and beat of one of my favorite songs. Adrenaline pumps through my veins as my body wiggles and jiggles as free as can be. Shaking my hips, jumping and twirling around, flipping my hair. I'm feeling myself right now. Killing two birds with one stone with dancing and air drying at the same time. My outfit consists of a yellow chuckie tee with black sleeve rims, a thigh high waisted black skirt and black knee socks. Face is freshly made up with the natural eyeshadow look, dark maroon lipstick, and perfectly winged eyeliner. Perfectly winged eyeliner is magic. Black squared framed glasses rest on the bridge of my nose and the summit of my ears. I finish straightening my hair and pose in the mirror with my fully glam look.

"Sabine, you are one hot spooky fox!" I flirt with my reflection.

Alistair: I'm here.

Last glance at the envelope with my name on it one last time before leaving the apartment. It could be anything in that envelope that has a chance to ruin a perfectly planned evening, not today, Satan. One handsome Alistair Barker sits in his car waiting for my arrival. He's wearing a maroon jacket over a pink tie-dyed hoodie, accidently matching my lip color. His pants are dark blue jeans with vertical white stripes down the legs. I haven't been out with a new friend in a long time, it's refreshing and nerve racking at the same time.

We talk about his life a little and that his parents are teachers and how he wanted to follow in their footsteps, but realized he has a different calling. He has one sister who owns her own business in the baby industry after having her son. Business is booming for her after making a deal on the Tv show Shark Tank with America's favorite shark. He played basketball since he was eight through his college years.

"So, you know what I do. What do you do for work?" I ask. "Great question. I am a substance abuse and addiction counselor. Far off from a teacher." He smiles to myself.

"That's why you're so good at this whole support group thing! To think I thought you were a natural. Not too far off at all, your job is to support and educate, right? What inspired your career choice?" I ask.

"Another great question. Growing up, I had eating disorders and an unhealthy addiction with the gym and working out. I had an offer to play professional basketball, but I wasn't right in the mind at the time. After college and basketball ending, came the alcohol addiction. Here I am today. I have never once regretted anything because I believe everything happens for a reason, you know?" His answer is the most honest one I've ever heard.

"Wow, thank you for sharing that with me. I have to say that looking at you and being around you lately, I would have never known. You're so golden." I'm in awe.

"You can paint anything gold if you wanted to. Everyone has things they struggle with and have to overcome. Trust me, I struggle too. What about you? What's your why?" He reverses the question back to me.

"I have always known I've wanted to help people and enter into the medical field. My father has always pushed aggressively, hard for me to follow in his footsteps in becoming a doctor, which led me to denying the doctor life all together. I became a nurse because it would be my choice and not something someone wanted me to do. To my shocking surprise, I fell madly in love with the NICU. Here I am today, everything happens for a reason." I feel gratitude towards my journey.

"Your dad still pushes the medical school thing, huh?" Alistair laughs.

"Oh yeah, hardcore!" I laugh with him.

We pull up to the venue and the outside is crowded with fans waiting to get into the show. The lines run long due to security, but we are early.

"I love your fit, girl," a random woman compliments my attire as we get in the back of the line.

"Thank you!" I smile.

"Yeah, you look great. Someone cleans up nice," Alistair finally comments on my look as he playfully nudges my shoulder with his fist.

Alistair gasps before I can thank him for his compliment. There isn't anything crazy going on, which confuses me. No one fainted or nothing shocking has happened. He looks as if he spotted a ghost nearby, his body stiffens. My eyes scan the area to figure out what Alistair is looking at. A rather good-looking man wearing a green beanie, white t-shirt, jeans and has a thick mustache growing on his upper lip.

"Is that...." I speak before the interruption.

"Lennox," he finishes my question.

"He's coming. Deep breath Alistair." My hand meets his lower back for comfort.

"Hey, stranger." Lennox and a woman approach us.

"Hi. Hello, Miranda. I didn't think I would see you here," Alistair greets them.

"What? Did you think I was going to miss it? It was my idea. I didn't think you would show up. Especially with a date. You move fast, Al!" Lennox has passive aggressive energy.

"Don't make a scene, enjoy the show," Alistair responds and shrugs off the attitude.

"First of all, you messed up, not him. Second of all, you move on fast. You lost with this tall, hunky, apple tree that can turn into delicious apple pie," I couldn't hold it in.

"This is my sister. This isn't your business anyways."

He gives the dirtiest look.

"It's nice to meet you, Miranda. I'm Sabine, Alistair's friend. I hope you two enjoy the show," I awkwardly engage and walk away with Alistair.

"Sorry, I couldn't let him talk to you like that. Are you okay?" I whisper to Alistair as we sit down.

"Hopefully, I will be after I start laughing my ass off in a few minutes. Do me a favor and don't try and fight my battles for me, it wasn't your place to do that. I appreciate you caring. I am really glad you are here." He his eyes grow serious for a split second.

"Me, too," trying not to let my embarrassment overpower me.

Lennox McCann is an attractive man with a bad attitude. He is not cute enough to be acting like that. It's awkward running into an ex, especially when it did not end on good or cordial terms. How is he so cool, calm and collected? Alistair's maturity showed up tonight, apparently, I have a lot to work on.

The lights go off and a bright spotlight turns on facing the stage. The audience quiets down because the show is about to begin. Bert Kreischer walks on stage with a microphone and a glass of water. He puts his water on the stool and dramatically rips his shirt off.

"What's up Oregonians! How are we doing tonight?" he asks and the crowd goes wild.

Bert Kreischer struts his stage with his microphone and does his thing. He does it well, this guy is hilarious. His poor wife and kids, they have to have some thick skin to be his comedy muses. Their household has to be a wild circus, sounds like a dream to me. This night out is exactly what I need. The laughs. The entertainment. The whiskey. The company. Lennox and Miranda sit a few rows up and to the right. Subtle glances back from Lennox to Alistair. This has got to be weird for my new friend. I keep on my best behavior and tame my inner lioness in order to not cross his boundaries again. Here we are a few drinks later listening to the final cheers of the audience as the comedian's set ends. To no one's surprise, Lennox hollers to catch up to us in the parking lot.

"Al, I'm sorry." Lennox's eyes have the same alcohol glaze as us.

"Thank you, but there's no coming back from it. I'm happy now. I've had all the closure in the world, babe." He obliviously yells out the world with his arms out to endless lengths.

"Lennox come on. The babysitter isn't going to stay all night."

Miranda nudges her guest in the whiniest of voices.

"I'm sure you're a great father," Alistair loosely spills the secret of his social media stalking.

"I'm sorry." Lennox eyes water.

Miranda yanks Lennox away without any further conversation. No boundaries were crossed on my end this time, but they left me speechless. Golden is an illusion of the mind. The golden boy is left here in the parking lot with me, heart's shredded to pieces. His sigh feels heavy in the air. We have to sit in the car for a few hours till the alcohol wears, might as well talk it out.

"Thank you for inviting me tonight, I couldn't sit in that tainted apartment alone again," I said.

"Hey, I'm here for you." I add when I notice his mind is elsewhere.

"Lennox doesn't have a sister." Alistair is overruled with sadness and for the first time, he is completely exposed in front of me.

CHAPTER 7

"Hey Martha, is there a program for volunteers to come and hold the healing babies? I know they get volunteers for the older kids in the playroom." Walking up to the front desk.

"I know there has been a few people who have come for that reason, but I don't think there is a program. You'll have to ask Dr. Hu about it because I was transferred to this department recently. Don't quote me on it." She generously shared.

"Thank you! That pumpkin sweater looks really cute on you, by the way." I smile and head for the back.

Today, the hospital is having a Halloween holiday party in the cafeteria for long-term patients and their families. Today is the only day the hospital approved for the party, even though Halloween is so close, but so far. We will take it. The holiday parties here are very successful events to boost morale. The cafeteria is heavily decorated, games are set up, treats baked, and low volume festive background music. Pumpkin walking is next to witchy ring toss, and face painting is across the area. Smells of fresh baked cookies loom in the air. Multiple people are working hard to finish putting the room together in time for the party goers to show up. Unfortunately, some nurses and doctors have to miss the party due to working and having have patients to take care of. Occasionally, they stop by on their breaks to mingle and watch the kids overdose in happiness.

"Hey missy, you're looking better these days. How have you been?" Ophelia side hugs my body.

"I am slowly doing better, thanks for asking. How are you? How are Bennet and Maddy?" I ask about her children.

"Girl, let me tell you. Bennet has his first girlfriend and Maddy is on her school's cheer team. Kids grow up so fast. I don't know where the time goes." She has disbelief written on her face.

"Thirteen and already a ladies' man huh? I'm glad your kids are doing great. Actually, speaking of kids, do you know if we have a volunteer program to hold babies?" taking the opportunity to see if she knows.

"That's a weird way to ask. A program to hold babies. We do have the cuddler volunteer program. I'm surprised you don't know about it." She laughs.

"You knew what I was talking about, didn't ya?" I laugh with her.

"I'm sure they have information on it in reception or maybe Dr. Hu does," she informs.

"Got it, thanks. Dr. Hu must be the man with the answer." I pat her arm and walk away.

A nine-year-old boy hooked to an IV, tugs on my pant leg. He's got a freshly shaved head and a feeding tube attached to the side of his adolescent stomach. The blue in his eyes sparkle as loud as his sweet crooked smile. His hand takes mine and pulls me towards the face painting booth. I look at the identification badge around his wrist, his name is Oscar. We sit down in the chairs next to the table filled with paint pallets. He doesn't let go of my hand the whole time he gets his face painted. I try to talk to him, but he doesn't want to speak with words. What he wants is comfort. Most of these kids crave affection because sitting in a hospital room all day every day is isolating and lonely. The faculty come to the hospital to work, but this is our patient's temporary home. Oscar smiles big when the lady shows him his reflection in the mirror. A big spiderweb and spiders cover the right side of his face. He gets up from his chair and wraps his skinny arms around my shoulders into a colossal hug and goes on his way. He never said a word. It's the little things about this job that brings light into my world.

"Hey, we've never seen you at one of these cheesy parties."

Raquel and Finley approach me with another man I've never seen.

"I love Halloween, what can I say." I awkwardly shrug my shoulders.

"Hi, I'm Duke Vaughn." The mystery man reaches his hand out to greet me.

"He's a real doctor. She's just a nurse." Finley informs the man.

"Just a nurse, have some respect kid. Hospitals couldn't function without our nurses." He gently puts Finley in his place.

"He's just mad, she rejected him in the kid play room" Raquel laughs at her friend.

"Where is Taylor and your other friend?" I ask.

"Taylor is sick today and Ying is a lucky one. He got to go home."

Finley answers with envy.

"You'll get your turn, don't worry. Both of you will," I comfort the teens.

"Who wants to get beat at webbed ring toss?" Dr. Vaughn proposes a challenge.

"You're going down!" Taylor turns competitive.

Suddenly, noises, gasps and yelling come from across the cafeteria. Everyone looks around for the source of the commotion. A woman lays on the ground in the middle of a circle of people hovering over her. Food is everywhere, she must have knocked a plate over trying to catch herself before she fell. She has no control of her body, it's stiff while involuntarily shaking. Her eyes roll back with sweat dripping down her face. The young children standing around begin to cry and whine from being scared, they go through enough. They don't need to see this. Taylor, Finley and the adults standing around guide the kids to the other side of the room until this situation is handled. The woman on the floor looks familiar, it's Karen Osgood. Duke and I rush to gently put her on her side. A man nearby takes his sweater off and places it underneath her head for safe comfort. She lays unconscious after her body stops seizing. Dr. Vaughn and two nurses help as she gains consciousness, while I finish clearly the area and kicking everything out of the way.

"Montgomery," Karen manages to get a word out. "Isn't that your name?" Dr. Vaughn questions me.

All three of them look up at me, Karen and I lock eyes. She falls back into the nurse's arms and becomes unresponsive. Why did she say my name? I think I heard her correctly. Why was my name the first thing out of her mouth? My heart is beating out of my chest, scared for her health, but feeling exposed. A gurney heads towards us to take Ms. Osgood to the emergency room. This is the best possible place for something medically wrong to happen to anyone, she's in good hands. After the staff wheels her away, it dawns on me to question why she is here in the first place, considering her son can't attend this party. Her attendance doesn't make sense, is she here for me? I start to follow them to the emergency room when one of the nurses taking care of Karen advise me to not visit her until they figure out why she called out my name. There is no way this woman can be a danger to me, I'm one of her son's care takers. Unless, she has ill feelings about me caring for her son more than her at the moment, but it's my job. A few minutes fly by and everyone has returns to a light and calm state of mind for the festivities. Made my rounds a couple more times before getting ready to head out for the night, feeling uneasy.

"Dr. Montgomery," a little girl tapped me on my lower back.

"Hi!" To my surprise it's Alma.

"I'm a nurse silly!" Our hands link together.

"Did you get the picture I sent to you? They never told me if it arrived or not." Her face is hopeful.

"Yes, I did get the perfectly colored picture. It was a wonderful surprise. Thank you, Alma. I hung it on my fridge at home. Are you enjoying the party?" I ask.

"I just got here. I saw them wheeling a woman away. Is she going to be okay?" She asks.

"She will be just fine. I will stop by your room to see you soon because I got you something," my face lit up.

"You did?" her excitement level went from thirty to one hundred.

"You're going to love it. It was nice seeing you Alma. Sorry, I have to go check on a friend of mine. I will see you later!" I promise. Alma gives me a big hug and we go our separate ways. I didn't need to check on Karen, but there is no reason to break the girl's heart. While it's on my mind, it has been a long enough time for Karen's test results to come back with what is wrong with her. Hopefully, it is nothing serious, Sebastian needs his mother. Walking to the emergency is a little nerve-racking thinking about the possibilities. My plan is to ask a nurse or doctor around if they have any information. The emergency team constantly have their hands full, but the selfish part of me needs to know what is going on. The first person I ask just started their shift and didn't know anything so I head for the floor reception desk.

"Hello Harpreet, could you tell me any information on a new

patient, Karen Osgood?" asking the nosey question.

"The woman who was just admitted a few hours ago? Who are you?" she's doing her job.

"My name is Sabine Montgomery; I am a nurse in the NICU. Karen is one of my patients' mother." I flash my badge.

"I'm sorry Ms. Montgomery, but you know out of all the people about confidentiality, the words spill from her mouth.

"Does it help that she is also my cousin?" I lie horribly through my teeth, but she gets the hint.

"You seem like a genuine woman, don't make me regret this nurse Montgomery. Now, family needs to know. She's going to need your support. Looks like she suffered a seizure triggered by stress. Great news, the baby was unharmed! Yeah, she's going to need a lot of support." The nurse seems to believe me and spills the tea.

Those words hit me like a ton of bricks, she's pregnant. Maybe she was coming to share her big news with the staff. That would make sense why she showed up without any reason. It's not healthy to carry heavy stress while pregnant, especially to the point of your brain malfunctioning. I wonder if she knows she is pregnant.

I hear Karen from across the hall saying "that's her."

A new nurse walks out of the room and calls me in the room for a conversation with Karen. I walk into the room with no expectations.

"Ms. Osgood, how are you feeling?" my tone is soft and sweet.

"I'm okay. I can't believe all of this is happening. I didn't know I was pregnant and yet I've been trying to lose weight. I've been trying for a new baby with this new guy I've been seeing. I want a healthy baby th........" Karen starts to seize.

I yell for help right away, without touching anything. She is not my patient. A few nurses and a doctor rush in and order me to leave the room for them to do their job. I comply and head for the door before a thought came to my head. There is something I needed to accomplish today.

"Hello again," I greet Harpreet.

"What can I do for you?" she asks pleasantly.

"Do you happen to have the flyer or packet on the Cuddler Program?" My spirit runs hopeful.

"I don't have any copies, but if you want to wait a few minutes I can print a copy." She offers.

"I would love that, thank you." I go and sit down on the bench in the hallway.

The short conversation with Karen runs freely through my head. She thinks that she should have another baby and hope for a healthy one because Sebastian is fighting for his life. That is one of the most twisted things I have ever heard in my line of work. I wonder where the conversation would have gone if she didn't have a seizure. She needs to pull through for not only herself, but for Sebastian and her new unborn child. No way she can abandon her first born son. Harpreet calls me over to retrieve the papers.

"Thank you for everything, you didn't have to bend the rules. I appreciate it. Don't forget to check out the party on your break." I give her a big thank you handshake over the desk.

"You seem harmless. Parties aren't really my scene, plus I'm heading out of town when I get off," she replies.

She might be my new favorite coworker, technically coworker. When I get to my car, I send a picture of the papers to Alistair letting him know that I have a present for him. He replies with the heart eyes emoji.

CHAPTER 8

"Sometimes when we are not self-aware enough, we won't realize some of the things we do can be self-destructive. For example, staying up till three in the morning, not showering for days, canceling on your plans often are all acts of self-destruction. Now, if you are now realizing these patterns, don't beat yourself up. We are all human. Your homework assignment was assigned to you to bring awareness to your action. Who wants to share what they do for self-care or a self-destructive pattern?" Maliha asks the group.

"I would like to share first," my hand raises itself, traitor.

"Cheers to your first time sharing first. Go for it, Sabine," she tries to hide her pleasantly surprised reaction.

"A few things I do for self-care is going on walks, drink water and rock some of my patient babies to sleep. They are babies in my NICU. I sometimes think they heal me more than I heal them. Some of my habits that can be labeled as self-destructive is staying in bed all day on my days off, drinking a bottle of wine at 10 in the morning after one of these wonderful meetings, or mentally beating myself up on a daily basis." I laid it all out there and told on myself, no shame in my game today.

"Wow, Sabine. A plus for you today. Can anyone relate to what she shared with us?" Maliha asks the group.

"Yes definitely," Alistair smiles at me.

"Yes, I struggle with mentally beating myself up and then I mentally beat myself up about mentally beating myself up," Gregory sounds stressed.

"Been there!" Luis theatrically snaps his fingers.

"Also, a self-destructive behavior is the act of constantly getting back with your cheating liar ex-boyfriend that never changes!" Hannah word vomits everywhere.

"Okay, want to unpack that?" Maliha encourages Hannah to talk about it.

"It turns out Jude was texting a few girls behind my back when we all went to breakfast and he said it was just coworkers talking about work issues. Then, one of them calls in the middle of the night and I answered, realized it was one of the girls he cheated on me with before. I woke him up straight away and kicked him out. I blocked his number and everything, haven't seen him since. I'm done." She huffs and puffs while crossing her arms.

"I am so sorry Hannah; he doesn't deserve you." I put my hand on her shoulder for comfort and she leans over to rest her head next to mine.

"The thing is I don't think I deserve better. No one wants damaged goods," she starts crying into my shoulder.

"Everything is going to be okay Hannah." I calmly caress her head while she cries.

"Everything will be okay." Luis walks over and take her from me to hold her.

"It's funny because the morning after I found out he cheated on me, I went for a run and had a full-blown mental breakdown in the park and a woman came up to me with her son and just sat there and held me while I ugly cried all over her in front of her son listening to the ABC's. I swore I saw an angel that day. Now watching Hannah, we need more space to just let go and release the built-up emotion. I'm not saying for everyone to start crying in each other's arms like crazy people, but maybe ask for someone you trust to hold you." My passion glows off my words.

"That is an outstanding suggestion!" Maliha looks at me with a proud mom look.

"So how do we just simply choose not to self-sabotage? I don't know about you guys but I don't know when I'm even doing it half the time." Luis speaks up.

"Great question, Luis. Unfortunately, we can't break bad habits we aren't aware of. The first thing is to start paying attention to yourself, be aware of what you are doing. When you start to notice the habits that you would like to change, it's simply a choice to stop doing it in the moment. For example, when you realize that you've been in bed for four hours during the day, take a second and get it. It's all about mindfulness and noticing and choosing," Maliha answers Luis's question.

"Why do you make it sound so easy? It's not easy," Hannah whines.

"It's far from easy, but each moment is a new moment. If you messed up today, then tomorrow is a brand-new day. If you messed up this morning, this afternoon is great for new healthy choices. When you find yourself wanting to binge drink or call your ex, stop and breathe, choose what's best for you in that moment," Maliha further explains.

Another hour goes by with everyone talking, sharing and learning. After the meeting is over, we all do our routine clean up session. Who would have thought I would look forward to coming to these meetings, I for sure didn't? There is an abundance of love, care and compassion in this group that is addictingly healthy. Before heading out, Maliha approaches me with a hug to let me know how proud she is of me. A part of me feels proud of myself, which feels weird because I am only in the first stages on recovery. Sometimes it really does feel like an AA meeting. Alistair comes over and wraps his long arms around me from behind when I open my car door.

"I will see you later, right?" he asks while I turn around to face him.

"Yes, you will. Are you excited for your first day as a cuddler volunteer?" I curiously ask.

"Hell yeah. I'm ready to get my cuddle on. Just you watch, you might start to get a little jealous," he smirks.

"In your wildest dream pretty boy. I have to go. My shift starts soon." I hug him and hop in my car.

"See you later boss," he salutes me as I drive away.

What was that? Alistair is an extremely friendly person, but I don't think I am blind. He was flirting. Am I going crazy? I drive straight to work and change my clothes in the employee locker room. This morning started my day off great with a great meeting and connection with my group of friends. A smile creeps up on my face when I think about it being Alistair's first day at the hospital. Ophelia approaches me in the locker room after I finish up changing, her face looks concerning.

"Are you okay?" I attend to her.

"You're going to want to sit down for this," she responds in a serious tone.

"Okay, stop. You're scaring me, O." My heart starts to race as I sit down.

"Sebastian fell really ill early this morning. He's even dropped weight. Dr. Hu said it's not looking good. I needed to tell you before your shift because you need to collect yourself to do your job, do you hear me Sab?" she's talking to me, but I can't hear anything.

"Do you hear me?" she repeats.

"Yes. Give me a minute alone, please," I ask and she grants the wish.

My heart sinks to my stomach and eyes fill with tears. There is no holding it all in, it all comes out. Sadness and anger flow out with the tears running down my face. I get up without thinking and kick a locker, the question "how is this fair?" aggressively flies out.

A few minutes before my shift starts, I collect myself and clock in for work. It's obvious I've been crying by the looks of my red and puffy eyes, but I don't care what people think about me today. It's not about me when my shift starts, it's about the patients.

My first question as I walk in, is if Karen Osgood been notified of the condition her son is in. She was discharged from the hospital a week ago and no one has seen her since. Dr. Hu informs us that he can't get ahold of Karen and has tried multiple times. My first instinct is that she abandoned her child, but I knock an ounce of logical sense into my brain. She would never abandon her son; she will be back. Sebastian doesn't look good. He has a sliver of hope in making it out alive. What was his purpose on this earth? He can't be destined to show up, suffer and leave. Dr. Hu took me off Sebastian's case because he felt I was too emotionally involved. There are no grounds to argue with him, plus he is my boss.

Tamara Lewin goes in for heart surgery today and we are all expecting good news for her. Hopefully, this surgery will help lead her towards going home with her loving parents. One of the machines attached to her starts to malfunction, we quickly swap it for a new machine. We always have machines on standby in case of situations like this happen. It's time to prep Tamara for surgery, wipe her down and wheel her to the operating room. My job is to prep her and send her off in good spirits, she's in good hands with Dr. Lujan.

"Hottie 3 o'clock," Ophelia nudges me.

"What?" I look up and see Alistair walking in for his first day.

"Oh, God!" I add.

"God is right baby." She can't take her eyes off of him.

"He's gay," I try to break her gaze, but it doesn't work.

"Hello. My name is Alistair Barker. I am here to volunteer in the cuddler program," he informs Pam before he notices us gawking at him. He looks up and waves.

"Don't tell me you know him." Ophelia's jaw drops.

"Yeah, he's a friend." I shrug it off like it's no big deal.

"Did you see the way he just looked at you? No way that man is strictly dickly." Ophelia body checks him again.

"Ophelia!!" Now my jaw is on the floor in embarrassment. "Sounds like you got a little thing for Mr. Cuddler." She smirks. "

And that's my cue to walk away." I walk away before that conversation gets too crazy.

Alistair Barker is the total package, but there is absolutely no truth to what Ophelia said. He has become my best friend and I am forever grateful for him and the bond we have created. He is kind of like a boyfriend without all of the drama, pressure and confusion. His title can be support group husband, but it's an anonymous support group so no know can know the title. He's my sponsor.

A few more hours go by of work and my shift is over. Today was intense to say the least. Alistair has another hour to go before he is done with his first day of volunteering. I look around to say my goodbye to him, and I see Xavier putting Sebastian in Alistair's arms. I immediately go into panic mode and race over there.

"Stop!" I quietly shout and Xavier pauses.

"What are you doing Sabine?" there is irritation in his question. "No, don't move him. He is too sick. Let him rest." Panic fills my voice.

"He is fine being held Sab; he could use it. Dr. Hu ordered it and who better to hold him then big Al here. You set this up," he continues to hand over the baby.

"Wait, no stop." I plead.

"Are you okay? What is going on?" Alistair looks worried. "Sabine." Xavier shoots a daggered look towards me.

"Okay, fine, but be careful." I motion with them like a crazy person.

"You need to go home now." Xavier orders me to leave.

"You are right." I say goodbye, grab my things and leave.

He is absolutely correct. My energy is drained and my body is exhausted from the whole day start to finish. Rest has to be one of the cures for sudden insanity. I pass out on my cot I've been using. The thought of my bed is revolting. The newfound energy after hours of sleep inspire me to clean up the apartment a little, then I rediscover the envelope with my name on it. I never opened it, until now.

CHAPTER 9

Sabine,

I am so sorry to be the girl your boyfriend cheated on you with. It has been eating at me to be that girl. We've been seeing each other for months and I never knew he had a girlfriend, until you walked in on us. I can't believe he played both of us. I don't know if you even want to hear from me, but I feel like I owe it to you. I would have never stepped foot in your home if I knew you two were a couple. Apparently, when you forgot things, he would leave to bring them to you at work because I was at your place. He told me his grandma needs a ride every now and then. To be honest, I knew about you at first, but he said you two were over. I swear I felt terrible about it. I told him he had to break things off with you or we couldn't be together. I hope you're okay and this letter helps. I'm sorry.

-Celia

irst of all, who writes a letter and delivers it to someone's home? It's 2019, isn't she supposed to write this all in an Instagram DM? She was here in my apartment, in my bed, with my boyfriend. I didn't have a clue. Why would she think I would have wanted to hear from her? Now, it makes sense why he took the time to bring me my things every now and then. How could she think this letter would make anyone feel better? I am such an idiot. I feel nauseous. I feel dirty. Disgusting. It feels as if my heart has been ripped out all over again. My pulse starts to race as my body begins to sweat profusely. The lightheadedness feeling presents itself and forces me to sit down. This letter took me right back to the moment I walked in on them naked. The self-work and personal growth I've worked hard for immediately goes out the window. It's just me in an empty apartment with a broken heart and a letter from a woman who helped tear it to pieces. Caring about self-sabotage is no longer an option right now, mindfulness is impossible, I don't know myself in this moment.

My mind begins to run irrationally, I completely lose it. This apartment is tainted, it's not mine anymore. I rush and grab the biggest sharpest knife from the kitchen and run to the bed and cut the sheets to shreds. The lamp on the bedside table gets thrown and shattered to pieces. Feeling angry, I snag the pictures off the wall and tear them until they look unrecognizable. My body collapses to the floor and I can't stop sobbing uncontrollably. My nausea suddenly reappears and my arm quickly reaches for the nearest trash can a few feet away. Everything put into my body today projected out into the can. As the vomiting stops, I lay on the floor paralyzed with numbness.

My phone rings and I let it go to voicemail. My body doesn't budge. A second later my phone dings with a text message. My scary reflection shows in the black screen before turn the device on. My mascara and eyeliner ran down my face, the lipstick is gone and my glasses are cracked. The screen turns on and it's a text message from Alistair with a photo attachment. It's a picture of him with a pouty face and a bottle of vodka.

Alistair: Can't stop thinking, please come help me drink this bottle. I need you girl.

Here I lay with the text that saves me. My text back to him involves a few pictures of the disaster I created during my mental breakdown. There has been a lot of these happening to me lately, mental breakdowns. He sends the shocked emoji.

Alistair: Come over, we can make pizza!

Me: You had me at Vodka. Text me your address.

Shame overpowers me after sending those pictures to Alistair. At least my intuition saved my night the other day from being ruined by a stupid letter from a homewrecker.

The shower is on and turned all the way to cold, I just need to feel something else. Jesus Christ, this water is freezing. It hurts so good. After a long cold shower, I throw on a pair of pumpkin pajamas and head over you Alistair's house to mindfully drink all my problems away. Alistair opens his front door and we both witness each other's freshly puffed eyes and laugh at ourselves. To my surprise, he has on a pair of black skeleton onesie, zips up to the top of his head.

"No way!" My jaw drops in awe.

"You like it? There was a 50-50 chance you would come in mysterious gear." He spins.

"I love the spirit. Now, let's drink the pain away!"

The smell of fresh bouquet of flowers fills the room, Alistair owns a four-bedroom, three-bathroom home, twenty minutes from my soon-to-be old place. It's silly to think my one-bedroom apartment is lonely after a painful breakup, he has this whole place to wallow in. The living room carries a cozy atmosphere with a sunken set up. The décor and build have a brick, wood, naturistic aesthetic. The patio opens up to a view of countless trees across a widespread of Oregon land. I don't think I've ever been in a place this fancy in my twenty-six years of living.

"This place is… breathtaking!" It's a lot to take in.

"Thank you, I've spent a lot of years creating my dream home. Hopefully, one day a family will make it less empty." He opens up. "Yes, this place is definitely untouched. It reminds me of a house where the parents threaten their kids if they touch anything," I laugh.

"Damn, you got me down to tee," he jokes.

After Alistair finishes giving me a tour of the most beautiful home, we start to set up a pizza station to dirty his squeaky-clean kitchen. Making homemade pizza could be a challenge while scarfing down shots of magic vodka to numb our hearts. After we finish setting up to start cooking, I pour two shots of alcohol in basketball shot glasses, while Alistair puts more wood in the fireplace. I down a shot before we take on to at least get a little buzz to catch up to him. The alcohol runs through my body and burns so good.

"I just realized something," he looks peculiar. "What's that?" patiently waiting for an answer. "We don't have pizza sauce!"

He laughs hard.

Hearing the words come out of his mouth was the straw that broke the camel's back and causes a huge laughing fit. Of course, there's no sauce. We both decide it's better to just order a pizza to be delivered instead of going anywhere. Drinking and driving is never an option. Plus, it saves us from a lot of work on an already exhausting day. While waiting for the pizza to arrive, Alistair shares about his first day as a cuddler volunteer. What he shares easily resonates with me, the feeling that holding the babies do more for us then them. He held four little ones today and fell deeply in love. It's adorable listening to a man share his love for babies or children. One veggie pizza and one meat lover's pizza arrive and we take another shot to celebrate food. The first slice tastes like heaven on earth, but the second slice lacks taste thanks to the liquid courage. By the fourth shot, Alistair gets up and asks me to dance. No one has ever asked me to dance before, bucket list check. I haven't told anyone that want because then they would possibly feel obligated to ask.

With one push of a button, Whitney Houston starts singing my favorite song. Joseph never liked to dance, but he humored me and danced to the music he liked. That's the only way he would join my dance parties. Happiness flushes through my system as my body dances in sync with Alistair, endorphins being released left and right. He takes my hands and spins me around before a dip. For the first time in my life, I feel seen. The feeling overwhelms me, I sit down and take a breather.

"Are you alright Sabi?" he's concerned.

"Yes, I'm just really glad I met you," taking a deep breath in.

"I'm glad I took pity on you and you stuck around," he laughs and nudges my arm.

Another piece of veggie pizza goes down before another shot gets launched down our throats. At this point our energy starts to dim down a bit. Being drunk yet responsible, Alistair grabs us a few waters from his weirdly, high-tech fridge. Water has never tasted so good then in this moment in time, refreshing and cool. I can't get enough of it. The fire place is a nice touch, but the alcohol is working overtime on the heat factor, feels like a sauna in here. We land ourselves into deep conversation until someone's phone dings. I reach for my phone, but it's notification free. Alistair's face drops, he got a text from Lennox. I'm guessing he doesn't get to many texts from him with the look on his face. The text read; I miss our midnight cuddles. The most dramatic barf sound comes out of my mouth a second after hearing what he said. For a moment, Alistair seems stunned. He lets out a big sigh, then throws his phone.

"Want to talk about it?" I ask.

"If I'm being honest, he is just an annoyance at this point. Like a fly that won't shoo, you know? It's kind of hard to fall for empty words numerous times, don't you think? Yeah, but I don't care. I'm over it." He looks at me.

"Would that really be the case for someone who is half deep in a bottle of vodka? Woah. Wait, can I ask? Alcohol and drug counselor. Are you not sober? Well, you're definitely not sober." I fall heavily concerned.

"Touché Sabi, touché. Like I said before, I'm not perfect. I'm an honest man, people slip. Tonight, was a conscious decision to drink. I'm not in any danger, it's just been a little rough lately. I will be okay." His eyes fall soft with his answer.

"I mean, I'm over him, just not over the time he wasted and my future plans going out the window." His brain bounces back quick. "Don't count your chicken before the eggs hatch now," I shoot a shot of vodka.

"I don't think that's the saying." He laughs and mocks.

As the night grows, the second bottle of alcohol has been opened. My worries about the man's drinking history fades away with the help of liquor. I can't even save myself tonight. Who am I to judge when I'm doing the same thing? Drowning my pain in vodka. Alistair brings out a karaoke machine to connect to the TV, little does he know I'm a legend at karaoke. Well, I like to think so. We both look at each other with our game faces on as the first song begins to play. "Don't go breaking my heart" by Elton John seems appropriate and ironic for the theme of tonight. Ironic and Iconic. To my surprise, Alistair gets deep into character and performs a show a long side me. Both of us scream, singing passionately at the screen of words and sounds. One could mistake this night for high paying therapy. The song ends and we fall into the couch as if we just performed a three- hour concert, it took a lot out of us. It's game on for round two after a break and shots; the second song set a different mood into the air. The karaoke highlighter starts filling the words to *You left me sad* by a band called Alkaline. This is fun, definitely therapy.

"But you're not the guy that I hoped you would be," Alistair sings with oomph.

"You broke my heart bad which helped me see," I sing.

"Thank God I didn't have my baby with you," we both passionately yell into the microphones.

"Cause you still around to only see what's in it for you," I finish the line before we both start laughing.

This song channels the suppressed energy buried deep inside us with the most relatable song. That was the first time I've listen to that song without bawling my eyes out on the spot. Two more shots get poured into the glass and down our throats. We dedicate it to the two scum bags that brought us together. I don't know if the alcohol is altering my sight, Alistair looks extremely beautiful right now. Who am I kidding, he always looks this good! Of course, the alcohol is altering my vision and my brain, laughter bursts from my mouth after my thought process. Beer goggles. My mind is past the point of no return, nothing serious, yet everything serious is going on inside my head. I get lost in tunnel vision while observing everything about the man sitting across from me. No thoughts, no words are running around in my brain while looking at him. My heart starts to feel things that I am too scared to admit, yet I don't want to sleep alone. "What?" he catches me.

"Nothing, just admiring how insanely flawless you are," my words slur.

"Oh, I have flaws. You just don't know them," he mischievously smiles.

"Well then Al, tell me all your secrets," the words come out more flirtatious then intended.

"First, I need to know something," he says.

"What?" my curiosity is peaked.

"Do you really think I am big apple tree that makes delicious apple pie?" he chuckles to himself.

"Well, that's embarrassing," my cheeks turn flushed while I laugh uncontrollably.

"Oh, come on, don't get shy on me now Sabi." He scoots closer and looks at me with his big goofy eyes.

"If I'm not mistaken, I'd think you're flirting with me Barker." My heart flutters.

"Well, I'd say you've got a pretty smart intuition there Ms. Montgomery." He gets closer.

"You tease!" My lips are almost touching his before I playfully push him away.

"You want a secret?" He mumbles through the vodka.

"I'm working really hard at making a choice to not self-sabotage right now." He smiles at his serious but sarcastic words.

"Sorry to burst your bubble here buddy but we are bottles deep in liquor at this point. Way passed the sabotage," I drunkenly admit. "I'm fighting the urge to kiss you, right now. That's my secret."

His voice becomes serious and seductive at the same time.

"Alistair, I'm still a woman when I'm drunk you know." I laugh out of confusion.

"Well, I'm bisexual. It's not a secret but being married to a man for years made the label unimportant to me. I didn't mean to make you uncomfortable, I'm sorry," he mumbles his confession.

"I'm not uncomfortable. Plus, my colleague called it. I don't understand how. There's no way to tell someone's sexual orientation by the way they look. How did she know?" I smile in my lost thought process. After cleaning up our mess, Alistair grabs my hand and leads me to his bedroom. Pizza stains and liquid spills filth my clothes, he lends me an oversized yellow tee to change into. Splashing cold water in my face feels like nirvana, my makeup smears everywhere. A few more splashes and scrubs do the trick. The king size Tempur-Pedic bed sucks me in for a warm hug. Spinning sensations begin to spiral in my head, my hands automatically grab my head before it gets out of control. Don't barf, Sabine. Alistair gets one look at my face and smiles at the clownish face painted on. We lay down and he puts his arm around my waist, kisses the back of my head.

"Thank you for hanging out with me tonight, I don't think I could have gotten through it alone," I flip around and meet him face to face.

"I think I'm the lucky one here." He pulls me in closer, he smells divine.

"You and me both." I bite my bottom lip as our faces are the closest they can get without touching, we begin to doze off.

"Can I ask you something?" Alistair whispers. "Yeah," I answer with my eyes closed.

"What happened with that Sebastian kid? What got you worked up?" he asks.

"No one deserves to die alone," I answer without even thinking about what he asked.

"He will be okay when he's got you on his side. You almost kicked my ass today for going near the boy. Maybe I should hire a bodyguard." Alistair lets out a tired laugh.

"Hey. Can I spend the night? I can't find my car. My eyes stopped working," I ask while half asleep.

"Yes, of course. Good night," Alistair mumbles.

CHAPTER 10

The pounding in my head wakes me up before my alarm is scheduled to go off. Looking around the room confused of my whereabouts. My heavy eyelids quickly shut when a merciless ray of sunshine burns my brain. A big yellow t- shirt easily wraps my body like a burrito and the bottom half is pant less. Where are my pants? Rolling around in the bed before I get up, it's just me in here. The smell of fresh coffee sends an invitation for a morning cup in the kitchen. A long-winded stretch takes over to relieve the overbearing stiffness in my structure. The bathroom calls my name before approaching a coffee gathering with Alistair. My reflection in the mirror scares the living day lights out of me when I see my face. I quickly grab a squeeze of face wash from the shower and scrub the horrid designed paint off my face. The cold water is shocking, yet refreshing and much needed. As I walk into the kitchen, my hair gets pulled up into an intentionally messy bun. Alistair looks as if he got hit by a truck last night, his eyes are puffy and a burden to himself.

"Good morning sunshine. Quite a night for not a party girl," he chuckles while sipping his black coffee.

"Morning. Can't claim the party girl badge without remembering the partying. I really needed last night though, what a sponsor you are,"

I laugh and give him a friendly pat on his chest.

"Want to carpool to group this morning?" he asks while pouring caffeine into a cup for me.

"Oh, I figured I would skip this morning with the whole letter thing, being hungover and all," I awkwardly reveal my plan.

"Sabine, this is exactly what the group is for. Let's carpool," he insists.

We sit outside for another hour before it's time to start getting ready for Infidelity Survivors Anonymous. Popped a couple of pain killers while listening to the chirping of the morning birds. A small nest sits in a nest in a tree near the fence, a family of three birds waking up together. The green and earthly view is incredible from his balcony, I could get used to this. It just dawns on me that I don't have any clothes with me, except dirty pajamas. Relaxing time has to be cut short in order to drive by my apartment before group. Alistair rushes to get dressed and ready for the day before we head to my place so I can clean up.

The moment I walk in; I'm reminded of what happened last night. We both gasp as we walk in because the place is destroyed, as was the result of my breakdown.

"Holy shit, the pictures you sent me didn't do this mess justice,"

Alistair is in awe of this disaster.

"Not my best moment. It doesn't matter because I'm not living here anymore," the words passively spilled from my mouth.

Twenty-three minutes later, I grab the stupid letter and we are on our way to help us feel less shitty. Alistair thinks it's important to restart the mood for the day with a concert in the car to his morning music playlist. Singing karaoke is the only thing I remember from last night, how crazy unfortunate. At least it's a good memory, I hope I didn't puke anywhere or embarrass myself somehow. He sings and bops his head to upbeat songs, belts out the emotional songs and laughs at the countless times he mumbles words to lyrics he doesn't fully know. I have to admit, it's kind of adorable to watch. It in no way helps my hangover, but whatever makes him happy. The dramatic shift in my life this past month has been an emotional roller-coaster ride, but choosing to sing on our way to group is worth it. So, this is what Maliha talks about with choices. Did I just notice my mind shifting? He catches me looking his way and he sticks his tongue out at me which tickles my funny bone. An overwhelming feeling of gratitude flushes through me, making my eyes tear up a little. Hiding it well, I pat my eyes as we pull in the parking lot. I take a deep breathe before walking through the doors to another emotional morning. The second we walk through the door together Hannah approaches us.

"You two look…… rough," she smirks.

"Hey, I've been called worse," Alistair chuckles and walks towards the refreshment table.

"Hey, Sabine. Can I talk to you for a second?" Maliha approaches Hannah and I.

"Yes, of course." I respond as Hannah leaves us to talk.

"Good morning. I just want to have a conversation with you about heading back into the dating scene so soon. It could open a lot of doors that haven't been closed and locked yet and could hinder your healing progress." Maliha lectures out of the blue.

"Thank you for your concern, Maliha, but I'm not seeing anyone."

I'm confused.

"I've been noticing how close you and Alistair are getting and it's just in your best interest to not get involved so soon. You've come so far," she kindly states.

"Okay, let's unpack this. First of all, Alistair is gay. Second of all, the point of a support group is to build connections with people who have the same experiences as you, right.? Third of all, I mean no disrespect but did you have this conversation with Alistair as well or just me?" I bombard her with questions after feeling attacked.

"I mean…. uhhh, no I didn't speak with him about it. I guess you're right, I should have thought to approach both of you. I'm sorry." She's stunned.

"I appreciate your concern, but there is nothing going on. You don't need to bring this up to him though because I think you've got the wrong impression." I tap her shoulder and walk away.

Is there nothing going on? People can like others with any sexual orientation, it's not a smart move but it happens. How is it possible to not like Alistair in every way? He is the total package: kind, smart, energetic, loving, funny, safe, perfect. The conversation with Maliha has me slightly bothered; did she open a can of worms? We are not drug addicts who need to completely quit the poison; we are people who fell in love with people who have broken our hearts. We are not in addiction recovery; our trust in people is mending back together after being ripped apart. People fall in love, that's what humans do and should do it big. Love, that's a massive word with huge fire power.

The meeting starts off with Hannah sharing about Jude begging for another chance as usual. She's proud for finally choosing herself in the relationship between them. It's a big act of self-love for her to leave him in the dust, she's growing. The group gives her a round of applause for her personal breakthrough.

Luis confesses about being in love again and how the woman makes him feel liberated and alive. He doesn't share her name, maybe because we all know her. I am convinced it's the beautiful bubbly queen who sits across me named Hannah. It's obvious there is a connection between the two of them, they look comfortable and happy when they are around each other. Maliha should be lecturing them about jumping into a relationship so soon, did she?

My train of thought halts when Alistair begins speak, he looks angelic and human when he's vulnerable. Oddly, we all seem kind of angelic and human when we practice vulnerability.

"Sabine and I went to a comedy show the other day and weirdly ran into Lennox. It's been a while since I've saw him and the energy was insanely tense. His words and actions were passive aggressive and for the first time I realized how toxic he felt to me. Then, last night he texted me like nothing bad every happened between us, I felt nothing when I read it. Lennox was a toxic drug my heart was addicted to for a long time and I have no interest in it. Now that I think of it, it's relieving." He smiles big.

Maliha's eyes feel like daggers from across the room, her face sends the I told you so message. She is still wrong. Friends experience life together and go out to create memories. If she is wrong, why do I feel guilty? The more Alistair spoke, the more nervous I get because it's my turn to share next. These people are going to judge the hell out of me from my actions last night, it's humiliating. But there is no point in being here if I don't talk about it and tell the truth. Tearing my apartment to shreds is evidence to support the argument of having a no dating rule. I mean, I'm not dating. Why does a part of me feel guilty? Every time the person before me pours their hearts out, I instantly regret showing up her in the first place. These meetings are like when you strongly don't want to work out but afterwards it feels like the most rewarding thing in the world.

I'm last, here is goes. Reading the letter to the group is saddening and telling them about my reaction feels exposing. Its uneasy thinking some of them are judging me or maybe it's me who is judging myself.

"Believe it or not but your reaction was quite common. There are healthier ways, but you were immensely triggered that your mind didn't fully process or communicate with your heart and in result, damage could happen. I'm glad it was your stuff and not you. Thank you for sharing that with us. I have to say, you are far from alone in that area. Can I ask what you did after self-destructive moment in your apartment?" Maliha attempts to comfort me.

"I went over to a friend's house and got black out drunk, hence the hangover I've been trying to hide, but clearly not doing a good job." I hate myself.

"Again, we all have those times" Maliha looks at Alistair and back at me, I avoid making eye contact.

My feeling of embarrassment is noticeable because people start sharing their psychotic moments after me. I could have never imagine feeling so seen by a group of strangers, well friends now. "I smashed the shit out of Jude's car one time," Hannah admits shamelessly.

"I stayed silent. I pretended to not know until I could financially move out and leave him. Okay, I did sign him up for the website that anonymously texts your partner that he might have an STD."

The shy new girl breaks a little out of her shell.

"Amanda!" Hannah's jaw drops.

"What? He was fucking around, maybe his stupid ass should get a wakeup call," she's blunt.

"I got black out drunk numerous times to numb the pain," Luis admits.

"I got drunk and slept with two of Lennox's exes after I left him."

Alistair opens fire.

"You guys are making me a feel a lot better about myself" I laugh with the group.

"I did not hear anything. Great work today, I think. No homework today. All I will say is to dress comfortably for our next meeting," Maliha dismisses the meeting.

Dress comfortably? That's an odd comment. Feeling ten times better after the meeting is a huge plus. The car ride is a little awkward due to my annoying problem of overthinking. When we get back to Alistair's place, I help him clean up from our first sleepover.

"I don't know about you but that meeting made me feel mad normal." He laughs.

"Normal is overrated. I will say that it's nice knowing that everyone is beyond out of their minds. So, you really hooked up with Lennox's exes? They were like rebounds right? Did it help?" I respond with the dramatics.

"My mind went really dark for a good minute. Turns out, it didn't make me feel any better. Have you had a rebound since Joseph?"

Alistair throws the last few pillows on the couch.

"I would be lying if I said it hasn't crossed my mind. I don't think I'm that type of person. Maybe a conversation for another time?" I speak.

"You got it Sabi," he replies.

Time is running out to get a run in before I go home and cleaned up for work. We say our goodbyes with a big hug. The hug is warm and comfy as always but something feels different this time. It's unknown how the feeling is but somehow the dynamic has suddenly shifted. Weird. My shift is in a couple of hours and my body needs serious damage control.

CHAPTER 11

"You came back for me!" Alma yells with excitement.

"I told you I would, didn't I?" walking towards her with my right hand behind my back.

"What are you hiding? Is that my present?!" she screeches when she realized.

"Great guess. Happy early Halloween, Alma!" I hand her the package.

"Stickers!" she said at the top of her lungs.

"Thank you!" she holds the packs of stickers close to her heart. "I figured you could decorate your room a little for Halloween.

There are enough stickers in there to decorate everything you own," I say dramatically with a raised eyebrow.

"I can't wait to show my mom! Maybe we can decorate my room before I go into surgery." Her voice cracks.

"When is your surgery happening? It's your last one, how exciting." I playful tickle her to see her smile.

"That's what they said about the last one. I just want to go home sometime soon. Mom said I can go back to school," slight fear shows in her eyes.

"Don't you worry your pretty little mind; everything is going to be okay. You have survived every day you lived so far, right?" I place my hand on hers.

"Oh yeah, I guess you're right." Hope flushes her fear away.

"You better start making a list of all the fun things you'll be doing when you leave this place. Big things are in store for you super woman," I caress her cheek.

"Want to make it with me right now?" she says with hope.

"I have to go take care of the babies across the way. I'm sure your mom would be honored to make it with you. It was great to see you again Alma," give her a tight squeeze again before heading out.

The nurse at the front desk gives me a slip a paper with the date and time of Alma's surgery. He gives me a heads up to check in a couple times due to the surgery having a good chance of being moved up. I leave a sticky note with my name and number for them to call me if the date changes, if they have the time or remember to do so. Poor thing, she's getting put through the ringer. She holds an abundance amount of love and light in her heart, she will pull through. Alma's light shines bright on my heart when I need it the most. She has no idea how magical she is.

Inhaling deep breaths to mentally prepare myself for a long shift in the NICU today. Alistair is sitting in the rocking chair holding Sebastian when I walk in the room. Two new babies have been admitted and one was discharged yesterday. Nothing stays stagnant at the hospital; this place is constantly changing. It's time for food and medication for the angels in their container homes. Sweet Miss Lewin lays peacefully as I hold up her feeding tube, food drains down her hose. Admiring how relaxed she is, brings bliss to my face. Life is precious and she lays in front of me fighting for a chance in this world.

I overhear the conversation between Alistair and Dr. Hu, they are talking about why he chose to apply for the Cuddler program. He says it fills an emptiness he's been feeling for quite some time, he feels as if he missed his shot for children when the divorce happened. Dr. Hu is giving him encouraging words regarding his longing for fatherhood. Unfortunately, the baby formula runs out and I have to go get more, it's not a conversation I should be hearing anyways.

Pam approaches me in the back to inform me that a couple to new parents requested a conversation with me regarding education about at-home care for their new baby. Pam switches tasks with me because the babies need to be nourished as I attend to the new parents. Providing support for parents and family members with at-home care education for their newborn is an important part of our jobs as health care providers.

After the education lesson, I walk back to get my lunch for break but Alistair stops me in my tracks to ask for a few minutes to chat. A million thoughts run through my head trying to figure out what he needs to talk to me about right now. Did Maliha end up having that conversation with him? Does he need to debrief about the conversation with Dr. Hu? He waited for me to go on break to discuss whatever is on his mind.

"Hey, what's up?" I approach him and sit down. "So, I've been thinking..." he says.

"Oh no. Not too hard I hope," sassy slips out.

"Awe she got jokes now. On a serious note, you mentioned how you are moving out of your apartment and I have a big ole house all to myself. I've got a room with your name on it if you want it." He generously offers.

"Oh, my God, Alistair. That is extremely generous of you, but I can't," the shock makes my heart race.

"Of course, you can. You will have your own room and bathroom. Plus, a view to die for," he tries to change my mind.

"Flattering yourself I see," my jokes stem from being uncomfortable.

"I meant the one from my balcony," he laughs

"Thank you so much for the offer, I really appreciate it. Honestly, but I can't. I have some things to do before I clock back in so I have to go. Thanks again," I jet out as fast as I can.

The only person that comes to mind is Maliha Patel, she's good. She saw it before I fully felt it and now, I have to call the friendship quits before I get myself hurt. Leaving Alistair in that waiting room after the sweetest gesture anyone has ever done for me was a dick move. The rest of my shift is just me working on human autopilot, my mind is busy. Except when working with the doctors, that always requires our full attention.

I finish cleaning up for the next nurse that takes over my section of patients and clock out for the night. Sebastian lays in his incubator with his eyes closed, he looks even tinier than before. My heart breaks to see him so sick, he has been ill for way too long. He has been fighting for too long, It's not fair. The sicker he grows, the more wires and machine we have to attach him to for his treatment and recovery. I run my finger in little strides across his tiny hand, humming a sweet lullaby. Nurses and parents come in and out, passively sending smiles in my direction. They all have great understanding for patience, love, compassion and hope. Sebastian's mom should be here comforting her son, not me. Although, time with him is time well spent. A couple of hours go by of me sitting here humming to Sebastian, a doctor stops by and suggests for me to go home and get some rest. It is getting late, but I don't want to go home, never again.

Bugsby's engine starts and an idea pops in my head to give Maliha a call. No one discusses if we can call her or each other for friendly advice, but I need it. There is a deep need for understanding what my heart is going through lately. Why won't I let myself move in with Alistair? What are the advantages and disadvantages to that proposition? To prevent crossing a boundary, I reach out to the wise woman.

Me: Hey, Maliha. Do you have some time to give me a call?

I could use some guidance.

A few minutes later, my phone rings.

"Hey Sabine, what's going on?" she asks.

"If I'm being honest, my mind is extremely noisy today with a variety of situations. Our conversation this morning made me realize a few things. Alistair offered me a place to live because I am looking to move and the scared little girl in me basically shut him down and ran away. Not literally but kind of. Then, I am judging myself because how can I move on so quickly from Joseph and…." "Sabine. Sabine, take a deep breath. Inhale and exhale three times," she interrupts.

"Yes, thank you," deeply inhales.

"It's obvious you and Al have created a special relationship; the two of you are beautiful beings with big hearts. It's no shocker how well you guys click. All I have to say about your feelings towards him are real, but that's a conversation to have with yourself and then him. I've been hearing from your heart for a while now and you need to be gentle with yourself. You have been mentally checked out of your relationship with Joseph for a while before the breakup. A lot of what I hear is your hurt and betrayal stems from rejection and the fact that he is your first love. What he did was shocking and all of your feelings and reactions are normal. I want to apologize now for having the conversation with you this morning," she offers.

"Wow, you articulated my mess brilliantly. I never thought of it like that and please don't apologize, it looks like you were right after all," my tone is soft.

"Right. That's where my apology applies is that the conversation, what I thought with you two was misguided. I think instead of running from new love and relationships, you need to figure out where exactly your hurt stems from to prevent your hurt bleeding onto the next person. Also, don't let your feelings get in the way of your friendship with Alistair. You two have something strong and he's a great person to confide in," she sweetly states.

"You're completely right. Thank you so much Maliha. This call was relieving and makes me realize I get stuck in my head too often, which makes me act like a weirdo. It's even more embarrassing to have this conversation when there isn't an option to move forward with him." I laugh at myself.

"Well, it's possible. I'm glad you called, Sabine. You are stronger than you think and remember to not be so hard on yourself," she advises and hangs up.

What does she mean it's possible? Far from possible. I am stronger than I think, that message went missing a couple weeks ago. For the first time in a while, life is seemingly less impossible to bare. There is only one more thing to do tonight and it's to apologize to an incredible friend that I don't deserve.

Scrolling through our text thread, searching for his address to surprise him. The address gets entered into the GPS on my phone and I stop at a gas station along the way. After putting the gas pump in Bugsby, there are a few things to get from the mini mart attached to the gas station. Flowers and a bottle of cheap wine make it to the register and then in my car. It takes a good ten minutes to figure out the perfect apology speech. When I park in his driveway, I am ready. Alistair answers the door and my perfect apology completely disappears from my brain. My mind goes blank with sunflowers in my left hand and the wine in my right. He stands there waiting for words to come out of my mouth.

"Hi!" My voice cracks. "Hi," he crosses his arms.

"I'm sorry to come unannounced, I just wanted to come and apologize for earlier. I understand if it's not a good time." My eyes are glued to the ground.

"Come in, Sabi." He grabs the gifts and lets me through.

"First of all, I am really sorry for the way I acted earlier. Well, all day. I was being a little weird." We sit on the couch.

"Yeah, weird is an understatement. I noticed. I want to apologize if I ever said or did anything that made you uncomfortable, that's the last thing I want to happen." His tone is sincere.

"No of course you didn't. I promise," I assure him.

"I was worried and thinking maybe I crossed a boundary last night or maybe it made you uncomfortable hearing that I'm bisexual," he looks worried.

"Bisexual? You're bi, not gay." Surprised as all hell.

"Uhhh, yeah. I told you last night," he squints his eyes in confusion which wrinkles his forehead.

"Of course, you told me the night I don't remember," nervous laughter seeps out.

"You were serious? You really don't remember last night?" his eyes grow wide.

"Last night is a giant blur, I swear. Shit, I'm so sorry Alistair. I promise I'm not uncomfortable with your sexuality." I put my hand on his knee for reassurance.

"But you're uncomfortable?" he looks hurt.

"How about we put a cap on that conversation for later." I divert.

"Okay, when you're ready I'll be here to listen." He smiles.

"Do you think God hit the perfection button when he created you?" I shake my head in disbelief.

"Yes, definitely. My offer about you moving in still stands. I would love for you to be my roommate. This house feels empty with just me." He offers again.

"I thought about it and I would be honored to move in, but I have a few conditions. This has to be done the right way. I will pay rent and you have to make me coffee in the mornings because I think you were a barista in a past life." I giggle.

"You don't need to pay rent," he shakes his head.

"That's not negotiable. It's my way or the highway buddy," I playfully rebuttal.

"You've got yourself a deal roomie. Don't be late on your rent or

I'm kicking your ass to the curb," he attacks me with a bear hug. "So, can I sleep here tonight?" I ask, secretly praying for a yes. "Mi casa es tu casa, baby doll!" His smile could light up any room.

"Voodoo doll!" I correct him and try and laugh as evil as possible from fail.

It's official! I am moving out of hell and into this beautiful masterpiece of a place. No one will know where I live or my address. No more worrying about Joseph showing up or any more surprise letters from the mistress. I can't wait for this new journey.

CHAPTER 12

One week later, the apartment I've called home for four years has been completely emptied. Memories flood through my head as I do the last walk through before closing this life chapter. The times filled with laughter and falling in love on the couch and cooking in the kitchen with Joseph. The room in which we slept in each other's arms every night no matter what our days were like. With three simple words, my world has been changed forever. I deserve better. My run in the park this morning allowed me to clear my head with everything that has been going on. The time outside helped me see more clearer and it feels right to move on. Of course, the wounds won't just heal on their own, but with time my heart will be stronger than ever. Joseph doesn't nearly come to mind as much as he used to.

"Cheers to the next chapter of my life!" I throw the keys on the countertop.

"Cheers to new beginnings and the life you deserve!" Alistair and Hannah snap their fingers as we all walk out the door.

"Thank you, guys, for helping me finish. It means the world to me to have your help and support," my eyes water.

"Of course, babe. Thank you, Joseph, for leading Sabine to us!" she giggles as we embrace for a group hug.

The three of us pick up lunch and head back to Alistair's house, well my house, too. That is going to take some time to get used to. There is a deli near the house called Sub Roulette, where they have a whole new menu for every day of the week. Sub Roulette is packed when we arrive, the line is out the door. It's time to see what the hype is all about, I pull up the menu on my phone to be ready when we get to the counter. The sandwich selection is wide with all sorts of food combinations. I order a sandwich called "Chicken out" with lettuce, grilled chicken, pickles, tomatoes, onions on a whole wheat bun. Hannah orders a sandwich called "Boulder in Italy" with three Italian meatballs, melted provolone cheese and sauce in a French roll. Alistair orders a sandwich called "Cheese Blast" with cheese, ham slices, lettuce, tomatoes on toasted sourdough bread.

The car smells like a fresh deli on a summer day with the heat blasting through the vents. The roulette theme continues in the car when we all each rotate picking songs to sing our hearts out to. The variety of songs playing through the speakers are exceptional, it's starts off with Whitney Houston, John Legend, Lauryn Hill, then to Fleetwood Mac, Backstreet Boys and Amy Winehouse.

Hannah does her happy dance as we pull into the driveway. Saying that food is exciting is definitely an understatement for most people. We sit our hungry selves at the table and dig in. Hannah dramatically moans after her first bite as if she's making love to her sub. This grilled chicken sandwich is divine, a work of art.

"Now I get it, I get the hype," Alistair's hypnotized by his sub.

"I wish I could taste it again for the first time," Hannah continues to moan and groan.

"Do you two need a room?" Alistair looks her Hannah with a disgusted face.

"I never thought you'd ask," she laughs.

"I'm very happy for the happy couple," they don't react. "Speaking of happy couple," Hannah adds.

"Yes?" I raise my eyebrow.

"I may or may not be seeing someone from group. It's a secret though so you can't let anyone know, especially Maliha," Hannah scolds.

"He finally made a move, huh?" Alistair responds. "Who?" Hannah looks guilty.

"Luis!" the name blurts out of my mouth.

"You guys know?" she raises her voice with surprise.

"It's obvious you two can't keep your eyes off each other!"

Alistair laughs and I smile.

"Oh, you two aren't?" Hannah gets defensive.

"Hey, I'm really happy for you two. Your secret is safe with me."

I ignore her comment and avoid eye contact with Alistair. "Also, there is something else." Her face falls sad. "Are you pregnant?" Alistair asks.

"God no! I've decided to stop coming to group. I feel cured and now I'm happy with a guy that I enjoy being with every second we are together." A smile forms on her face.

"Oh Hannah, I am so happy for you. We will still see you outside of group, like today." Alistair hugs Hannah.

"Yes of course. I'm happy for you!" Hannah hugs me next.

Hannah goes on about the plans her and Luis have made for their future together. Her face lights up every time his name comes out of her mouth. She seems genuinely happy. It looks good on her. Happiness looks good on everyone, if only it was easy to achieve. The world would be safe and healthy if people were happy beings. It shows if you do the work, the outcome is worthwhile. Her journey offers hope to anyone looking for healing in their broken hearts through infidelity.

After lunch is well into our bellies, Hannah heads home as the day grows later. I have no place to go as this house is now my home. Looking around brings butterflies in my belly when the energy feels right. The energy in this house is light and feels clean, not because Alistair is a neatnik. It's a long week ahead to get situated with settling into my new home.

My new room is filled with boxes of things I wanted to keep, purged what I didn't need. I've got my work cut out for me in the upcoming hours. This space is tremendously bigger than my old one, even the bathroom. The theme in the bathroom is inspired by a pink sunset. Sunshine shower curtains hang low in front of the tub, a fluffy, pink rug rests in front of the marble sink. Light blue towels hang on the racks to represent the ocean; a white cup of colored washable markers sit on the sink next to a box of tissues.

The markers are for writing messages and affirmations whenever I feel inspired to do so. It puts a smile on my face to see a message left for me, especially a positive inspirational quote.

A much-needed break arrives when Alistair interrupts me with a home cooked meal. Its dinner time already? Time got away from me. The smell instantly makes my knees fall weak as I walk into the dining room. He made Shrimp Puttanesca with warm bread rolls and a vinaigrette salad.

"Oh my God! Where did you learn how to cook like this?" impressed after I take my first bite.

"Lennox is a chef actually. We used to cook all the time together and my skills have been mastered," he answers truthfully.

"Oh sorry. Hey, at least you can cook for the next special person that comes along. Grab a plate and come sit down already," avoiding the awkwardness from my previous question.

"Actually, this is for you. I wanted you to have a nice meal your first official night here." He rubs the back of his neck.

"This is all really sweet of you. Are you going to have a seat? Wait, are you going out?" Curiosity hits my brain hard. "Yes, I have a date," he hesitates to say the statement. "Oh! Do I know this lucky person?" I ask.

"You might, I met him at the hospital the other day. His name is Roger Briones, he's an X-ray technician, I believe." He answers while putting his jacket on.

"Never heard of him. Well, don't let me stall you. Have a great time! Thank you for dinner, it means a lot," my tone comes out overly enthusiastic to avoid the sting.

"I will have a great time, thank you. You are very welcome Sabi. Don't wait up!" he smiles before leaving the house.

Alistair leaves and I am all alone in a house I've only been in a hand full of times. Its intimidating being in a place by myself for the first time ever. Alistair leaving me with this beautiful meal for a date slightly knocks the wind out of me. There is enough food here to feed a family of four, plenty of left overs. The realization hits me that I don't know where anything is when I scan the cabinets for

Tupperware to pack up the rest of the food. The perfect time to explore this house is now when the place is a ghost town.

Before I do anything, a change into more comfier clothes is a must, let's not forget the music. My hair is up in a high ponytail, wearing an old oversized white button-down shirt of Josephs, tight boxers and crew socks on. All I need to complete the look is a pair of sunglasses and a broom guitar to rock out with. Dance party for one takes place in the front of the castle. Out of breath, I grab my glass of wine and lay sprawled out on the couch. An hour goes by and the night evidently turns lonely. I grab my phone to text Hannah and Luis with an invitation to come over and hang out. Twenty minutes later, the happy duo shows up at my door step with a carton of vanilla ice cream and a card. The envelop isn't glued shut, it's a congratulations card with heart felt messages written inside from them. We grab our scoops of ice cream and get comfortable on the couch.

"Where's Alistair? Is he not here?" Luis asks.

"No, he's out on a date," it feels physically awkward to say.

"Ouch," Hannah gasps.

"Yeah, can't feel good for you Sab," Luis adds. "Me? I'm fine," I lie.

"You can fool yourself, but not me. I see things," Hannah eyes me.

"Time to get your eyes checked, girlfriend," sass leaks out.

"Do you know who it is?" Luis asks.

"Some guy he met from doing the volunteer program at the hospital," I take a bite of my dessert.

"You know the guy?" Hannah's eyes grow wide.

"Never heard of him. Do you guys want to watch a movie or play a game or something?" I divert the unwanted conversation.

It took us some time to find a movie the three of us wanted to watch. Horror is our genre of choice, no brainer. Halfway through the movie, Alistair walks in drunk and stumbling over himself which ends movie night early. He looks off, Hannah and Luis gently drag him to his room and I grab him a cup of water from the kitchen. He must have had hardcore first date jitters, happens to the best of us.

Hannah talks to Alistair in his room while Luis helps me clean up the kitchen.

"You guys don't have to leave. I'm sure he's just going to fall asleep. At least finish the movie," I say to Luis.

"We can always come over another time. We want to respect his space especially when he is in that state. We love you but we really should get going," he respectfully declines.

Hannah comes out and lets me know I've been summoned. I thank them for coming over and bringing thoughtful gifts to celebrate an important event in my life. Hugs and cheek kisses before they depart. I walk to see my new roommate in his bedroom.

"Hey!" I stand at his door.

"Will you do me a favor?" he slurs. "I'll see what I can do," I stand still.

"Will you sleep with me tonight?" he gently asks with warm eyes.

"Is everything okay?" my heart softens.

"Yeah, I just want to be held." His voice is vulnerable.

"Hey, how did you get home?" nervous for his answer.

"Oh! My car is out still. Definitely not making it back for curfew.

My friend, Uber, came and got me," he laughs at his poor joke.

"Alistair, when should I be worried? The drinking. I'm here if you need someone to lean on." I turn the lights off and crawl into bed with my friend.

"I'm good, it's out of my system after tonight. I promise." He responds.

Alistair lays back down and slightly curls his legs up into a comfortable position. My arm wraps around his upper body and the same with my leg on his. My chin is gently placed in the back nook of his neck. I hold him tight from behind and don't let go. I don't need to know what's going on or what happened, it's not about me right now. It's my turn to be his safe space.

CHAPTER 13

My morning is stacked with loads of tedious paper work to fill out in the office. Every once in a while, the nurses spend a couple of hours doing office work. Some nurses prefer to do more of the equipment set up and maintenance rather than performing tests and being more hands on with the patients. Everyone has their preferences but we all have to do the job at the best of our abilities. The day has been non-stop busy and full of running around and consulting with parents. Basically, today is like most days here at the hospital. After consulting with my last set of parents, it's time to prep a little one for surgery.

"Sabine!" Ophelia hollers jogging towards me.

"What's wrong?" My mind immediately thinks something happened with a patient.

"I don't know how to put this but Ms. Osgood is here and wants to talk to you." She seems uneasy.

"She's here again? What does she need me for?" I ask while walking with her to our patient's mother.

"I'll just let you two to talk." Ophelia leaves me alone with the woman.

"Hello Ms. Osgood, I hope you are doing better from the last time you were here. I hear the news that you are expecting, congratulations," I congratulate her.

"Thank you. Uhh, that's kind of what I need to talk to you about nurse Montgomery. Can I call you Sabine? Sabine, this is going to be a quite uncomfortable conversation. The thing is I'm having a really hard time right now and I can't afford to be a single mother of two kids and not to mention that Sebastian is extremely ill. I don't think he's going to make it." Karen starts to dramatically hyperventilate.

"Awwww, don't say that, he is a warrior. Everything is going to be okay. There are resources for people who are struggling financially and mentally." I interrupt her rant.

"No, no, no I don't need them. The hospital bills are just too much and I clearly can't deal with it all the stress. He needs a stronger mother and parents who can be there for him." Tears fill her face as she feels her baby little baby bump.

"What are you saying Ms. Osgood?" My heart starts racing when I assume what she's doing.

"I just can't. I'm sorry. I can't raise Sebastian. I can't," she's erratic.

"Ms. Osgood!" I try to calm her down as I panic.

"I mean you're so good with him and I see how much you love him. You can adopt him, please take him!" she pleads like a crazy person.

"You can't just leave your sick son. He needs you, he needs his mommy. Is this what you were coming to talk to me about at the holiday party? Why me?" I catch on to her plan.

"I'm sorry, I can't. I have to go" She begins to walk away and I grab her hand.

"Karen, you can't just abandon your son!" I aggressively yell as she walks away from me.

"Nurse Montgomery!" Dr. Hu approaches.

"Karen! You can't just throw him away and make another one! That's not right, that's not what mothers do. He needs you!" I am the crazy one now.

"Nurse Montgomery! Go take a walk, now!" Dr. Hu sternly orders.

Ophelia grabs my shoulders and pulls me through the hospital exit doors. The more I try to calm down, my breathing gets frantically worse. My brain refuses process what just happened. Holding me tightly, Ophelia, starts to rock with me and hum like I am a mental patient. To my surprise, it's working. When I first started working here it was hard to not get too emotional with the babies. Nurses wouldn't get into this line of work if they didn't care. Some are good with disconnecting their feelings and avoid becoming emotionally attached. I don't want to live that way. They need all the love and care they can get. It's unheard of to abandon your sick child in the hospital to go have another baby with a new guy.

Ophelia begins to tell me how sometimes parents are physically and mentally unable to care for their sick babies. Giving up your sick baby for adoption is uncommon but not unheard of. She's been a nurse working in this hospital for over twenty years, running the place.

Trying to bring my breathing back to normal, Ophelia wipes under my tear-filled eyes. She gives me one last hug before we go back inside.

Dr. Hu pulls me aside when we walk in to discuss my behavior towards a mother in front of everyone.

"I understand your reaction, but please tell me you know that outburst was completely unprofessional and unacceptable in this work place," he lectures.

"I am a million times sorry. I don't know what came over me. It will never happen again. I'm so sorry Dr. Hu," I plead Our discussion doesn't last very long considering I apologized profusely and acknowledged how highly inappropriate my actions were. My shift was over a half hour before the whole fiasco in the lobby. All I want to do now is sit with Sebastian, he needs someone in his corner. Sweet sleeping sounds come from his container. He's lying there so peacefully.

"Hey sweet boy," I lean over and whisper to him.

"You're doing so good baby. You are strong, you're going to get through this, you hear me?" Tears calmly run down my face as I grab his little hand.

"You have to fight, beat the odds," I continue.

One of the moms nearby walks up to me and puts her hand on my shoulder, her husband follows and holds her hand. A few nurses walking around join holding hands around the baby. I stand up and grab hold of the woman's hand next to me. No one says a word to each other, it happens natural. We all surround the sick baby in silence before someone starts speaking a prayer.

"Lord, we trust in you to watch over this baby boy as he is in a fight for his life. Take hold of his hands until he is recovered and healthy. We lift this child up for healing and comfort.

Jesus, please grant us strength and patience as we wait for his full recovery, In Jesus name we pray, amen," Nurse Pam prays.

"Amen," everyone speaks out loud and opens their eyes.

Is God watching over and paying attention to our prayers? I can't remember the last time I took a few minutes to pray in stillness. Is God paying attention? Hugs happen all around to complete the moment filled with hope and compassion. Everyone departs and goes their separate ways while I sit back down with Sebastian. When he wakes up, his little body wiggles as he opens his delicate eyes. I carefully pick him up and hold him in my arms for hours on end, long into the night. Sleepiness hits my system all the sudden and I pass out in the chair in the mist of all the babies in the NICU. Waking up the next morning stiff and sore leaves me confused for a quick second before I realize where I am. Someone must have taken him from my arms at some point in the night. My phone has seven missed calls and four texts from Alistair. It's nice to have someone check up on me once again when I don't make it home, granted it rarely happens. It's disappointing to have missed group for the first time since I started going. It's a good thing today is my day of because I probably would have missed my shift or at least have been late even though I'm already here.

"Sabine?" a familiar voice sounds from a far as I stand up. "Sabine," I hear again. When I turn around, I see Alistair. "Hey," I stretch while still waking up fully.

"You didn't come home last night, I was worried," he says.

"Oh my, you two are living together?" Xavier overhears and interrupts to gossip.

"Roommates. It's good to see you man," Alistair and Xavier pound hug each other.

"Damn girl, get it," Xavier smirks at me.

"It was a long day yesterday for Sebastian and I fell asleep here last night. Now, I'm going to go home to take a much-needed shower. I will catch you later, Alistair" I smile and head for the parking lot.

My phone starts to ring as I sit down in the driver's seat, it's the hospital. An exhausted sigh escapes my lungs when the thought of going back inside appears. It's the nurse from the pediatric wing letting me know Alma's surgery is in thirty minutes. The news pumps adrenaline into my veins and I put my tennis shoes back on to make a run for it if I plan on making it on time. The pediatric wing is on the opposite side of the neonatal intensive care unit.

The smell of fresh hospital coffee hits my nostrils as I run past the cafeteria, it slows me down for a second to contemplate on grabbing a cup. Deciding to skip the coffee is depressing yet the right decision. When I get to Alma's room, she was already gone for the prepping stage. I get to the desk and the nurse apologizes for the late notice; he just started his shift. Still being in yesterday's scrubs with my identification card attached has its perk to get through to Alma.

"There she is!" I approach Alma winded and smiling like a crazy person.

"I didn't think you were coming," she vulnerably states.

"Wouldn't miss it for the world, girl! There was lots of traffic", I lie to spare her feelings.

"Ready to get wheeled into surgery missy?" her nurse arrives. "I'm scared, Sabine." She quickly grabs my hand as panic flushes her face.

"Don't be. Your mom will be right here when you wake up. You're a strong independent woman remember?" I squeeze her hand and reassure her, "And you are too, right?" her eyes shine with hope.

"Of course, I'll be waiting with your mom." I let go and she gets wheeled in.

"You look exhausted, why don't you go home and get some sleep and I will call you when she's in recovery," Joan offers.

"You are a gem, but I am here for Alma and you. I got you. I will let you buy me a cup of coffee though," I smile.

"Coffee is the least I can do," her energy radiates gratitude.

For the next four hours, Joan and I become well acquainted with each other. Joan is someone I would hang out with if I met her under other circumstances, it's nice getting to know her and Alma. She shares about what her life was like falling in love and being young and free before having a child.

"Alma's battle with cancer took a huge toll on my relationship with Alma's father, Rob. When he left, I had to get a second job and take a second mortgage out on the house just to pay for the hospital bills. The amount of pain and stress I was under felt unreal at times. The even more unreal thing is we got an anonymous donor for her hospital bills out of the blue. I thought it was a joke." Joan breaks down a huge part of her life story.

"That's insane! You have no clue on who it is?" I'm shocked. "No idea. They also paid for three other kids. I sobbed for a while when they told me. I got to go back to my career and show up for my daughter again.

I'm telling you Sabine; angels are out there."

Joan bares her heart.

The strength this woman has is unbelievable, admirable. People underestimate the toll it takes on parents who have sick children. Even I have underestimated it. Hearing about her husband leaving and giving up on them reminds me of Sebastian's mom. Her story and experience compel me to share what happened yesterday with Karen trying to give her sick baby up for adoption.

"I couldn't imagine being a position to give my child up. The mental state someone has to be in to choose a different life for their child, it's heartbreaking. It takes an insane amount of courage to admit you are not what is best for the child. Don't you think?" Joan asks.

"I didn't think of it like that." Shame comes up.

Was I too rough on Karen Osgood? Should she be given the benefit of the doubt because the pain is somewhat unbearable? Giving your baby up for adoption isn't a decision to take lightly, it's a heavy life choice. Maybe the strength Karen has to give her child away will be the best thing to ever happen to him.

"But to give your child away to make room for the next one and hope they are healthy. How is that fair?" I ask.

"It's not fair. Alma's father left and he now has a new family. It felt like the end of the world at the time but him leaving seems like the best decision for her now. I can't tell you what it would be like if he was still around but I can look at and appreciate the good that comes out of that situation. I do understand your point though, your reaction was really just out of love for her son", Joan offers insight. Joan wraps up the deep conversation before we head back to the waiting room. Alma should be waking up any minute now. The surgery was a complete success and the smile on her face is priceless when she notices us walk in.

"You did amazing, sweetheart! Final surgery before you can go home. You're almost there." I hold her hand.

"I didn't do anything Sabine, they put me to sleep and I laid there." Alma's drugged personality is a literal person.

"Alma, Sabine has to go home. She has been here since yesterday with no sleep. I'm sure she will be back." Joan breaks the news to her daughter for me.

"Thank you for coming," she gives me a faded smile.

I say my goodbyes and I leave them to have their space as I head to Bugsby. As I walk to my car, I see Alistair standing outside talking to a man I don't recognize. It dawns on me that he is standing with Roger Briones, the man he went out on a date with. Alistair locks eyes with me across the parking lot as I pass near them on the way to my car. He quickly says his goodbyes to Roger and runs to catch up with me. He taps on my shoulder and my body collapses into his arms. He holds me tight and I melt in his embrace. I close my eyes and ignore my surroundings for the next thirty silent seconds.

"You need a shower," he breaks the silence.

"I need a lot of things before I go home and ignore the world. Did you need to get your car? I can take you but it needs to be now," I offer.

"Nope. Go home and get some rest woman," he demands.

"Who was that guy?" I'm sleep walking at this point.

"Please drive safe." Alistair ignores my question and gently pushes me towards my car.

CHAPTER 14

There is plenty to do before Halloween arrives next week. I've been out shopping this morning, getting materials for my costume before support group. Grabbing the coffee and bagels at a nearby café is my last stop before heading to the high school. Saturday mornings are always a busy time in coffee shops, well every morning is. Waiting in this long line makes me wonder if I should have called ahead with such a big order. I get to the counter and order ten bagels with a ninety-six-ounce coffee traveler box. It's a good thing there is an hour 'til show time because the wait will be twenty minutes. Time flies by with me people watching. College students doing homework, people grabbing coffee before a long day at work, love birds flirting with each other on a cute coffee date. People watching gets put to an end when I spot a familiar face walking through the entrance door. Weeks have gone by without seeing the man I once loved and surprisingly nothing resurfaces. It's quite of an aha moment.

"Well, hello, stranger," Joseph approaches me with an inviting energy.

"Good morning, how are you?" I genuinely ask because his energy right now is one I've never witnessed.

"I've been better. I stopped by the apartment the other day and was stunned when it was empty. You moved out?" he seems hurt by it.

"Yeah, I did, I needed a change. Turned out to be one of the best decisions." I smile at the thought.

"Where you staying now? Maybe we can hang out some time, I miss you Sab." He tries to touch my arm and I discreetly dodge it.

"How is Celia?" I try to change the subject.

"Turns out I made a huge mistake. She cheated on me, hurts like hell. Maybe it's my karma. You seeing anyone?" he pauses before the inevitable question.

"I'm sorry to hear that, it doesn't feel good to be on the receiving end. I've got my eye on someone, but I'm in no rush," I vaguely respond.

"Well, I hope he treats you better than I did. You deserve it. If it doesn't work out, give me a call and maybe we can Netflix and chill." He chuckles.

"Order ready for Sabine!" the barista announces.

"Hey, there is this support group for dealing with infidelity. It changed my life and could do some good for you too. Good luck out there, Joe." I hand him Maliha's card and grab my order.

The awkward run in with Joseph had my mood skyrocketing into bliss after realizing there are no feelings left for him. I kind of feel sorry for him. Tons of energy flows through my body with excitement to share with the group. Unfortunately, giving Joseph information about the meetings pushed my exit date up, but I feel ready anyways. Music blasts through the car radio as I sing and cheer to celebrate feeling so good. Paramore always does the trick.

All I can think about now is Alistair Barker. Let's be honest, he is rarely not on my mind. A few people were already inside when I arrive with the refreshments. This will be the first meeting without Hannah's bubbly presence, Luis is still showing up.

Me: Hey, meeting starts in twenty minutes. You're usually

here by now. See you soon!

Me: Fifteen minutes, Al. I hope you are bringing me the strongest cup of coffee.

Me: Ten minutes, I'm saving you a seat.

Me: Alistair, I hope you're okay. We are about to start.

Every five minutes goes by with me checking the time on my phone, waiting for Alistair. I send him a couple of text messages, but he doesn't reply. It doesn't look like he opened or read them either. The meeting is about to start and Alistair is nowhere to be found, this is probably what he felt like the morning I missed. My first meeting without Hannah and Alistair feels different, too weird. I grab a cup of coffee and sit in the seat next to Luis to greet him good morning.

"Good morning, everyone! Today we will be discussing ......anger. But first, let's check in. How are you doing? Whoever wants to share, go for it," Maliha opens the discussion.

"I will go first. As you all know, Hannah and I have started dating and it's going great, but we are experiencing a few hiccups. When we get into arguments, she has been accusing me of cheating or telling me I will cheat on her and break her heart. I don't know how to handle it quite frankly. It's a challenge. Honestly, I've never had a girlfriend react this way so much. It helps to know her past but still., Luis opens up first.

"Well, I wouldn't cheat on her that's for sure," Gregory jokes. "Good advice. This is a good area to practice patience for you. Positive affirmations and healthy reassurance can help someone feel more secure when prior infidelity trauma. It will help her feel important to you and maybe even desired. It works on people with that love language, but especially people who have a past of infidelity," Maliha shares her wisdom.

"Also, I think it's important for you to state how you're not Jude and you would never hurt her. Deep down she knows your eyes won't wander," I put my hand on his shoulder.

"I struggled to not text Sarah and won. I can't seem to stop missing her. I can't get her out of my head even though she cheated on me numerous times," Samira takes her turn.

"It's normal to miss someone you love. There is nothing wrong with that," Maliha responds.

"Also, the more you regain love for yourself, she won't appear in your mind as much," Luis adds. "I hope so," Samira sighs.

"I would love to share next. For the first time in forever, I feel liberated. This morning on my coffee run, I ran into Joseph and there was no hurt or pain coming up for me. He asked me to Netflix and chill like nothing happened between us. That moment made me recognize what a blessing his infidelity was. I'm not happy it happened, but it opened a whole new life for me that I am in love with. I have amazing friends, a beautiful place to live, good mental and physical health. What more could I ask for?" My face lights up. "Time for a new man," Luis jokes and I laugh and nudge his shoulder.

"You don't *need* a man, Sabine. But, it's okay to want one. This is incredible news, I'm happy for you. You earned it all," Maliha says.

"Unfortunately, with all being said, I am ready to move on and graduate from Surviving betrayal. Maliha, thank you for everything you do to heal our broken hearts. I couldn't have done it without all of you," I get emotional.

"Oh God!" Maliha blurts out with terror.

The nine-month pregnant professional quickly gets out of her chair and rushes to her phone. A small sized wet spot displays in Maliha's chair, she could soon go into labor before her anger lesson is supposed to start. Everyone jumps out of their seats to attend to the woman panicking in the heat of the moment. Luis grabs her phone to call her husband and leaves with her to the hospital. My last support group meeting is cut short from a baby arriving into this world. Today is filled with an abundance of good news.

I scurry to get home and tell Alistair about my morning; he should be awake by now. Dropping my purse and keys by the front door to deliver the news when my eyes start to burn from seeing a naked stranger in the kitchen. Roger Briones is standing butt naked in the kitchen.

"Woah!" I quickly cover my eyes.

"Oh shit, sorry." He grabs a plate to cover his private area.

"So, this is what he skipped his morning for?" I say feeling disappointed for a few reasons.

"Was he supposed to be somewhere? We've had a busy morning. Alistair is in the shower," Roger winks and disgust flushes over me.

"Okay, remember he doesn't live alone for the next time you want to play the nudist role,"

I dish him attitude and race to my room to get ready for work.

Thirty minutes later and I'm rocking purple skeleton scrubs for today's shift. The kitchen is empty when I return to fill my travel mug with coffee before heading out. Coffee is running my day, I'm past the point of no return.

"Hey! Just read your texts. What's the amazing revelation you had this fine morning?" Alistair greets me.

"Oh, it's nothing. You missed Maliha going into labor mid meeting though," I decide to keep my news but share hers.

"Holy shit! That's a good story for the little one. Is everything okay?" he taps my arm with concern.

"Everything is great, just running late for work," I lie through my smile and escape out the door.

Bugsby's engine revs a couple times but doesn't start, this day is turning bad quickly. My body freezes and the palms of my hands catch my face as it falls in despair. A knock on my window startles me out of my position. Roger motions for me to roll my window door for conversation. He offers me a ride to the hospital since he is heading there anyways. It's embarrassing but looks like there are no other options than to go with the nudist man dating my roommate friend. Conversation is nonexistent during the ride; heavy metal music fills the silence between us. What does he know about me because all I got was his name? He should be thanking me for his new situationship with Alistair due to them meeting at the hospital. What is this feeling, bitterness? What's wrong with me?

"So, you like Alistair huh?" I blurt out.

"Definitely, what's not to like? Have you seen him?" he looks at me with crazy eyes.

"Yes, I have," nervous laughter comes out.

"You're a little hard to read Sabine," he bluntly states with a calm tone.

"What are you trying to read?" confused, that came out of nowhere.

"Well, my new man talks an awful lot about you and I don't see what he's talking about," he says with no hesitation.

"Excuse me?" My face scrunches up.

"Well, he says nothing about you and I see why. Thanks for the ride, I guess." I open the door.

"Wait, that came out wrong. You just seem closed off to me," he tries again.

"You're allowed to feel whatever you feel. It's okay, I know who I am. Have a great day. Thanks for the lift by the way," I smile and quickly get out of the car.

Something about that guy sends creepy chills down my body. It feels like I need to shower being around him. Let's hope it's not going to be often, although unlikely to happen since his man and I are close friends and roommates. His man.

A few people compliment my festive pair of scrubs on my way into work. The NICU is overly crowded today with specialists, nurses and new parents. Heavy machinery sounds and lights fill the room as usual. This place is never quiet, which comes to a surprise to parents arriving for the first time. Frankly, when I first started here it was a surprise when the place, I imagined was an opposite illusion to the reality. My shift starts as its time for the infants to receive their round of medications. The back-medication closet has a large organization system, easy to track what we need. Looking around for a few more types of doses, Dr. Vaughn approaches me.

"Can I help you find something?" Dr. Vaughn asks.

"No, I've got it. I get medications in here all the time. Can I help you?" I ask.

"Actually yeah, that would be great. I'm looking for Dr. Hu." He rubs the back of his neck.

"I can take you to him." I grab my tray of medications.

"Duke Vaughn, Geneticist. It's nice to meet you." He grabs the tray from me while we walk.

"Sabine Montgomery, nurse and almost nurse practitioner. Nice to see you again." I reach my hand out.

"I do remember now. So, this is your department. Now I know where to find you if I figure out a way to ask you out," he flirts.

"So, what patient were you called into see?" ignoring his pass at me.

"Patel. Fresh to the world with a birth defect I need to check out." He's charismatic.

"Patel?" My brain is stirring for the similarity.

"Maliha Patel?" I realize.

"I don't know the first name, just the last." His head tilts.

"No, that's the mother. She went into labor this morning," I inform.

"Wait, you guys meet parents before babies come into the NICU?

There is already enough on your plate, don't you think?" he asks.

"She's a friend of mine. I was with her this morning when her water broke. Long story. Hello, Dr. Hu. This is…." I start to say as we approach the doctor.

"Dr. Vaughn," he shakes Dr. Hu's hand.

Baby Patel lays in her container with the biggest brown eyes staring up at us. She's here, ready to follow in her mommy's footsteps. Overhearing their conversation, she has down syndrome. Maliha must have known her baby would have down syndrome because it can be detected during pregnancy. We happen to be overstaffed today, escaping to see Maliha for a few minutes is manageable.

The warrior woman looks exhausted, she just gave birth to miracle for the world to have. A tall, bald, Latino man with dark brown facial hair sits beside her, holding her hand. He is not what I would have pictured her husband to look like. I sneak in their room and Maliha's face lights up like a Christmas tree.

"Hey!" she whispers.

"Hi! Your daughter is so precious. Her piercing brown eyes are beautiful. She's in the best possible hands." I hug the new mother. "Girl, you look good in uniform! No wonder Alistair wants to volunteer in your department." She smirks and seems to have warmed up to the idea of Alistair and I, like the rest of the group.

"Hi, I'm Vince." He stands up and shakes my hand.

"It's nice to meet you, Vince. Congratulations on becoming a father! Your wife is amazing, I was in the meeting this morning when her water broke, so it's a little funny how today is turning out." I smile.

"Happens in a small town. Thank you for your work," he laughs.

"Did you choose a name yet?" asking like I do with all the new parents.

"Arya." Maliha smiles.

"Arya Patel, welcome to the world. What a beautiful name. I better get going, just wanted to sneak over here and bring some love on your special day. It's nice to meet you Vince and congratulations to you both," I say my goodbyes and leave.

CHAPTER 15

Alistair sits shirtless in the rocking chair with Sebastian in his arms. Skin to skin contact healing has never looked this good in the NICU. He is a popular man with the nurses and doctors around here, including a few new moms. We should put a stack of rags out for the people drooling over him. If they only knew he was the most incredible person on top of looking like a God, they would try to find a way to clone him.

Sebastian's eyes are glued to Alistair's face, admiring the man who spends all his time holding him during the fight of his life. He has been responding really well to his oxygen treatments, recovery is slowing getting back on track. Thank God. He had us all scared for a hot minute, lots of prayer circles surrounding the baby boy. Everyone realized how amazing the prayer circles feel, they have a few a day for some of the children.

Karen hasn't showed up to see him since the last time she was here to give him away, and it drives me crazy. Dr. Vaughn walks in as I'm feeding Arya. He's been here a few times since baby Patel arrived. He's a rather tall man with a long face, big round tipped nose, pirate like facial hair. His energy feels cocky yet confident, flirty yet professional and sweet yet masculine. He's one of those guys that needs to walk around with metaphoric caution tape wrapped around them. Alistair looks at me as I look at Duke, he catches my wondering eye and smiles quietly with his condescending smirk. My eyes roll to the back of my head in response to his nosey presence in this room.

"Nurse Montgomery, good afternoon," Duke smiles his pearly whites at me.

"Afternoon, Doctor," I respond without eye contact.

"You've got a bit of a hard shell don't you," he smiles and squints his eyes.

"Why does everyone keep saying that? Do I have RBF?" I ask as our eyes meet.

"There are those beautiful eyes." His eyes meet mine and catches my smile.

"Don't tell me you're a man who tells women to smile," my tone turns sassy.

"Not at all. You don't have to smile, but maybe ease up on the death stares Montgomery," he chuckles.

"No promises," a nervous laugh escapes my smile.

"I'm aware that its very inappropriate to ask you out in your workplace, but I promise I'm great with rejection. I would kick myself if I didn't take the shot. You seeing anyone?" Duke puts himself out there.

"Highly inappropriate, Doctor." I smile and move to feed the next patient.

"You like rock climbing?" he moves closer but still respects my space.

"Is that where you bring all the women you date?" I tease.

"Most definitely, but you'd be the most beautiful one." He's smooth talking now.

"Lucky for you, rock climbing is on my bucket list." I look up at him.

"I knew I woke up feeling lucky today. What else is on that list?"

Duke asks as he scans paperwork.

"I have a day off on Monday, I'll get a hold of you and maybe we can climb some rocks. I mean, if you're lucky that day. I can put my number in your phone." It kills me inside to flirt back, but I'm enjoying it. He hands me his phone and my digits get entered.

"Yes ma'am. See you then," Duke dramatically body checks me before going on about his business.

Alistair raises his eyebrow towards me when Duke leaves the area for good. My facial expression tells him to not make a peep about what just happened before his eyes. He laughs which accidently wakes Sebastian up, the baby starts crying. Quite frankly, Sebastian crying is celebratory. His cry is getting louder by day, which means his lungs are getting stronger.

My phone vibrates in my pocket, the hospital is calling. I'm confused at the caller identification because I'm here. It's a nurse over in the pediatric wing. He mentions Joan put my contact information in Alma's notes and to get down there immediately. My shift is over in fifteen minutes, but Dr. Hu lets me go early so I head to the pediatric department. He's pretty great to us nurses and staff. Alma's room is empty when I walk in and panic sets in, where is she?

"Boo!" Alma jumps out behind the door in orange dress and black leggings.

"Oh my God, you scared me! Alma, your clothes. You look stunning" She jumps into my arms.

"Wait, are you going home?!" I add as realization sets in.

"Yes!" Alma screams.

"Oh, sweetheart, I'm so happy for you," I hug her tightly as my eyes water.

"Don't worry, I'll be back. I will be working with you when I become a doctor to help people, like you." Her eyes sparkle. "That's a great dream, I can't wait," my hand caresses her cheek.

"Ok baby, it's time to head home." Joan says as she walks in. "Hi Joan. Congratulations on this special day!" I hug Joan. "Thank you. Thank you for everything. You have such a big heart Sabine. Sorry about the scaring you part, it was her idea," she playfully blames her daughter while she hugs me tighter.

"You two take care. I can't wait to see what life has in store for you guys. You have my number, right?" I proudly ask and Joan nods.

Alma joins in our embrace for a little group hug before they leave the hospital, hopefully for good. Tears of joy fall down my face as I look around the room Alma called home for over a year. It's always a joyous occasion when a child gets discharged from the hospital. Before heading back to grab my things, I stop by the desk to thank the nurse for calling me. I need to go home and take a nice hot bath with a chilled glass of wine. A sudden gasp hit my lungs as I realize I got a ride to work this morning and have no plans on how I will get home. Most of adults probably think ahead and plan more than me. My things still sit in the place they have been in all day when I get back from the pediatric department. A folded piece of paper falls out of the jacket, it's a note from Alistair. As I unfold the message, Duke interrupts.

"Hey, I didn't know you were still here. Thought you'd be long gone by now," Duke approaches again.

"Forgot I got a ride to work this morning," I giggle and crumple the paper and shove it in my pocket.

"Oh, then let me give you a ride home. I'm about to head out," he offers.

"No, thank you. I can just call someone. I appreciate the offer though," I reject his suggestion.

"Nonsense Montgomery. On the way to your place, we can go do something," he persistently said.

"On the way? I'm in my nasty work clothes and I'm exhausted.

A hot bath is calling my name," I persist as well.

"As am I. We can see a movie, all that is required is sitting, relaxing and enjoying. How does that sound?" he respectfully pushes harder one last time.

"You really have an answer for everything don't you?" I try not to smile.

"Not everything." He smiles back.

"Okay, we can see a movie. Just a movie," I concede.

A part of me wanted to say yes from the beginning, but the other side is screaming no for unknown reasons. Something about his energy is too charming and smooth, although his smile is to die for. Duke finishes up his paperwork and grabs his long dark grey peacoat jacket before we head out.

We run to his car in order to stay as dry as possible in these Oregon showers. A tingling sensation hits my stomach as we jump in the car, it could be butterflies or my intuition being skeptical. Skepticism is a natural trait I was brought up with, given my history with Joseph and my parents. Deep breaths form, curtesy of my healthy lungs to clear my head with a spiral of fear and doubt. There must be a war in the heavens because it's pouring up a storm outside.

"Dr. Vaughn, tell me about yourself. What inspired you to become a doctor? Why genes?" lighting up conversation. "You can call me Duke," his smile is as charming as ever. "Duke," I correct myself.

"Well, I have amazing little sisters who have down syndrome. They are twins. I grew up very different than them and I was obsessed with finding out why they were different. The answer is simple, I fell in love with science. My mother was in the military and I was old enough to help raise them when she went off to do her thing. They grew on me over the years and I couldn't imagine a life without them. They are a huge inspiration in what type of medicine I chose to practice and here I am," Duke opens up.

"That is a beautiful reason why. You should feel fortunate to be their brother. I can only imagine how they keep you on your toes," I playfully tease him.

"Hey now, I can keep up," he laughs.

Seeing a soft side to him creates warm sparkles in my chest, I'm a sucker for good hearted men. The whole ride, I sit in the passenger seat admiring the structure of his face as he spills his life out for me. Small wrinkles hug his eyes when he smiles big at the sweetest parts of his life story. My pocket buzzes when Duke pulls into a parking spot near the back.

Alistair: Hey, did you need a ride home? I'm done. I forgot your car broke down on you this morning.

There was no way in hell I was going to tell him I'm out and about with Duke Vaughn. I can already picture the thoughts of him mocking me, stirring up in that brain of his.

Me: I got a ride from a coworker. Thank you for thinking of me!

A little fib doesn't hurt anybody. Well, could it technically be a truthful fib?

Duke takes my hand and helps me out of his light blue Jeep Wrangler. He is presenting as the perfect gentleman, he pays for the tickets, food and drinks. It's been a while since I've sat in a theater chair, eating hot fresh buttered popcorn, watching a loud movie on the big screen. This is my first official date ever, well as an adult, outside of a long high school sweetheart relationship.

"I'm really glad you came," Duke whispers as the lights go out. "Thank you for the invitation," I speak truthfully.

The movie starts to play and begins with the stereotypical dance team trying to win a competition to raise money for their team. Nothing compares to the classic Channing Tatum dance movies, even the ones following his exist. We share a medium bag of popcorn and a small carton of Dibs. The nostalgia in this Dibs bites bring back fun memories.

Halfway through the movie, Duke slowly slides his hand into mine and intertwines our fingers together. Such a sweet and simple gesture, kind of hard to hide my smile. Suddenly, silence smashes into the theatre room along with total darkness. The storm outside the takes power right out of the building, maybe the city. Gasps and chatter begin to fill the room, a few children become startled from the dark. A few people yell out of irritation with the movie being shut off. Others are grabbing their things to leave. Two men in uniforms walk in with sizable flashlights, to keep the crowd calm and informed. They inform us that a powerline nearby has been hit, which affects a wide twenty-mile radius. The older gentlemen employee offers us an opportunity to stay inside until the storm clears up and the power turns back on. There is no rush what so ever, and Duke and I decide to stay in the high up seats 'til the storm clears.

"Sabine!" a familiar high pitch voice screeches from a distance.

"Huh," I look around in confusion.

"Ha, I knew it was you!" Alma slowly runs up with her mother's phone flashing light.

"Alma wait, I can't see where I am stepping," Joan desperately hollers as she walks closer.

"Alma! Hello!" surprise marks my face.

"You don't have regular clothes?" Alma looks repulsed after wrapping her arms around my waist.

"Hey. Hey, I would have dressed up if I knew I would be running into you," I humor her disgust.

"You must be Alistair. Nice to meet you, I'm Joan. I've heard great things about you!" Joan reaches her hand out to shake Dukes.

"Duke Vaughn. Nice to meet you, Joan."

He smiles and makes direct eye contact as I die inside.

"He is a colleague of mine," is the only thing my mind could think of because I want to run away.

Joan catches the aftermath of her comment and says her goodbyes and best wishes. Alma gave her mom a little pushback on leaving, but gives in after Joan insists on leaving. Her hug is the tightest she's ever given, maybe she thinks she will never see me again.

When they are far enough away, Duke and I look at each other and burst into laughter. Laughing seems to be the only way through an extremely awkward situation. I'm starting to rethink staying a little while after Joan leaves a huge elephant in the room, we both feel it. On the contrary, Duke falls back in his chair with no other care in the world. His hand reaches out to grab mine and pulls me down to the seat next to him. I'm relieved he seems unphased about Joan's comment, we are in the clear. I think. I hope. Duke grabs one flake of buttered popcorn from the bucket and throws it up in the air to catch it with his mouth. Me being impressed, I give it a try and it pokes me in the eye and he makes fun of my attempt. Another flake gets tossed in the air and misses the target once again, maybe third times a charm.

"Focus! Envision the popcorn. Be the popcorn," he dramatically jokes before I throw it in the air.

"I did it!" the volume of my words fly out a little loud.

We cheer and stand up in excitement as if we won something extravagant on a game show. The popcorn eventually runs out and we debate on getting more but choose not to. The theatre has cleared out a good amount since the power went out. People have things to do, but I'm on a date. Holy shit, I'm on a date and it feels natural.

"Your tattoo there on your left arm was showing from your long sleeve earlier. Can I see it?" Duke asks me to lift my sleeve.

"It's not just one tattoo actually, I have a sleeve. On both arms."

I pull my compression sleeve up as far as it will let me.

"That's pretty dope Montgomery. I would love to see them all sometime, tattoos are attractive as hell," Duke flashes his phone light to see.

"I love the dark Halloween witchy theme, its hot. I mean, you are one beautiful woman." He runs his finger over my arm, his touch feels like fire.

"Thank you. Well, I will say that you have good taste. That's a plus for you," I laugh and nudge his arm. The sexual tension is too thick at this point.

"I have a sailor duck tattoo on my calf that I got in college. I wish I could say it was a dare," he moves quick to lift his pant leg up.

A few hours of talking, laughing and playing flies by before an authority worker comes in with the weather news. It's dark and gloomy, but the rain has transitioned into a pace that is a lot less scary. We casually hold hands walking back to the car and reconnect them as he drives. The truth is, we could have left when the lights went out but I'm glad we didn't. A good time continues until the very last second when Duke pulls into my driveway. Our bodies don't budge for a moment of silence.

"I can't remember that last time I had this much fun," Duke's hands fall from the steering wheel into his lap.

"Yeah, I don't have many days like this either. I needed today, thank you, Duke," I put my hand on his forearm.

"Just wait until Monday when we go rock climbing. It's going to rock your socks off!" he said with a dramatic effect to support his pun.

"I am really looking forward to it actually. I'll text you. Thanks for the ride too." I kiss his cheek before I open the door.

Duke pulls me back in and his lips almost meet for the first time.

"May I?" he whispers.

"Please do," I answer honestly, eyes his lips.

He grabs the side of my face, pulls me closer and softly presses his lips into mine. He pulls away too quickly and I pull him right ack into my embrace. Our noses passionately smash into each other while Duke rests his hand on the back of my head. The windows fog up as our breathing gets simultaneously heavier in the heated moment. He grabs my hair and gently pulls my head back; his eyes stare right into mine before his lips caress my neck. My head starts to spin, then a loud thunder strike brings me back into my body. The thunder strikes at the perfect time to stop us from getting to carried away.

"I have to go," I wish I didn't have to.

"Yes ma'am. I will see you Thursday. Well, probably at work

first," he corrects himself

I kiss his cheek for the last time today and climb out of the Jeep. Turning back to wave at him before I enter my house. Seconds after closing the door, I lean back against it to collect myself. My heart is racing and my body is jelly, my breath has been taken away.

CHAPTER 16

A listair walks through the front door at the crack of dawn after his weekend long ski trip. His eyes grow wide when he notices me cuddled into the comfy couch with my hot cup of coffee. It feels like a whole month since we have been alone in the same room, there is always someone around. I haven't seen Roger around here since the last time he spent the night and woke up for a morning of naked leisure, courtesy of Alistair Barker.

The coffee pot beeps to turn off just as he grabs a landscape painted mug, perfect timing. He gets his fresh coffee and wiggles into the spot right next to me in the couch cushions. I don't budge when he practically sits on the left side of my body, I miss him. The tiny bags under his eyes are evidence of a badass fun filled weekend. My head naturally rests on his shoulder, he moves his arm and wraps it around me into a warm cuddle. No words between us, just affection. Life seems serene whenever he's around, feels safe.

"Can I tell you something?" Alistair breaks the silence. "Yes, of course." I break our cuddle to face him.

"It's a big deal and I'm a little nervous how you'll react," his voice shakes.

"You can always tell me anything. No judgments here, I promise," my heart drops to my stomach. "Uhmm.. urrr," he adjusts his body.

"You okay? Did something happen? Do I need to kick someone's ass? Is it Roger?" I dramatically ask as I rest my hand on his.

"What do you think about me adopting Sebastian Osgood?" he asks with serious direct eye contact.

"Woah," I'm speechless. I never thought in a million years those words would come out of his mouth.

"What do you think? Would that be okay with you? I mean it's not a for sure thing, it's just a thought right now," his speech speeds up from nervousness.

"Is it okay with me? You don't need my permission. You would be the perfect parent for him," I pause. "You are an angel sent from above Alistair Barker," tears start to form when I gently grab his face.

"I was really worried you'd be upset at the idea." He looks down with a deep frown.

"That baby deserves you," I tilt his head back up and look him straight in the eyes.

"It's going to be a process and quite the journey," forehead wrinkles form as he smiles. "Are you ready to be a father?" my thumbs cup his cheeks.

"More than anything," a tear falls down his cheek.

My thumb swipes his tear and my lips comfort the middle of his forehead. The sexual tension between us turns exceptionally thick moments after Alistair's big revealed secret. What is wrong with me? There's no way to hold it together any longer, we simply chop the tension with a machete. His lips brushed mine, softly, delicately, like the stroke of a feather, just long enough to feel the warmth of my skin. A slight pause occurs when our foreheads rest against each other, we close our eyes for our hearts absorb every second of this present moment. Something about his kiss feels like something I've never felt before, it radiates love. Feels like home. For the first time, my heart truly feels his, it's breathtaking. Alistair kisses my forehead one last time before he heads off to get much needed rest in his own bed. He takes my breath away then leaves me alone with loud scrambled thoughts. He knows what he is doing by leaving me here like this. It's unheard of for me to kiss two guys within the time span of days, what has gotten into me? I laugh at the thought of what my life has quickly turned into, it's bizarre. A lot of processing my life needs to happen for me to catch up with myself.

After finishing the cup of joe resting in my lap, I rinse my dish and get ready for my morning run. It's time to do something about this built-up sexual frustration, hopefully running will get the job done. Moving into a different place allowed me to choose a more challenging direction. It's refreshing to get a change of scenery, just now am I starting to get used to it.

The nature trail is just as beautiful as the last and the path before that. The importance of running on cement, pavement or gravel when it's been raining is crucial to avoid slipping in mud or falling. It's messy to say the least. The air is freezing leaving the grass and rocks with frosty tips. The time is early enough before the sun fully rises and melts the winter wonderland aesthetic away for the day. Red and Yellow leaves decorate the trees and ground, natures finest autumn décor. The strong cold air makes it easier to breathe while running long distance but stiffens my muscles a little too much. Stretching is key. A lot of muddy spots along the trail, just as I suspected. If only it could be possible to be traumatized by too many slips and falls in the stupid clay material dirt. I've got too much adrenaline pumping thorough my veins, my pace is fast and my legs can't stop moving.

Just to think a couple of years ago I couldn't even run a full minute without dying from lack of oxygen. More people walk this path than the last few ones I've stepped foot on. Just the right song starts to play and leaves a nice background melody for the thoughts circling my mind. All I can think of is watching Alistair chase Sebastian around the playground when he's six or holds him at night when he gets his first nightmare. His dream kills mine to raise my favorite kid in the world. Alistair is more qualified for the role, he's the one. It's not like I won't be able to see the little guy. Where would that leave Duke and I? A nearby scream breaks the fantasy scenario thriving in my head, a woman slips in the mud. Go figure. She's covered in mud after a hard fall, you can barely see the colors in the front side of her outfit.

"Jesus Christ, are you okay?" I race to help her up and easily slip on my back side. We both burst into laughter at our embarrassment. I lay stiff for a few seconds to catch my breath.

"Are we okay is more like it, we are a mess. Can you help me up darling?" she asks as she braces herself.

"Yes, I'm a nurse. Let me take a look at you." I quickly get up and reach out my hands to assist. I recognize her from somewhere, but I can't quite put my finger on it. By the look on her face, she could possibly have the same idea.

"Thank you, sweetie, but I will be okay just a little banged up. Hey, you're the girl that was crying on the park bench with the cheating boyfriend." She states the past, then I realize who she is. "Yes! Diane, right? Maybe now you can remember me as the girl who slipped in the mud with you." An awkward giggle comes out.

"Sorry, I didn't mean it like that. Thank you for helping me. How weird to run into you again, especially on the other side of town." Diane raises an eyebrow.

"Yeah, what are the odds. I actually just moved around here and it only made sense to run in a park closer to home. Do you live around here? How is the little one?" I remember she has a son.

"Oh wow, congratulations! My brother lives around here and I thought I could get a walk in before we meet for breakfast, think I should reschedule now." She chuckles as she tries to move her sore body.

"Lots of ice and rest today and tomorrow!" I advise.

"Oh yes, lots of care. How are you? You seem to have a light and bright energy this time, looks good on you. I hope you didn't take that guy back," Diane bluntly says.

"Oh no, I would never in a million years. I kind of fell for someone else," a smile escapes my lips.

"Get it, girl! He must be doing something right because you are glowing. If he doesn't act right, I'll come and kick his ass. It seems like we have a habit of finding each other," she laughs.

"If he doesn't act right, I'll kick his ass! Well, I better get going and get cleaned up, now. It was nice running into you again Diane." Extending my muddy arms out for a hug.

"Have a great day, Sabine. Thank you for helping me girl!"

Diane starts to slowly walk away.

A little chuckle pours out when I process the fact that I am covered in mud. I must have manifested it because I know better than to move to fast in unstable ground area. Everyone passing by have sympathetic looks in regards to my outfit and it being obvious what happened. I really need to start finding a new way to workout, running in the cold is not for me anymore. The sun is out and shining bright by the time I reach the front door of my house, our house. I start to get butterflies in my stomach before I open the front door, I can't stop thinking about that kiss. Both kisses.

"Look who is alive." I'm surprised to see Alistair awake.

"Just needed a twenty-six-minute power nap. Twenty-six minutes is all you need to be revived from the dead. Didn't you know? Plus, I have somewhere to be that involves food. Want to join? Woah, what happened to you?" he offers an invitation until he looks my way.

"What? You don't like my new look?" I pretend to be offended.

"You should definitely fire your stylist," he laughs too hard.

"So, you mean to tell me the men I saw this morning weren't checking me out?" pretending to act surprised.

"No, they were definitely checking you out." Alistair body checks me and dramatically bites his lip.

"Shut up!" I laugh and lightly shove his shoulder.

Alistair tries to dodge my dirty hands and complains about getting mud on him. He nudges me back and demands I get straight into the shower. A few more jokes about slipping in mud fall from his mouth, and I decide to run and jump into his arms with my filthy clothes. I fall to the ground when he doesn't try to catch me. Alistair makes fun and holds out his hand to help me up, and I pull him to the ground and his body falls right on top of mine. His hands hit the ground to prevent his figure crashing too hard onto mine, he could crush me. The playful mood quickly turns serious

and heavy. His eyes get me every time, it's easy to get lost in these pretty browns. He rests his face in the crook of my neck and sighs in defeat to the shared dirt between us. The weight of his giant physique starts to hurt mine, especially after my previous fall in nature earlier.

"As much as I would love to stay like this, you're hurting me," I desperately say.

"Oh, my bad mud monster," Alistair gets up on his knees and reaches out a hand to help me up.

"Now, you're a mud monster." I take his hand and he yanks me and I fall into his lap.

"How's this?" our faces closely meet once again as my thighs straddle his lap.

"This. This doesn't hurt. This is good." My heart feels as if it's beating out of my chest and my body feels weak. I don't move a muscle as I feel his breath on my lips.

"Sabine," he quietly speaks as his eyes are piercing through mine.

We know this can't happen. I clear my throat as I break the moment of our endless possibilities, it's not our moment to have while he is with Roger and I with Duke. Alistair's face reads slight disappointment but he seems to cover it quickly before I could possibly notice. I notice.

Even I am disappointed in myself for stopping whatever was going to happen between us.

Trying to avoid awkward tension, I bring up what happened in the park today, and how I ran into the woman who held me the day after I found out about Joseph's second life. Of course, I left out what I shared with her regarding a man I have unexpectedly developed feelings for. The hard part is who should have come to mind when I told her the secret, Duke or Alistair? I guess one could say I'm dating Duke Vaughn, I rather not be open about it.

"How's your boyfriend?" I ask Alistair while I redo my hair.

"I don't have a boyfriend, how's yours?" his response is sharp. "I'm a single pringle." I keep my answer short and sweet. "Right, that's not what I hear through the grapevine. Hey, did you ever read that note I put in your jacket?" Alistair is curious as ever.

"No actually. It's still in that jacket. What did it say?" I refuse to tell him I lost the note.

A sudden knock at the door, jolts my body off his. It's Roger Briones, Alistair's non boyfriend showing up kills our conversation completely. My shower awaits me.

"Why the hell are you two all muddy?" Roger speaks before I could escape fully.

"We went on a run and I accidently slipped in the mud and tripped her. I wouldn't recommend it," Alistair surprisingly lies. "Gross. I don't run and certainly not in mud. I enjoy lighting my weights in my clean gym. Wait, you went running after our long weekend and early morning arrival," Roger seems suspicious.

"Dedication at its finest!" I randomly blurt out and run into my room.

I quickly close my door and get undressed but stay near the door to eavesdrop on their conversation. Alistair seems caught off guard that his beau showed up unannounced. Roger sounds annoyed we went running together when they have a lunch date. Boring, I thought I would hear the good stuff.

"Do you have to go see that sick baby again? I want to go out tonight!" Roger whines inconsiderately.

"First of all, I am a volunteer. Second of all, we just spent the whole weekend together. How are you not sick of me yet?" Alistair responds.

"I mean he's not even your kid, I'm sure the child's parents feel some type of way," Roger steps out of line into disrespect.

Roger doesn't know anything? Why hasn't Alistair told him about Sebastian? I gasp at the thought of Roger being another one of Alistair's meaningless hookup rebounds.

CHAPTER 17

It's the day before Halloween. Duke brings me to his rock-climbing gym for a holiday gathering event. This is the third time I am climbing this gigantic rock wall with multicolored stepping stones bolted in. Each climb up feels heavier and heavier which makes my hard work over the past few years so worth it when I hit the top. The energy in the building is vibrant and festive, the room is full of mostly young adults. I make it to the top and all I see when I look down is Duke's handsome face smiling big at me. He shares his favorite hobby with me and takes me to his happy place, I'm honored. His face lights up in this place, his smile is wide around the people who share his passion. I didn't realize how much fun it would be and how amazingly friendly everyone is, underestimating the community aspect. I mean I wasn't expecting ogres, but I also wasn't expecting the all-inclusive small community vibe.

The way down from the top is a semi scary moment, yet quite exhilarating. I never thought I would be able to physically do an activity like this. A dream come true. Duke proudly takes my hand when I ditch the harness, can't help but smile at it. He's naturally giving me the simple things I've always wanted from Joseph.

"What?" Duke catches my smile.

"Nothing," stopping my face from blushing is impossible at this point.

"What? Is there something on my face?" he laughs and wipes his face.

"It's nothing....you're just cute. I was just thinking of how happy I have been feeling lately with everything going on in my life. I feel great." I smile big.

"I hope I'm involved in the category of "everything going on","

Duke puts air finger quotations while saying everything going on.

"Yes, of course you are. You know you are," I playfully knock his shoulder and my smile widens from ear to ear.

"Good, I like what I'm hearing. My turn, I'm going up!" Duke attaches his harness to the rope and begins to climb.

Of course, Duke climbs his wall with ease. To be fair, he's done it over a million times. They have extreme walls on the other side but we all know I could never climb those right now. He's pretty much a good sport other than showing off for everyone. It's daring, he loves his passion for the rock.

"Hey, your Duke's girlfriend, right?" a really fit, brown skinned woman covered in tattoos and gold jewelry approaches me.

"Hi, I'm Sabine. No, we are good friends. What's your name?" I greet her.

"Zara. Sorry for being nosey, we've just never seen him bring a girl to this gym before. He invites people all the time but not like this," she states her disbelief.

"Are you a friend or ex or….," I ask.

"God no. I mean, no to exes. I've been climbing here ever since this place opened. It's always nice to see new faces here," she smiles.

"Zara, back off woman. She's taken," Duke puts his sweaty arm around me while he catches his breath.

"Good friends, is how she put it," she one ups Duke.

"Ouch. That cuts deep Montgomery," his tone is playfully sarcastic.

Zara says her goodbyes after their pissing competition. Her delicate gold chain hangs from her nostril piercing to her ear is one of the most beautiful pieces of jewelry I've seen in a while. She's my first friend other than Duke at this place. I'm starting to feel like I blend in here, feels good. Duke steps out of his harness and squirts water into his mouth. He's hot and sweaty.

"You need my towel to wipe your drool?" He jokes, but I can tell he likes it.

"You aight," I joke back knowing he's hotter than hell.

"What are you doing tomorrow night? I would like to do something with you," he asks his flirtatious question.

"I would love to but I have plans with Alistair." I awkwardly look away.

"Ahhh, Alistair. Will there always be competition with this guy?"

Duke isn't afraid to be blunt.

"We made plans to hand out candy to the trick or treaters because it's my first Halloween at the house," I brush off his energy.

"I see the way you look at each other," Duke sassily shakes his head.

"I'm here with you. That's got to count for something. I wouldn't be here if I didn't want to Duke," I push back.

"Roger was right about you." He snickers and sighs.

"Roger?" my mind boggles.

"I want someone who is all in with me. I am too old to be chasing someone who is chasing someone else," he continues.

"Roger Briones?" my mind is stuck. "I mean you…" Duke keeps talking.

"Stop, stop, stop," I interrupt him. "You know Roger? You guys talk about me, why?" I ask.

"Yeah, I mean we all work in the same hospital, Sabine. I like to get to know everyone and we became good friends," he responds. "With an agenda, I see. Why are you two talking about me? I barely know him." I'm confused.

"It's nothing. It slipped anyways," he sighs.

"Duke Vaughn, spit it out already." I glare at him hard

"He wanted me to take you out and see where things go because you are into Alistair. He thought the more time you spend with me, he can spend with Alistair. He warned me that you're uptight and cold most of the time. I could agree, but there's a lot more depth to you than he knows. Coldness comes from walls and boundaries. I just didn't expect to have a great time with you," he tries to backtrack.

"You asked me out because someone else told you to, and you think you're too old for games?" my voice softens.

"We have a good thing going, you know? You can't deny what you felt when you kissed me," he softens his tone to match mine.

"I should get going. Thank you for bringing me here and sharing your hobby with me. It's been a lot of fun and I guess I'll see you around sometime." My head hurts.

"Don't go," he grabs my hand as I turn away.

"I really should. I'll see you around Duke." I grab my things and walk out.

Leaving Duke inside the rock-climbing gym is the best decision to stray away from causing a scene. Uptight and cold. They don't know anything about me. My blood is boiling after his little immature secret comes to light. Of course, he had to ruin a good time. Who does he think he is? Who does Roger think he is? I knew something was off about him, that conniving crazy jackass. The music is blasting loud enough to make Bugsby shake to mask the words I scream at the top of my lungs. It's beyond me how grown men can act like this, especially well-educated men who should know better. My brain will explode if Alistair has been in on this plan all along, only time will tell. He can't possibly know; it would shatter me. All I can think about is giving the next person I see a piece of my mind.

The house is dark when I first walk in, then I see the two men I didn't want to see. They sit at the table eating dinner with wine and candles on a fancy set for two. I see Roger, then I see red.

"Heyyy," Roger prolongs the greeting.

Before I know it, my hand meets Roger's right cheek with hard force. Yes, it did make me feel better. I know it's immature to slap someone out of anger but my body had a mind of its own. What's the harm in meeting him on his level?

"Sabine!" Alistair grabs my arm before I strike again.

Roger looks straight into my eyes with no emotion, he's figured out the source of my anger. "No, stop. I deserved that." He stands still.

"No, you didn't. Sabine, what the hell is wrong with you?" Alistair responds quickly.

"Let your NON-boyfriend tell you," I raise my voice.

"Oh honey, boyfriend is definitely the title!" Roger's aggressive tone is sassy.

"Where do you find these guys? Why do you attract people like this?" the anger is loud in my voice.

"What the hell is going on? Someone, tell me right this minute!" Alistair raises his voice.

"Tell me he's not your boyfriend, Alistair," my eyes start to fill with tears, but I have control. For now.

"Sabine, please," he responds softly.

"Your boyfriend told Duke Vaughn to start a relationship with me to get me away from you. Funny thing is that he had nothing to worry about all along, huh?" I scrunch my nose and the tears start to fall. I hate that I cry when I'm mad.

"What?" Alistair's face falls.

"What? I wanted more time with my man and I got you a man. What's wrong with that? Duke is a gem. He mentioned he met you at the party and I ceased the opportunity," Roger tries to downplay the situation.

"I don't need you dictating who I hang out with. We aren't in a relationship, you know that. We are all adults here, there was no need for scheming, babe," Alistair's hand graces Roger's cheek.

Watching Alistair with Roger makes me sick now that I know what a deceiving person Roger is. I've always had a bad feeling about him and I was right, my intuition was right. The only thing I can muster in my brain is that I don't want to spend the night here under the same roof as them. My overnight bag sits on the bed as I stuff random clothes and toiletries that I'll need. Staying somewhere else tonight is an overdramatic move but I just can't be here right now.

There is a knock at my door that opens the cracked space wider. Alistair stands alone in the frame of my bedroom door. He doesn't say anything at first. Once he realizes I'm packing, he freaks out and tries to stop me.

"Don't leave. Where are you going?" he panics.

"I'm going go stay over at Ophelia's house and help her finish the costumes for her kids," I made it up but it's not a bad idea.

"Please don't go. I sent Roger home." His tone seeps with sadness.

"High five," I sarcastically raise up my hand. "I deserve that." He laughs.

"Don't laugh, it's not funny," I say as I continue packing. "Then, don't be funny," he sits on my bag full of clothes.

"Hey, get off! Alistair!" I try to push him off but his body doesn't budge.

"Sabine, please stay!" his voice raises but not loud.

"Give me three reasons why I shouldn't leave." I stand with my arms crossed.

"Roger is gone. Tomorrow is Halloween, and because I don't want to lose you," his eyes are peeled to the floor.

"Roger is gone. What does that mean? He's not here? You broke up with him? You killed him?" I give him full force attitude.

"He's gone. I'm done with him," he states.

"I still didn't hear a reason to stay," I pout and try to hide my smile.

"Roger was the easy choice because nothing serious could come from it. I got so drunk on our first date because all I could think about was you, but I can't fail again. I thought Lennox loved me and I was wrong. All I want right now is to adopt Sebastian and give all my love and energy to raising a family. I knew I was going to have to let him go after I made the choice to have kids on my own. I don't want to lose you, you're one of the best things in my life. I don't want to lose my best friend." His voice is strong.

"Okay. I'll stay, but you have to give me a foot massage." I smile. Alistair's face has a grateful yet devilish smile right before he sweeps me off the ground and carries me into the living room. This is the first time anyone has ever picked me up like this, I'm shocked, scared and aroused at the same time. He throws me on the couch and I can't help but laugh because I'm feeling too much right now. Alistair glares at me before breaking out into laughter himself, seems we both need the energy release. I get comfy on the couch and suddenly a pillow hits my face before his body falls directly next to mine. I playfully throw my feet onto his lap with a smug look on my face, chills shoot up my body when his hands grab my right foot. My eyes roll to the back of my head and followed by a dramatic moan when he starts to dig deep with the foot massage.

The dumb smirk on his face gives my stomach butterflies, I can't help but melt with his touch.

"Do you think I'm cold?" I can't get that label out of my head. "No, I wouldn't say cold. You know who you are and you have little space for bullshit. Uneasy people can be intimidated by that. That's on them, not you. It's okay to hold your cards close," he responds as he switches to my left foot. He tells me what I needed

to hear whether he truly believes it or not.

"Thank you for that. I love you too, by the way. You're going to be the best father a kid could ask for, especially Sebastian," I plant a kiss on his forehead.

CHAPTER 18

"There you are," Alistair says as I walk through the front door.

"Sorry, a nurse called in sick and I had to cover some of his responsibilities. It's okay because it's still a little light outside. Cute costume," I try and hide my smile at his cuteness.

"Don't I make Sully look good?" he holds out his hands and does a three sixty spin.

"That's the cutest thing. I just remembered your nephew is Mike Wazowski. Is he coming over?" I ask.

"Something like that. Go shower and get your costume on, girl. Time is ticking!" he pushes me towards my room with his hands on my hips.

"Hey, hey don't rush me." I swat his hands away.

The cold shower water hits my hot and sweaty skin creating steam, which radiates off my body like a freshly hot frying pan getting rinsed after cooking. Chilling liquid washing away todays hard work, patient's pain and suffering, and my hardcore feelings for the grown man dressed as a cartoon character for his nephew. Goosebumps fill my outer layer when I get out of the shower, and I shiver as I run to my room wrapping a towel around me. Music bounces from the stereo, which triggers a full-on solo, naked, dance party. I am pumped for Halloween. My outfit hangs on a clothes-hanger in my closet, a black hat sits on my dresser, and black booties are in front the shoe rack.

After getting dressed, I check myself out in the mirror for a final time before I meet Alistair at the front door. My costume is more of a sexy, but classy outfit, Ms. Krueger. I have long black stockings

under my thigh high black flared skirt. My cropped top sweater has thick pink and black horizontal stripes with designed ripped holes across it. The black hat and booties top off the outfit.

"Damn you look good, girl! Freddy better not come for me tonight" Alistair walks in my room at the right time.

"Why thank you Mr. Sullivan. Just don't fall asleep," my voice is playfully seductive followed by a beautiful make upped wink.

"You ready? We have to leave in a few minutes." Alistair adjusts his costume.

"Leave? No, we have to hand candy out to the kiddos," I'm confused.

"You see, that was a great cover plan for the actual plan. Huh?" he smirks.

"Cover plan? What's going on you big blue monster?" I tug on his outfit.

"I guess you'll just have to wait and see. I'll meet you in the car."

His smile is devious as he taps my nose and leaves.

I'm watching him as he drives with the endearingly smug look on his face. Where are we going? Am I under dressed? Am I overdressed? My outfit isn't too promiscuous, but it's not wholesome either. I mean, he went all out in his costume. We could be going somewhere to meet his nephew, or maybe we are taking the little guy trick or treating. Looking this good makes me contemplate not having plans with Duke. Should I feel guilty for thinking that? It has been thirty minutes and he's still driving. It dawns on me that we might be headed to The Halloweentown event in St Helens, the miles sign that says St. Helens is a dead giveaway. My smile grows wide from feeling extremely touched, I hold back my words in case I am mistaken. Alistair looks at me when we are eight miles away, and I can't hold my excitement any longer. I clap and break into my happy dance.

"What?" Alistair's smile becomes as big as mine.

"Nothing," I'm overwhelmed right now.

"You know where we are going now, don't you?" he's still smiling.

"This is the sweetest thing anyone has ever done for me!" my eyes water.

"You better stop crying or your makeup will get messed up, or maybe you should mess up your makeup to add the wow factor." He chuckles. I quickly peck his cheek the second he puts the car in park. Looking at him, I know I have the most amazing best friend a girl could ask for.

Witches, warlocks, zombies, monsters, fairies, mythical creatures loom around the vicinity, sharing the same love for their favorite childhood Halloween town. Background sounds from the movie play through the speakers that surround the place, roaming sounds. My heart is substantially warm and the little girl inside of me is elated as if it's Christmas morning. Props and set items from the movie are placed out for the public to celebrate and take photo memories.

Then, the most important thing before my eyes, it's picture perfect, the giant Halloween town pumpkin. It glorious, magnificent even. Alistair takes his phone out and tells me to stand in front of spooky monument, but I grab his hand and take him with me for a selfie. A young teen girl nearby offers to take a full-length picture for us, he sneaks a kiss on my lips when the picture is captured. He takes my breathe away, completely unexplainable. There is plenty to see and experience to fill our evening of fun. I can't wait to go in the Haunted House.

"Can I buy you a caramel apple?" Alistair puts his arm around my shoulder.

"Alistair! There you are," a familiar voice hollers behind us with a shriek of a toddler.

"Diane?" I'm shocked to see her yet again coincidentally; Jackson is wearing the very costume Alistair bought his nephew.

"Sabine? Girl, you look hot!" Diane has the same look on her face as I do.

"That's what I said!" Alistair responds.

"You two are related? Roz? Your costume is legendary. Your family costume idea is the best," my eyes grow wide and my jaw drops.

"Wait, you two know each other? Diane is my sister and this little guy is my nephew that you hear so much about." Alistair' confusion begins to match ours.

"Diane is the woman from the park," I say still in shock.

"And Sabine is the woman you can't shut up about?" Diane's smile grows bigger than James Giant Peach.

"Alistair volunteers at the hospital I work at. He is one of the popular volunteers with the babies and the mothers." I smirk towards Diane while ignoring the dig she took at her brother.

"Now it makes sense that we kept running into each other, fate. How adorable! You better keep this one. The only one I met at breakfast the other week, he's got to go. What's his name? Robert?" Diane throws the right amount of shade, I knew I liked her.

"Roger," I snicker.

"Hey, hey now. Well, we don't have to do introductions, Sabine is a friend and the woman who is renting a room from me," Alistair breaks up our jokes on his love life.

"Friends," Diane scoffs.

"Best of friends," my eyes meet Alistair's when I smile.

"Diane wasn't even your other surprise, but my game is on fire tonight," he rubs his hands with a matching smirk.

"Another surprise?" What else could a girl need?" What does he have up his sleeve?

"Carmel apples anyone?" his offer extends to his sister.

As the night goes on, we've taken the cutest photos of great memories. Bennie the cab driver, Gort's messy house of everything lost, and Marnie's first broomstick. I lost count of how many people commented on the adorable Monsters Inc. duo. The sun goes down and a band begin to play the traditional Halloween tunes with a dance floor in front of the stage. A group of children gather in the front row dancing their carefree, little, costume butts off. The band performs *Thriller* by Michael Jackson, Diane grabs our hands and drags us to the dance floor. She is serious about her dancing, that woman can move.

This moment is it, it's real happiness. Alistair is a giant blue monster dancing his tail off, Diane has joy written all over her face while dancing with her son in her arms. His face says it all, his face looks how I feel inside. I've never felt such intense love and admiration as I look at the people surrounding me. It's different, It's new, I can't get enough of it. A little girl dressed as a pumpkin, walks towards us waving her arms smiling, she looks like Alma but I'm not taking chances in case it's not. My head turns quickly when Alistair waves both of his arms at the pumpkin girl and her mom who is dressed as a doctor. It is Alma!

"I was waving at you! You didn't wave back." Alma approaches us with her mom by her side.

"I wasn't sure it was you. Hi!" I wrap my arms around her. "Surprise!" Alistair winks at me. Alma laughs hysterically at Alistair in his costume.

"What a great surprise you are! How are you?" I wrap my arms around her.

"Great! I made it into the spelling bee at my school! Can you come? Mom can she come?" she sounds elated.

"Heck yeah you are. I am so proud of you! Hi Joan." My arms reach out to hug Joan after giving Alma the most enthusiastic high five.

"Should we go get our face painted?" Diane cheerfully asks the group, but the question is aimed more towards Alma.

"Yes!" Alma shouts and starts jumping up and down. This is the most energy I have seen her have, it's incredible.

The six of us get in line for a wicked face painting to humor the cutest six-year-old pumpkin girl. The woman who paints Alistair's face thought he needed a blue face to really tie his costume together. Joan gets a haunted pumpkin painted on her right cheek and Diane has a smiling pumpkin on her left cheek. Alma and I are getting matching designs with a broomstick, cauldron and of course, a pumpkin. Diane's son passed on the activity considering he is passed out in his stroller next to his mama, poor guy. Alma pauses the artist and roughly coughs into her elbow. Panic rushes through my veins and my head shoots straight to Joan. She meets my eyes with a calm reassuring smile, maybe it's just tickle in her throat, it is pretty cold out tonight. After we all are done being made into freshly painted Halloween sculptors, Diane has to get home to put the baby to bed. Mom life.

"At this point, I hope to see you again Sabine." Diane hugs me tight.

"You will, we live in the same house," Alistair chimes in.

"You better not mess with her, I will kick your ass, little one," Diane threatens her much younger brother, which makes everyone laugh considering he's a giant and she's not.

It's sweet how much Diane cares enough to look out for me. I'm sure she has put two and two together from what I've secretly told her and what she sees. The line is too long for the haunted house, we decide to kill time for the line to shorten. Alma wants to play games and have fun rather than spending an hour in line. Us adults agree. We explore Halloween Town with Alma, taking crazy pictures, laughing at how many kids want a picture with Sully, aka Alistair. His face being painted really did tie his costume together. I think he secretly likes it.

"Woah, Look guys! Can we go in there, mommy?" Alma politely asks even though she knows the answer is yes.

Alma points to the tunnel of glowing lights with a path that takes you to what they call the Pumpkin King. They had me sold from the tunnel of lights, it's sort of breathtaking to walk in the middle of it all. Joan takes out her phone after Alma asked for a picture with only me underneath the lights. Her smile is as wide as ever on this incredible Halloween night.

"Your turn," Alma pushes me towards Alistair without any warning.

"Yes, ma'am," he humors the little one.

Alistair wraps his arm around me and smiles for the picture. Such a beautiful and surreal moment. I look into his eyes and the rest of the world melts away. He lives in the moment and presses his lips against mine. Feeling is mutual. Alma's excited squeal breaks our embrace into laughter. She really can't help herself, always one hundred percent alive. Alma struggles to catch her breathe halfway through the walk; her inhaler doesn't help as much as it should. The look on her face when her mom suggest we go back breaks Alistair's heart. He doesn't hesitate another second and picks her up and carries her the rest of the way. Her face lights us like she's on a ride at an amusement park. Yeah, there is no doubt. He will be a great father.

We finally get to the Pumpkin King, but the throne is empty. Seconds later, a giant man jumps out and scares the living day light out of all of us, including the people behind us. That's a great way to shoot adrenaline into our systems after a long walk. Surprisingly, Alma isn't afraid to be spooked. I knew she was special.

"Seems to me we have an imposter or are you from the same patch as I?" The Pumpkin King tries to speak in riddles to Alma and it goes right over her head.

"I am the queen of my pumpkin patch, Mr. Pumpkin." Apparently, she understood his riddle very well.

"What would be the first letter of your name pumpkin queen?"

He asks her with a tiny pumpkin in his hand and a knife.

"A!" She replies with enthusiasm.

Oddly, this isn't the weirdest conversation I have witnessed in my lifetime. The Pumpkin King comes with a secret talent, he quickly carves a beautiful calligraph "A" into the tiny pumpkin and hands it to Alma. Bravo, pumpkin man. By the look on her face, this has to be the best night of her life. Maybe, mine too. We say our gratitude and goodbyes before Alistair picks up Alma and we head back towards the haunted house. My favorite part, besides everything else tonight. Alma stares at me with puzzling eyes.

"What are you?" she asks as her brain is turning.

"The scissor man's wife?" she adds.

"The scissor man?" Alistair laughs at me because he knows she got it from a previous conversation of ours.

"Have you heard of Freddy Krueger? You are probably way too young to know but he is a scary man from some movies that will haunt you. I am his wife tonight." Now I am laughing at myself.

"Oh. So, are you Alistair's wife sometimes? Or the guy at the movies?" She's trying hard to understand what's going on, her and I both.

"Alma, let's talk about something else please," Joan tries to stop her daughter from creating awkwardness within our group. With Alistair and I.

The giant blue monster man looks at me with a gentle smile of compassion. It doesn't have to be awkward if we don't make it awkward. Another thing to appreciate about him. The walk back doesn't feel as long because we take less time admiring the lights, we've been staring at for the past half hour. The line for the haunted house attraction is a fifteen-minute wait, not bad at all. Joan stands in line and waits with us even though she isn't going in. Spooky isn't her thing. Alma squeezes my hand harder and harder the closer we get to the door. I can only imagine she's doing it to her mom with her other hand.

"Alma, it's almost time. Are you sure you want to go in? You don't have to." Joan tries to give her daughter an out but she's adamant about going in with us.

The witch takes our tickets and Joan takes some of our belonging before we enter the house. The spooky sound track gives me life. Alma doesn't let go of her grip on my hand and she quickly grasps for Alistair's hand. The place is crawling with scary evil. The most well make upped clown ever hangs from the ceiling in the pitch-black walk way. We only get glimpses of him from the strobe light. Alma's face looks like she is witnessing murder, but she's doing a lot better than I thought. The clown drops down and Alma screams bloody murder. Now, this is what I thought.

"I want out, please let me out," her body is paralyzed clinging to my leg.

"Alma. Honey, we have to keep walking babe."

I try to soothe her off my leg but she doesn't budge.

"Keep moving, little girl," the clown helps but tries to stay in character.

"I want my mommy," Alma cries.

A person dressed in all black pops out and quietly guides the three of us out of the emergency exit. Should we have brought her in? Probably not. We have scarred her for life. I start to feel guilty and we search for Joan, but Alma bets me to it.

"I'm so sorry. I ruined it. I wanted to be brave like you guys," she cries more from being disappointed I herself.

"Don't be. Thank God you helped get us out. That might have been too scary for me," Alistair attempts to make her feel better and she falls for it.

"Mommy!" Alma takes all the energy left in her to run into her mother's arms.

"Yeah, I had a feeling it would go as such," Joan comforts her daughter.

I hug Alistair for being a great guy all the time. Before the rest of us head home, we stop by the drink stand with a huge sign that says "Wicked hot chocolate." Alistair generously pays for everyone's drinks before we sit at a bench and catch up on our lives. Who would have thought that I would be sitting here having hot chocolate with Alistair, Joan and Alma at the Halloween town event on Halloween? Feels like fate.

"Wait, so how did you two meet?" I ask them.

"I don't know if you know this about me but I work at the adoption agency," Joan answers first.

"Yeah, and I was shocked when I realized she was Joan from Joan and Alma. She is working with me on my process with Sebastian or another child if that doesn't work out." Alistair smiles after thinking about baby Sebastian.

"No way! We really do live in a small town. Joan from Joan and Alma sounds like a band," I laugh at my own joke.

"I'm cold, mommy," Alma interrupts our conversation.

"Okay, we can go in a minute." Joan wraps her arm around her daughter.

"You can take her home." I help Joan out. "You sure?" she asks.

"Yes, of course. Thank you so much for coming. I've had a lot of fun and it was amazing seeing you again little one," I tap her nose before she coughs again.

"Yeah, you get her home and under many blankets. Thank you for coming. This was the most fun I've had in a while. I will be seeing or talking to you soon, Joan." Alistair chimes in.

Alma jumps into my arms before I stand up and reminds me about attending her spelling bee. We all say our goodbyes and go our separate ways, it's just Alistair and I at this point. Tonight, is a night to remember for me, my heart is completely full.

"Did you want to take another crack at that insanely scary house?" Alistair offers.

"I would love to but I'm exhausted and tonight was perfect," I answer honestly.

We take one last picture with our face painting before we walk back to the car. The whole ride home Alistair is cracking jokes about his fear that the face paint won't wash off. He is skeptical that makeup remover wipes can do the job of making him a grown man again. It's late when we get home, I am ready for bed. I pull out extra makeup wipes for the both of us to wipe off the temporary art.

"Can you, do it?" Alistair's tone is adorably innocent. "Yeah, sit down." He sits down on the edge of the couch.

"Close your eyes," the energy between us is calm while I stand between his legs in the silence.

I take the wipe and slowly swipe the blue gunk of his handsome face. As I expected, the paint comes right off. It might take a few wipes, but the job will get done without a problem. Alistair's big hands naturally rest around the back of my legs while I clean his face. He opens his eyes for a second and smiles, I shyly look away so he can't see me smile, but he knows. I know he knows by the smirk on his half blue face.

"Close your eyes!" I try not to smile but it's impossible.

"Yes, ma'am," he chuckles.

I take my time cleansing his face because I don't want this sweet moment to end too soon. He opens his eyes again and I softly shut his eyelids with my fingers before he starts tickling me. I scream from being completely stripped of control over my body, stopping my laughter at this point is impossible.

"Stop. Stop." I laugh hard, trying to catch my breath.

"Well, hurry up so I can take your makeup off," he stops the tickle torture.

"You're crazy if you think I'll let you cleanse this masterpiece. I do this daily. I think I got this, sir."

I finish cleaning his face and he is himself again.

"Come on, let me." He grabs a wipe.

I give in and let him take my makeup off, what could actually go wrong? I thought he was going to scoop my eyeballs out of the sockets at first before I take his hand and show him how to graze my face. He looks embarrassed but I act like it's not a big deal. It's not a big deal. My hands are itching to touch his body, yet I have nowhere to casually place my hands on him. He is on his knees to match the height of me sitting down. He is taking as long as I did, maybe we are on the same sensual page.

"I'm all done. Just as new. Beautiful as can be." Alistair seems nervous.

"You sure? Why are you looking at me like that?" nervous laughter leaves my mouth.

"I think I missed a spot," he pauses.

"Well, then what are you waiting for? Get it" I laugh.

Suddenly, Alistair kisses me. Our lips meet again, they are strangers no longer at this point. The last time we did this here, he left me hot and panting. It's going to be different this time, I remove his costume hat and unzip the body suit zipper. I'm too in the zone to pay any attention to the silly costume. He helps me by taking it off which leaves him in his boxers. Our faces hardly leave each other during the whole strip tease.

"Good night," I smile and start to walk away.

"No, you don't. Get back here," he pulls me back and I can't help but giggle.

"Someone doesn't like the taste of his own medicine," I smirk. "Everyone makes mistakes," he bites his lip and looks at mine.

He starts to pull off my shirt while multitasking; kissing, stripping and walking to the other side of the couch. All I have left is my bra, panties and stockings. I push Alistair's almost naked body onto the couch and place my foot between his legs. Then, I slide one finger on each hand around my leg in the stockings and slowly take them off. He sits there making eye contact the entire time, he bites his bottom lip when I finish the first leg. Then, goes the second leg stocking before I climb on top and straddle him. He wants me, I can feel how much he wants me.

"Jesus Christ," he moans.

CHAPTER 19

It has been quite some time since baby Patel has been discharged from the hospital and sent home to her loving parents. Maliha took her daughter home on my day off and I didn't get to congratulate her. Here I am in line at the coffee shop, bright and early to bring coffee and bagels to Maliha's support group I used to mentally depend on. Congratulations are in order and it's only right to bring gifts to celebrate such a beautiful occasion. The last time I was here, I ran into Joseph, feels like ages ago. My order is called and I am out the door within five minutes after ordering, very impressive.

Walking into the gymnasium after a while brings up a weird but thankful tenderness feeling inside. Maliha's face lights up when she notices me walk in with my hands full of food and gifts. There are two early birds for the meeting, just like old times. I congratulate the new mother with a gift bag filled with diapers, the softest green blanket and a personalized onesie that reads 'Baby Patel.' She loves the gifts and thanks me a few times until I got distracted with a woman, I never thought I would see here again, Hannah.

"Sabine?" Hannah and I walk towards each other and greet one another with a hug.

"Hannah! How are you? What on earth are you doing back here? Or have you never stopped coming?" curiosity fills my brain with slight disbelief.

"Did you know the average woman goes back to her abusive significant other at least seven times until she's done for good?" she asks.

"No. Jude. Damn, I am sorry. You're a survivor because you never stop finding your way back to yourself. I'm proud of you. What happened with Luis?" I ask hoping she doesn't mind me being nosey.

"He actually ghosted me. There's no recovering from infidelity and ghosting." Hannah looks uncomfortable.

"No!" I shout a little too loud and then apologize to everyone when I realize my volume.

"Yep. That did it for me and I hit rock bottom and here I am." She starts to shut down, so I wrap up the conversation.

"Some men can't handle a queen as powerful as you." I wrap her in my embrace.

"Wait! Sabine, your ex-Joseph. He came to a meeting not too long ago. He sure does mention you quite a few times and it was only a matter of time before I put the pieces together. I know it's against the rules to share that info but you did guide him here. All I can say is…. I wouldn't ever give him another shot. He sounds like bad news." Hannah shares the news and pats my shoulder for comfort.

"Wow, good for him. Girl, that ship has sailed. I better get out of here because I rather not have an awkward run in with him. It was great seeing you, Hannah! Don't be a stranger. Come over sometime or text me". One last squeeze before I head out to work. A man leans on Bugsby and I believe I know exactly who it is as I walk closer and closer. So much for trying to avoid an awkward conversation with an ex- boyfriend. The funny thing is that he looks normal, you'd never guess that someone would claim he is unstable. Unstable, what even is stable?

"There she is! I was surprised to see dear Bugsby here," Joseph speaks first.

"Honestly, I didn't think you would come to these meetings."

Avoiding eye contact feels right for this conversation.

"Yeah, I didn't either but you seem genuinely good the last time I saw you and I would like to feel the same. I would still like to get coffee sometime, if you're up for it?" he extends his original offer.

"I actually brought coffee and bagels for the meeting. It's all inside, please help yourself." I wonder if he's going to get the hint. "Aren't you coming inside? You go to these meetings still, right?"

Joseph grabs my arm.

"No, I have a shift to get to. I hope you enjoy your meeting." I move to open my car door but his hand doesn't budge.

"Then maybe we should play hooky for the day and go do something. Want to catch a movie? You've wanted to do that in the past." His grip is slowly getting tighter.

"Is this guy bothering you?" Unexpectedly, Alistair walks up and interrupts. "What's going on here Joe?" he notices the grip on my arm.

"What are you doing here?" I ask Alistair, his answer is the only thing I am thinking about.

"All good man. This is Sabine, the girl I talk about in group. My beautiful ex-girlfriend. The one that got away." Joseph removes his hand altogether and begins to play cool for a second.

"Joe is your Joseph?" Alistair's eyes grow wide, his mind is blown.

"Are you attending meetings here still? You told me you

stopped." Currently, my mind is on one track.

"It's not a big deal." He rubs the back of his neck.

"Don't tell me that she's the girl you've been talking about. She's mine to earn back. I'm sorry, are you having sex with him Sabine?" Joseph turns slightly aggressive and steps closer to me but Alistair steps in between us.

"You need to back up from her. Have some respect" Alistair says while I back up.

"Wow, you really move on quick Sabine. Who else in these meetings have you fucking slept with? Why am I here trying to get you back when you turning into damaged goods?" The mean words fly out of Joseph's mouth.

"Who even are you anymore? I've never met this version of you."

My heart is racing.

"You're not going to talk to her like that, not now and not ever.

Back up before I do it for you," Alistair threatens.

"Alright. Alright. She wasn't worth it to keep in the first place,

clearly. This group is bullshit anyways," Joseph backs down.

Alistair balls up his fist and the look on his face is anything but good. I grab his hand and he unclenches his jaw. He cares about me enough to physically get in the middle, but hitting the guy doesn't solve anything. It shows a great deal of maturity to have self-control in a heated argument and that's something I like about him. I know I lie to myself when I call him my best friend but it's all my heart is comfortable with, ignorance is bliss. A sadness hits me after finding out Alistair is still attending these meetings, why doesn't he feel comfortable confiding in me or even telling me he attends?

"Are you okay?" Alistair asks.

"I'll be fine. Are you okay?" I return the question. "Peachy," he winks then hugs me before walking away. "Alistair," I call out.

"Sabine," he turns around.

"Have a great meeting," I smile and wave.

I'm at war in my head, going back and forth to question why he goes to support group still but he didn't need to be interrogated on an already annoying morning. Plus, I trust him to talk to me if he needs to. I want him to. This morning started out incredible and slowly transformed into a major disappointment, not a good way to start a shift.

Ophelia is the first friendly face I see walking into work, and I instantly feel better. She is supposed to show me her kid's school pictures that came in the mail yesterday. They are growing up too fast.

"I've got some gossip that your ears would love to hear," Ophelia lowers her voice.

"Oh yeah? What's that? Is someone getting fired?"

Unfortunately, gossip cheers me up.

"I overheard the doctors in the break room talking about how Sebastian's crazy mom is really going through with giving him up, and your homeboy wants him," she whispers.

"What? No way!" I act surprised. I can't believe she's really going through with it, and I already knew the second part.

"Yes. This kid is going to have one hell of a story when he gets older," she pops her last grape into her mouth, gets up and goes back to work.

It would be the best thing for Sebastian to get adopted by Alistair. It would be the worst for him to get dragged into the foster care system, no kid deserves that. It just dawns on me that if it really does happen, would I have to move out? We never discussed that far into the possibility. Has he thought about it? Do I fit into that equation? Does he want to kick me to the curb? The best way to clear a busy mind is to drown myself back into saving the babies. Dr. Vaughn is here today to examine a new born boy. Everything stays professional, awkwardness has no space in this hospital today.

"Dr. Vaughn," I nod.

"Nurse Montgomery." He nods back and trying to hide his smile.

"Some of the people at the rock-climbing gym have been asking about you. Zara misses you." He relays the information.

"Are you sure you didn't have to convince all of them to be my friend so I didn't have much time to spend with Alistair?" My reply may be on the bitchy side, but it's the truth.

"I deserved that. To be fair, it drained my bank account to pay them all. Thousands are gone," he jokes.

"Shut up!" I can't help but laugh at the handsome goofball.

"When are you coming back?" He sure is persistent.

"I'll only come back if you stop flirting with me Doctor." I smirk. "Impossible," his smile is good as gold.

"You'll cry yourself to sleep when you realize what you lost," I play.

"Do you have cameras in my house? How did you know? I have to change my pillow cases every hour." He plays back.

"I did really like it there. You're okay if I come back?" I ask.

"Of course, I really am sorry about my intentions in the beginning. You are nothing like Roger said. I hope you can forgive me," he seems genuine.

"You are forgiven. If we are going to be friends, I would like you to try and become friends with Alistair because he is my closest friend and the animosity between you two will be the death of me." I pray he complies.

"You're asking the world of me, Montgomery," Duke says before being pulled away.

My shift runs a bit over which cuts out my time to go home and change before Alma's school spelling bee. It's adorable how proud she is of herself; she should be. She has already conquered something greater than most kids her age, cancer.

By the time I get there, the auditorium is more crowded than I imagined. Joan waves at me from a distance with a saved seat for me. The more people I walk by, I become more self-conscious about being in my scrubs.

"Cute scrubs," Joan compliments. "Thanks," I laugh to myself.

"Who is this empty seat for?" I point to the one next to me. "Alistair said he was coming, but I haven't heard from him,"

Joan whispers as the announcer begins the program.

Alma's hair is short and soft like peach fuzz, ruby red jewelry hangs from her ears, which match her beautiful frilly red dress. She looks stunning for the competition. She notices her mom and I in the crowd and smiles big with a wave. The guy in front of us looks back and shoots a sweet smile our way. Some of the words they are giving the kids seem advanced for their age, but they all seem to be ready to get their spelling on. Newscast. Pioneer. Machine. Wheelchair. Whistling. One by one, contestants start getting eliminated and Alma makes it the top three before she gets eliminated.

The event doesn't last for more than an hour, after we take Alma out for some ice cream to celebrate. The good news is she doesn't ask where Alistair is. Disappointment on a child's face is hard to see. The Freezer Factory Ice cream shop is around the corner from the school and the place was a ghost town considering it's winter. We grab our frozen desserts and sit in an inside booth to keep warm.

"Metamorphosis. Metamorphosis. How could I have gotten that one wrong? I should have studied more." Alma metaphorically kicks herself.

"You're too young to know how to spell that. Don't be too hard on yourself. I still have trouble spelling that and I'm like ancient. I think the generations are getting smarter. I think people ate glue at your age back in the day," I joke with her to raise her spirits.

"Yeah, you're right. There is always next year!" Alma takes a bite of her bubblegum ice cream before coughing.

"You're still coughing?" I look at Alma and then at Joan.

"Yeah, she should be at the end of it by now. She has a little cold,"

Joan responds with no hesitation.

"Awe, poor thing. Are you feeling okay at least?" I turn back to the little one.

"Yes, I'm fine," she takes another bite of her ice cream.

A few others from the spelling bee competition walk in with the same celebratory idea. Alma clings onto her mom and hides in the crook of her arm. Joan laughs to herself and looks at the group and back to me. Seeing parents with only boys, I catch on. Alma has a crush on one of those boys. A red headed boy with a shaved ginger head approaches us while his dad keeps a watchful eye.

"Hi Alma, you did really good today," he is shy as can be. "Thank you, Charlie." She speaks with the sweetest voice.

Charlie smiles and runs back giggling to his dad. We all smile and giggle at their wholesome interaction. Oh, young love. Joan waits an hour until their group leaves to spill the tea on Charlie.

"A few girls at school were teasing her about her hair and he went home that day and asked his dad to buzz all of his hair off. It's was long, to his shoulders! The sweetest thing," Joan has a bright sparkle in her eye, thinking back on the story.

"He likes me," Alma shows her toothless smile.

The three of us spend almost two hours having girl talk and gossiping about Charlie and Joan's work. I catch her up on my drama situation with Alistair and Duke. Alma's list is more than a page full of fun bucket list activities to complete. It's way past the little one's bedtime, we exchange hugs and go on our way.

Before I know it, I am back at home in an empty house. Where is

Alistair? Five hours later and I have my answer when the man of the hour stumbles through the front door, plastered. Hesitation stops me from encountering a conversation with him, but he has different plans. He walks straight up to me and mumbles a few words that no one would be able to comprehend. I look up at him filled with confusion, he gets the hint from my perfectly groomed eyebrow.

"Lasss partay night cuz we getting a baby, baby" he slurs. "You're getting a baby? Who did you knock up?" I laugh and play off the awkwardness I feel inside.

"Not final, but crazy Karen isss apprishtive that I want to raise Bashitian." He smiles proudly without the ability to open his eyes in the moment.

"Wow, that is really amazing. I am so happy for Bashitian. I thought the last time drinking was your last time drinking, Alistair." I mock him and lecture him all in one.

"Hey, hey, hey. You're making fun anddd that's not nice. I thought we were friends. I'm fine, it's all owe now." He playfully acts offended while grinning the whole time.

"Friends we are, baby daddy!" I raise up my hand for a high five and he reaches over, misses and gently collapses on me.

"Babyyy daddy has a niceee ring to it," Alistair mumbles softly against my stomach.

"I've always wanted a little one to call me Auntie Sabi," I chuckle while placing my hand on his head for comfort. Suddenly, calmness chases my awkward butterflies away.

"Mommy Sabi sounds more like you," he chuckles and passes out on my lap.

My heart races hearing those words leave Alistair's rank mouth. This has to be his last time because God only knows what I would do if he ever put Sebastian in harm's way. I keep still and hold my drunken munchkin of a best friend for a while. Best friend? Roommate? Lover? Definitely, confused.

CHAPTER 20

Stiffness stills my body from being in the same spot for the past seven and a half hours. To my surprised, Alistair lays motionless on top of me until I slowly push him off. The second my body is free; it seems as if every bone in my body cracks simultaneously. The time on the clock reads half past eight, but I have nowhere to be today. Alistair starts to stretch with his eyes closed before a lightbulb goes off in his head.

"Shit! What time is it?" He pops up off the couch and checks the time.

"Woah, it's okay. You need a glass of water or some painkillers?"

I try to help.

"I have a meeting with my adoption attorney in thirty minutes. I've got to go!" He looks at me with a peculiar gaze, then quickly snaps out of it.

The new dad to be, moves quicker than I have ever seen him. He doesn't appear hungover; he hides it better than I ever could. I've never seen him so intoxicated before. Fifteen minutes later, Alistair walks out of his room wearing a fancy dark blue suit. His pants and suit jacket are dark blue over his white button up shirt, topped off with a black tie. He looks in the mirror approximately ten times before saying a word to me, the man is definitely feeling himself.

"How do I look?" Alistair asks extending his arms before doing a three-sixty spin to show off his fit.

"You… ummm," nervous laughter follows the first two words out of my mouth.

"You good?" he laughs.

"Great! You look great." Every word I've ever learned, leaves my brain the moment I see him in that outfit.

The expression on his face leaves me slightly embarrassed. A few minutes after being home alone, someone knocks hard against the front door. I open the door expecting it to be Alistair, who could have accidentally locked himself out, but I's a package. It completely slipped my brain that the bookcase I ordered was expected to be delivered today. Putting this thing together by myself as an ambitious thought. After trying to build it for the past thirty minutes, I'm overwhelmed. It's just me here surrounded by all the bits and pieces in the world.

Another knock at the door, I have no possible clue who it could be this time. I open the door and Duke stands awkwardly rubbing the back of his neck when I open the door.

"Duke?" I'm surprised.

"Hey," he continues to awkwardly stare at the ground.

"What are you doing here? How do you know where I live?" my arms cross during questioning.

"I'm going to the rock-climbing gym and was wondering if you'd like to come. Also… I've dropped you off before, remember?"

He responds.

"That could have been a text, but can't because I have to build a stupid bookcase. I thought it was going to be a simple task." My body loosens up after laughing at myself.

"Well, let me help! It's the least I could do," Duke offers. "Yeah… I don't know," I sigh.

"Please, Sabine. I want to make it up to you." He looks adorably hopeful.

"Fine, but only if we can still go rock climbing after. Plus, you've already apologized. We are cool, I promise. Stop being all awkward and weird now," I smile.

"Deal." He lets go a breath of relief with a grin.

I somehow forgot how kind his smile is, how kind he is. Duke comes in and sits on the couch while I go to the kitchen and make a pot of coffee. This project is going to take some time, so I need caffeine. Hell, I would need coffee if I had nothing to do. The only work I've done is unwrap and unpackage the boards and screws. My only job now is to hold boards together and watch Duke screw them together. What a sight to see. I like the way his hair flops in front of his eyes, how his tongue hangs out a little when he's concentrating. A screw drops out of my hand as I'm handing it to the man with the power tool. He is a lifesaver. I bend quickly the same time he does and his head knocks right into mine causing my body to tumble down. He lets out of a loud grunt and places his hand directly on the target spot. Laughter pours out of both of us until the pain kicks in after the adrenaline filled seconds are over. My head hurts as if my brain is physically rattled.

"Are you okay? Let me see." Duke gets up and gently touches

both his hands on the sides of my scalp.

"Yeah, I'm fine." My hands cover to move his, but he doesn't budge.

"I'm a doctor, I think I know what I am doing. People trust doctors." Duke smiles.

"Oh cute. I bet that works on all the woman who don't know you're a baby doctor." I move his hands from my face, but he doesn't let go of mine.

"Key word is doctor, Montgomery." He smirks.

"So, where were we?" I drop is hands and get back to work.

"Screwing," he laughs and picks the power tool back up.

There is no question of chemistry between the two of us. The question is why do I want to act on it? I am a single pringle even though I don't feel like one. The more we finish and the less parts on the floor helps the stress in my brain disburse. I would've had a mental break down if he didn't show up. His hand touches a part of mine for extra security before he drills the spot. I like his touch.

"Water?" I gulp.

"Yes, please," he responds without breaking our gaze. I break it.

"Can I run something by you?" Duke asks as I hand him a bottle of water.

"Yeah," I respond with no hesitation.

"I've been thinking about this for a while now, but I guess I'm a little on the scared side. Everything in my life is going great, but I feel stagnant. What better time than now, I want to open my own practice." Nervousness pours out of him.

"Really? That's a great idea!" I encourage.

"Really? You don't think I will be in over my head?" he asks. "Even if you are, new things will always have a learning curve. Owning your own practice is a huge accomplishment. Especially in medicine. Plus, don't you already own half of the rock-climbing gym? A business mindset has to be pumping through your blood somehow," I support his dream.

"Thank you for that. This is exactly what I needed to hear," he lets out a sigh of relief.

Two hours and a pot of coffee later, we have a few more boards to put together before a beautiful auburn bookcase is ready to be moved and filled. It shouldn't have taken this long, but what's an activity without amusement? Bonding with him today made me dislike him a little less, but he doesn't need to know that. I catch myself staring at him and immediately grab my empty coffee mug and bring it to the kitchen.

Alistair walks through the front door yelling how amazing his meeting with the attorney went and then, silence.

"Duke Vaughn....... in my house," Alistair states the moment he lays eyes on the man he isn't too fond of.

"Alistair Barker, it's nice to officially meet you," Duke stands up and reaches his hand out to shake Alistair's. "Yeah," he shakes his hand.

"Duke came over to see if I wanted to go rock climbing and saw me struggling with this beauty," I hope my tone doesn't sound as guilty as I feel.

"Yeah, we better get going anyways," Duke speaks with a cordial tone.

I have never changed my outfit so fast in my life, the tension between them is thicker than a bowl of oatmeal. They both need to find something in common and bond over it if they are going to be my friends. Before I leave, I tell Alistair we will talk about his adoption meeting later. He hugs me and after I let go and turn, he grabs my hand and pulls me back.

"I'll see you soon," his right hand holds my face and his lips touch mine for a kiss of passion, right in front of Duke.

"Yeah, we will talk later," I push him off me without being obvious how uncomfortable he just made me.

Duke's face says it all, but fortunately he keeps his mouth shut. My blood starts boiling changing my mind about one thing. I didn't want to talk about it later, and needed to say something now. We get into the car and my excuse to go back inside is how I forgot my water bottle inside. Duke stays in the car while my conversation is waiting for me in the house.

"Alistair!" I shout for him as I walk inside.

"What? Is everything okay?" he walks out of his room in sweats and a tee.

"Listen to me. Don't ever do that to me again. You and him have this weird competition or whatever it is and you put me in a very uncomfortable position with that kiss. You knew what you were doing. I understand there is something special and confusing between us, but we are not in a romantic relationship. I get it you need to entertain the toxic masculinity nonsense, but don't violate me to do it. That is not being a good friend. Do you understand?" My words come out loud and clear.

"Yes, ma'am." He looks afraid but apologetic.

"Anything else you want to say?" My voice is shaky from being upset.

"Yes. I'm really sorry, Sab. It will never happen again, I swear. I put my feelings before yours, and it was highly inappropriate." He sounds sincere in his apology.

"Thank you, now I have some rocks to climb. I will see you later, okay?" This conversation helps my chest feel lighter. I catch my breath on my way back to the car.

"Sorry," I say while getting back into the Jeep.

"Where is your water?" He asks.

"Of course, I forgot to grab it. We can just go." My cheeks run hot and turn red from embarrassment.

"No, I get it. Good for you, girl." Duke smiles and drives off.

The car ride is filled with silence in the company of blasting music. The only thing I can hear are my own thoughts, they seem louder than the words in the songs. What Alistair did is mind boggling, but he did it because of what? There is only one explanation to why a man would make that power move in front of another man. Alistair likes me and he thinks Duke likes me. Never in a million years would I have thought to be in a position like this. I don't want to be that cliché girl from the movies, do I have to choose? Do both guys really want me? What is so special about me? What's special about them? The thing is, in the movies there is always a saint and a bad boy. These two men are both amazing, genuinely good guys. So, who do I choose? Who do I want more? "You know what, I have an idea!" Duke abruptly stops my dark train of thought.

"What's that?" I ask.

"We skip rock climbing today and do something more important that could be a great gesture." He pauses. "I'm listening." I pause for him to continue.

"Let's go get a crib and stuff for a nursery. I think Alistair needs a baby room set up for Sebastian. Don't you think?" Duke finishes. "Duke Vaughn, you have just completely melted my heart. Let's do it!" I quickly kiss his cheek before fastening my seatbelt.

To execute this plan perfectly, we need Alistair to be out of the house for the night.

Me: Diane! Call me ASAP

Within a few minutes she calls and I excitingly pitch the idea for him to babysit while her and Craig go out for date night. He's about to become a parent, he can use all the practice he can get. The used baby store is bigger than we imagined, but being overwhelmed isn't going to stop us. We are on a mission. Where to begin? We need a crib, blanket, changing table, clothes and a few cute comfy decorations. It's not much, but it's a last-minute start. The first thing we need to decide is what color theme fits Sebastian's personality more. How well can you really know a baby? My eyes immediately scan the cribs and spot the perfect warm green crib. It's the one. Duke decides the complimentary color to green will be yellow, he throws a yellow duck themed blanket and mattress cover in the cart.

"Hi there! Can I help you with something?" a kind woman approaches us with a smile and a sweet southern accent.

"I will admit, I was lost for a second but who knew this would be so fun!" There is no stopping this excitement pumping through my veins.

"Yeah, it's addicting spoiling the little ones. How far along are you?" The woman asks which leads to Duke and I bursting into laughter.

"We are making a baby room for our friend who is adopting a baby boy very soon. It's a surprise," Duke answers.

"Friend?" I look up at Duke with playful puppy dog eyes when I hear the word.

"Well, her friend," he winks at me.

The store is filled with a variety of things we didn't even think to put on our list. Alistair is going to need a stroller, car seat, bathing essentials, a rocking chair, toys! We can't forget the toys. Man, children are expensive. Sebastian is worth every penny. Baby clothes are selling for buy two outfits and get two free. What a steal. Fifty outfits later, we are past essentials.

"Look how cute this little duck bath towel is!" I'm obsessed.

"We should do a baby duck theme. I don't see many of those these days," Duke has a brilliant idea.

"Hell yeah! That's so cute! I wonder if they have those really soft couch chairs made into animals. Do you know what I'm talking about?" I ask.

"This version of your is adorable but a little scary," he laughs.

It takes us another thirty minutes to finish our shopping and check out; we have three hours until Alistair comes home from babysitting his nephew. Going overboard in the baby store is an understatement. The room across from mine is an unused spare bedroom, with only a bed and a white dresser. The white dresser will go great with the green and yellow furniture and bedding, but the big boy bed is going to move into my room until after the home visit. It's a good thing Duke drove his pick-up truck today, otherwise none of this would be possible. The crib is one of the heaviest things I've had to carry, maybe I should have stretched. We ran with the duck theme down to the bank. Ducky decals for the walls to match the bedding; one big duck and three little ones came home with us. The bedding is light green and yellow to tie the color scheme together. They did not have a duck chair but I will keep it on my list for next time. I put together a green three drawer shelf and place it beside the dresser for clothes or medical supplies he will need. I grab the large load of baby clothes from the dryer and fold them before I fill the drawer with clothes. When we finish, I take a moment to digest the life coming into this room. Duke finishes vacuuming and I roll out the big baby duck rug in the middle of the room. My eyes begin to water, thinking about Sebastian's journey. This kid is already the most loved baby I know.

"It looks incredible in here," Duke puts his hands on his hips while observing the space.

"I love it. He will love it. Thank you so much. This is the most generous gesture I've ever been a part of." I wrap my arms around Duke and he returns the motion.

"We all know that baby deserves this," he kisses my forehead. "Yeah, he does. Now get out of here before your friend gets home," I look up and smile from ear to ear, proud of my comment. "Now that's the best idea you've had all day. Can we do some rock-climbing this week?" his hands drop to my hip. "Deal!" I gleefully shout.

"It's a date," he looks at me for a reaction.

"It's a date." I roll my eyes and hide my smile.

Am I dating two men at once without actually dating two men at once?

CHAPTER 21

Anita Bridges from the adoption agency is going to be here any minute to do a home check to make sure it's a safe and healthy environment for a child. One of the last steps before the big day. Joan needed to reschedule to attend a personal matter and passed the inspection off to her trusted friend and colleague. Alistair brews coffee and boils water for tea. The prettiest charcuterie board rests on the counter waiting to be devoured. There isn't much to stop the adoption process, but I understand how he can still want to make a great impression. Anyone could tell how tense he is from a mile away; his body immediately eases up as my hand touches his shoulder. I place the snacks and beverages on the coffee table in the living room as he changes his outfit for the fourth time.

"I know I had you check all the rooms yesterday, but can you just double check they are all perfect. She will be here any minute," Alistair yells from his closet.

He can count on me for the job. Little does he know; the rooms have been perfect since last night. I got little to no sleep last night worrying if he was going to spontaneously check the rooms himself. He is a spotless guy who trusts himself. The odds were in my favor. A knock sounds at the door.

"Hi, I'm Anita Bridges. You must be Ms. Montgomery." She reaches out her hand to shake mine.

"Nice to meet you. Please call me Sabine. Come on in," I shake her hand and motion her inside.

"Hello Ms. Bridges, it's nice to see you again." Alistair walks out in a navy-blue collared shirt with black slacks and dress shoes.

The three of us sit down on the couch and enjoy the refreshments while creating small talk before business. Anita is far from shy when it comes to asking questions, she has to know his whole life story by now. After the interrogation with Alistair, she turns her questions to me. I tell her about my career and how I know Joan and Alma, plus my relationship with Sebastian. I'm surprised she hasn't asked how I know Alistair, but maybe they've discussed it in a meeting before.

"So, what is the relationship between the two of you?" Anita asks the question we all knew was coming.

"Friends," Alistair answers.

"Also, I rent a room here. Tenant," I nervously offer too much information.

"You live here?" she asks.

"Yes ma'am." I'm becoming more and more nervous.

"How is the environment here? Do you bring outsiders here often? Do you have children of your own? What is your lifestyle outside of your career?" Ms. Bridges bombards me with questions. "I'm a nurse at the hospital, I work all the time. I've worked closely on Sebastian's case before they removed me from being too emotionally invested which makes sense. A conflict of interest.

Alistair and his home are the place that boy belongs." I hope I add positivity to his case.

The last and most important part of this visit is to check the environment of the soon to be home for baby Sebastian. Anita has already seen the kitchen, dining room and living room area. She asks permission before taking a quick peek in my room, then she quickly opens the door and closes it. Alistair's room is spotless as usual, including his bathroom and walk-in closet. My heart begins to flutter before the moment of truth. It's hard to hold in all my excitement.

"This room is one of the two spare rooms. There is just a bed and dresser in here." Alistair opens the door, turns the light on and gasps.

"How cute, I don't think I've seen a duck theme before." Anita reacts.

"Surprise!" I hold out my hands with a surprise motion of spirit fingers.

"Wow! I'm... how did... this is the nicest thing anyone has ever done for me," He struggles to find the words of gratitude as he takes in the moment.

"You're going to be a great mother, Sabine." Anita smiles. "Oh, no," my eyes grow wild.

"No, it's just me. Single father for table one." He giggles.

"Oh. Well, it will be nice to have a prenatal nurse and just a friend living here while you raise a sick child. If he even makes it." Anita gasps when she realizes what came out of her mouth.

"Oh, I'm sorry. I didn't mean..." She immediately says.

"No, it's okay. I'm prepared for that news,"

Alistair interrupts her with ease.

Ms. Bridges comments about how beautiful and clean the home is and sits down for another cup of tea. She has an abundance of wisdom for new parents in the adopting process, Alistair is trying to absorb it all, like a sponge. He is about to embark on one of the most precious journeys life can offer, fatherhood.

"Alistair, I have one last question for you," Anita says. "Yes, ma'am," he answers.

"Are you ready to be a father?" she asks.

"More than anything," he takes a deep breath.

"Well, sir, congratulations are in order. Sebastian is going to have a wonderful home to come to," Anita shakes his hand and walks out the front door.

Alistair closes the door behind her and presses his back up against the door. He looks at me with a look in his eyes I've never seen before from him. He walks up real close to me, his demeaner doesn't change.

"Sabine," he intimately says.

"Yes?" my heart starts to race as he gets up close and personal. "May I kiss you?" Alistair asks while trying to hide his smirk. "Ooooo, consent How sexy!" I bite my lip and reach up to pull his head for his lips to meet mine.

"Thank you for the nursery, thank you for walking through those infidelity healing gym doors." His lips meet mine again.

"You're welcome, it was actually Duke's idea. You'll have to thank him later when he picks me up in forty-five minutes." I can't help, but smirk.

"I'll have to thank him, but mention him again and I don't think I can do what I'm about to do to you." He picks me up, my legs wrap around his hips as he walks to his bedroom.

Alistair throws me onto his bed and starts unbuttoning his shirt. I lean up on my elbows and watch this smoking hot man get undressed before my eyes. Our eyes don't break contact, all I see is fire in his. He gets on top of me and starts kissing my neck. I struggle to take my clothes off underneath him, he rolls us over and I end up on top. Sex with him is breathtaking, every time. Forty minutes later, we are gasping for air, butt naked under the sheets.

"I love you," Alistair says while trying to catch his breath.

"I...." My phone begins to ring, which interrupts our moment.

"Duke is around the corner. Come on, get dressed. You have some bonding to do with your new friend." I laugh.

"Can't you just tell him we aren't home. I can't wait to thank him, but maybe when I don't have the most beautiful woman laying naked in my bed. I am down to stay in bed for the rest of the day." He gets out of bed knowing what he said isn't an option.

"I've got some climbing of rocks to do!" I quickly get out of bed and put my hair up into a messy bun.

We run around getting properly ready to face Duke like teens rushing to clear the house before their parents get home. There is no way I want Duke getting any hint of what just took place in this room. Then, I think of what went on in this room and considering canceling plans myself, no. Well, what goes on all around this house. I throw on a black skeleton tank, black leggings and my white Nike tennis shoes. Alistair throws his previous outfit back on and heads to the kitchen for some water. A couple pumps of perfume and swipes of deodorant will do the trick. I wash my hands in the kitchen and squirt soap into Alistair's hands to do the same. Duke walks up with a happy filled energy as I open the front door.

"Hey man!" Alistair approaches Duke as he walks inside.

"Hey." Duke waves.

"Thank you for putting the nursery together. It's the most kind hearted thing someone has ever done for me and I heard it was your idea, so thank you. How much do I owe you for it all?" Alistair asks.

"You're welcome. Don't worry about it, it's a congratulations gift to you and Sebastian," Duke generously replies.

"Thank you, I appreciate it more than you know." Alistair hugs Duke. Duke looks at me over Alistair's shoulder with help me eyes. "Good job guys. Fighting toxic masculinity one step at a time.

You ready to go? I'm ready to beat you up the wall." I smile and walk out to the car.

We get to the car and once again I forget my water, silly me. I run back inside the house and kiss my man one last time. I don't forget to grab a water bottle this time and head back out to the car. Duke and I discuss how well the home visit with Ms. Bridges was and how priceless Alistair's reaction was to the nursery. The gym is emptier than usual; we take advantage of all the free wall space. I remember how intimidated I was when I stood in front of this wall for the first time, now it's practically a new hobby.

"Sabine! I thought I was never going to see you again. Duke has a tendency to scare women away," she teases the man.

"Yeah, I can totally see that. You sound like a woman with that experience," I joke back without knowing their history.

"Duke and I had a thing for no more than a hot minute. Then, I realized I wasn't into pretty boys. Women are where it's at," she love taps his cheek with the tips of her fingers.

"Women are in fact the best." I support her case.

"Oh, I see. Montgomery plays for both teams?" Duke is intrigued.

"No, unfortunately it's only men," I laugh with Zara.

"Alright ladies, keep your trash talking to the wall. You'll be grabbing tissues when I hit the top." Duke put his harness on.

I copy him and put my harness on for a little friendly competition. Stretch, Sabine. Stretching will get me loose enough to climb faster and beat daddy long legs. Duke beats me on the first race up the wall, his legs are longer. He was born for this sport.

"You should just give up now, I've been doing this for years."

Duke talks trash.

"Not a chance!" I shout from across the wall.

The people surrounding us cheer as we both fly up the artificially constructed wall again. I don't even glance at him this time, my full focus is between me and these colorful grips. All the sudden, I hear the bell and he's done. What the actual hell, he's a speed demon. I'm out of breath and tired more than usual, but I still finish like a champ. Maybe I went a little too fast then my body can keep up with. The adult exercise I got earlier could have done a number on me. When I get back to the ground, Duke high fives me with both hands before I reach for my water.

"Uh oh, something's wrong." Panic overruns me as I feel dizzy.

"You okay?" Zara asks.

"I think I'm going to faint," I say right before blackness takes over. A few seconds later I come to with Duke hovering over me with panic. The weird thing is, I feel fine when I wake up. The small crowd surrounding us is relieved when I get up without a scratch. I try to convince Duke that I'm fine but he will not take no for an answer. He insists on taking me to the emergency room to get checked, he's over reacting. I only agree to go on the condition that he has to drop me off because I want to go see Sebastian after.

There are a few people in line at the check in desk when he drops me off, I decide to go see Sebastian first. There's no harm in holding a baby in a rocking chair with nurses and doctors around. I turn the corner and see the chair already being used and Sebastian is taken care of by his soon to be father. Alistair sits in the chair holding his soon to be son. His smile is so pure as he strokes Sebastian's tiny hand with his thumb. An unknown warm feeling hits my stomach as I watch them, and I realize I've known my answer all along. It's Alistair, he's the one I want.

Choosing to not disturb them, I uphold my end of the deal and check into the emergency room. The line has shortened a little by the time I walk back. They check me in and give me a bed before drawing my blood to run tests. I have to pee in a cup for more tests. It's feels awkward being the patient and not the nurse. Being hooked up on an IV and machines isn't comfortable one bit. An hour later, a doctor comes in.

"Good afternoon, Ms. Montgomery. I see that you're one of us, it's nice to meet you. First of all, how are you feeling?" she genuinely asks.

"I'm feeling better, a little nervous if I'm honest," I reply.

"You are in good hands. A couple of questions. How are things at home? Do you feel safe at home? Have you had any recent major surgeries? Are you Diabetic?" the doctor repeats the questions they ask every patient.

"I am safe, no surgeries and no," I answer quickly to get to reason I fainted.

"Let's see what's going on. You guys are going to be okay. You are severely dehydrated. As a nurse and health care provider you should know how important drinking fluids is. Your iron levels are on the low side but you should be fine if you put more meat in your diet or other foods of your choosing. Sabine, because you are now providing for two for the next nine months, you need to drink plenty of fluids and eat for two." The doctor looks up from her clipboard.

"I'm pregnant?" my heart drops to my stomach in disbelief.

"Is this the first of you finding out? Congratulations, Ms. Montgomery. Considering your career, you're going to be a great mother. I will have one of the nurses give you information and papers before you get discharged. They can set you up with a fantastic OB/GYN to see how far along you are and all that good stuff," the doctor kindly informs.

Happy tears run down my cheeks; reality is going to take a second to set in. Then, it sets in and the freaking out part begins. Holy shit, I am going to be someone's mom. I don't even have a place of my own, how am I going to support a child right now? The doctor leaves me alone to ugly cry all to myself. I'm still in shock. Getting pregnant was just a fantasy, it's irresponsible to get pregnant this way. Oh God, how is Alistair going to react?

How am I even going to tell him? He's adopting a child any day now, what if he doesn't want two? Can I do this on my own?

CHAPTER 22

Alistair lounges on the couch wearing his reading glasses with his MacBook resting on his lap. Shirtless is always a good look for Alistair Barker, this is what got me into trouble in the first place. I've always wondered what working from home could look like, comfortable I see. Sitting on the couch with a laptop and headphones could also be code for I'm busy, don't talk to me right now. He looks hot, modeling the modern work life. I sip my coffee and admire the cold morning view from the balcony.

"Stop staring at me and get over here," Alistair keeps his eyes on his computer screen.

"Staring is a rather strong word." A nervous laugh escapes. "So, I've been thinking…..," he starts his idea.

"Uh oh!" I dramatically sip my small cup of caffeine.

"Wait, you can still pick me up from work before your shift tonight, right? My sister has already taken my car." Alistair has worry in his eyes.

"Yes and no. I work the night shift tomorrow night. I'm off today. Yes, of course I can pick you up from work." I smile runs wide for some spontaneous reason.

"Okay, great! Do you have plans for today?" he asks.

"I see your wheels turning, Barker. What's up?" I speak.

"The roller-skating rink opens in five minutes and I think we should check off another one of your bucket list items today before I go into work at three. What do you think?" he proposes his thoughtful idea.

"I think you spoil the hell out of me." I feel warm inside.

"You're worth it. Plus, I can't remember the last time I've been roller skating. I hope I still got it." He pushes his work off and jumps up.

"The rink opens at seven thirty in the morning?" I'm in shock when I see the time on my phone.

He ignores my question and walks to his room to get ready. I'm worth it, that man is something else. What do I wear to go roller skating? I'm over the top excited, rushing to my room to find an outfit. People wear flannels around their waist when they skate, I think. Is that a thing? I take the safe bet and go with half black half yellow and black checkered pants over my oversized black shirt tucked in. My face is naturally made up as my hair hangs straight. Perfume looms the space, which freshens up my look. One more peek in the mirror and I am ready.

"You smell divine. You look even better than you smell. And she finally lets her arms out to breathe," Alistair calls me out.

"She is me and I am right here. I'm not afraid to show of my flappy wings." I try to not get defensive because he means no offense.

"I know, wearing compression Under Armor shirts can get tiring at times too. I just love the body of the beautiful woman standing before me is all," his voice is flirty sweetness.

"What's not the love?" I shake off this sweet yet uncomfortable conversation and grab his hand to drag him out the door.

Alistair offers to drive, but I think it's because he's secretly in love with Bugsby. Should I be jealous? He bumps his tunes on the louder side to mask the volume of his terribly goofy singing voice. He loves to sing while driving. Well, everywhere. To be fair, who doesn't? We arrive at our early morning activity and the parking lot is completely empty, except one car. Yeah, I didn't think a lot of people would be able to show up this early.

"Is it just us two? Anyone else showing up as a surprise this time?" I ask.

"Nope. Just the two of us. Disappointed?" he shoots back while he extends his hand out to take mine.

"Not one bit." I smile and reach up to tap the tip of his nose with my index finger.

"Good to kn...'" he grins.

"Alistair!" I shout and interrupt him.

"This place doesn't open until noon!" I read the opening schedule label on the front doors.

"Well, it's a good thing the owner gave me these," he jingles the keys in front of my face before unlocking the entrance doors.

He never ceases to amaze me. Having the whole place to ourselves is something not everyone has the pleasure to experience. Plus, eliminates the stress of accidently bumping into people when learning how to skate. Two pairs of roller-skates sit on the counter when we enter the lobby. His are significantly larger than mine, pretty obvious which pair is for who.

The roller rink area is dark except for the neon lights and disco ball hanging from above.

I finish lacing up my boots and take a second to mentally prepare myself to walk in skates for the first time. Ready or not, here I come. Of course, I didn't budge after that brave thought. Alistair gets up first and extends his hands to help guide me to the floor.

"I'm a little nervous. I don't want to fall." My hands are shaking. "You will fall, but I got you. Think of falling as your right of passage into the realm of funk". He helps me stand and we take baby steps.

My steps are wobbly at first until I tighten my grip on my human walking stick. People make this look easier than it is. The wooden floor is slippery compared to the carpet on the other side.

"You're doing great!" he pulls me as he slowly stakes backwards.

"I feel like a five-year-old!" I laugh at myself through my fear. "Loosen up, Sabi. Steady your balance," his patience eases my nerves.

"Okay, okay, let go!" I regret the words I speak.

Alistair stands in full steady control of his body while I wobble to catch my balance. He extends his right hand to take mine and gently pushes off to start the rolling. His hand is for comfort only, not stability. I push off with my right foot and my left foot automatically follows. I'm doing it. *This is how we do it* by Montell Jordan plays through the loud speakers to match the vibe. The energy in the rink feels how I've imagined it to be. Slow wind brushing my face with my smooth strides.

"I figured ya'll could use some beats! Good morning, you two," the owner says through the microphone in the DJ book.

"Hell yeah, this is incredible. Thank you!"

I yell to the man at the booth.

"Diane's husband owns this place. Craig." Alistair fills me in.

"Haven't skated in forever huh? Don't know if you still got it. Oh, the lies, the coercion." I play around.

I skate as fast and confident as I can into Alistair arms. He catches me and spins us both in circles. The bright lights spin around with us into pure euphoria. I'd go flying if it wasn't for his steady tight grip. The first few laps back and forth are extremely slow as I learn to roller skate for the first time in my life. My balance isn't perfect, but it's damn near.

"There you go. You're getting the hang of it," Alistair encourages.

"I think I'm ready to race." I'm surprisingly optimistic or my competitive side is showing.

"Slow down, speed racer," he laughs.

"I'm serious." I'm afraid but I can't turn back now.

"You are cute when you're serious. Let's eat first, I'm starving."

He kisses the tip of my nose.

"Where did you want to go?" I ask.

"Follow me." He takes my hand into his with a big smile.

We roll out of the rink together. Considering we have a few hours before opening, I take these death trap shoes off to walk. Alistair does the same. As we get closer to another room in the building, Alistair covers my eyes with his mighty soft hands. To my surprise, a beautiful candle lit breakfast presents in the room for birthday kids. I won't have a heart much longer if he doesn't stop melting it. A gasp escapes my lips as this man leaves me speechless once again.

Candles, Orange Juice, omelets with potatoes and avocado.

Chocolate covered strawberries. Am I being punk'd? Someone wake me from this impossible dream. I flip around and wrap my arms around my angel. A few kisses later and we sit to fill our bellies with this delicious meal.

"I don't even know what to say. Never in my life have I been treated like this. I guess I never realize how content I was with being content until I met you." I struggle to get out the perfect words.

"That's not true. You stopped settling for being content when you took the first step to take your life back, multiple times I believe. When you treat yourself better, the world will know to treat you better." He spits his wisdom while shoving potatoes in his mouth.

"I suppose you're right, yeah. I never thought about it like that."

I begin to think.

"Can I ask? What made you want to change your lifestyle and get fit? Was it health? To fit society's standards? Feel better? Perhaps, all of the above," he asks bringing up the earlier conversation again.

"Yes. It wasn't long after I started working in the NICU that I had an epiphany. It was never about the way I looked. I didn't do it for the attention of men because I always felt attractive. Joseph loved the way I looked. He never once made me feel otherwise. I had always felt trapped in my body and silently begging for someone to save me and when I started working with the babies, I realized it was me who needed to save myself. I showed up for them every day so why couldn't I show up for myself. Also, there's nothing more I want than to be a mother and having my previous life was risking my chances of that. The doctors said I couldn't get pregnant until I was healthy enough to do that. Healthy was the goal, not skinny. Skinny just happened." I begin to tear up and Alistair hands me his napkin, the guilt in holding in my secret is intense with these hard-hitting questions.

"Yeah, most of the time that all it is about. Choosing you. It's simple, but most of the time the hardest thing to do." He scoots next to me.

"Is that what it was like for you?" I ask hoping to shift the conversation to catch myself in my vulnerability.

"Oh, yeah. I was at the point with drugs to where it was overdose right now or choose better because no one is coming to save me. It's funny how we all are conditioned to hope for a hero to show up. The more I self-sabotaged and got high, the more my loved ones wanted nothing to do with me. I was all that I had left at that point." He opens his heart.

"Thank God, you pulled yourself out. I'm thankful you're still here. This world would be incredibly dark without you." I've never felt closer to him.

"Yeah, me too. It was pretty scary. The journey is not over. Like nutrition, addiction is a lifelong battle. Yes, it's great when you're on your *A* game, but the low days are really low. As we all know. I've been falling down the rabbit hole lately, I'm human. It's been two days since my last drink and I'm proud of that. I know you were worried, but I got this. Okay, I'm full and ready to win that race. You ready to get back in the rink?" he asks while holding my hand.

"Thank you for sharing pieces of your life with me." I stand up with him.

"Back at you babe. Thank you for listening." He kisses me with gratitude which gives me butterflies.

He takes my hand in his as we walk back to the rink, then I spot a room I haven't seen in years. An arcade. What a waste it would be to not hit the arcade when the place is a ghost town. It's thrilling to feel like a kid again, no responsibilities, no drama, no pain. Air hockey, pinball machines and the most incredible of them all, Dance Dance Revolution. I keep my cool before I accidently reveal my love for the game.

We race in the car racing game, Alistair wins. We battle in air hockey, Alistair wins. We take turns punching the strength bag, Alistair dominates. The screen flash with music blaring out as the quarters fall down the shoot. Alistair rushes the random selection button because we don't know a lot of the songs. A song called *Bizarre Love Triangle* pops up and I almost loose strength in my knees. We do what most adults do and ignore the awkward situation and hit the button again. The song *Let's Groove* sounds more like it. Right foot. Left. Right. Right. Up and down.

"Girl, my feet are way too damn big to play this game. I see you."

Alistair quits and rests his eyes on me.

"Oh, come on you have to give it a shot," I keep going to attain my perfect streak.

"I rather admire how you move those legs," Alistair flirts and I step off the machine to hide my embarrassment.

"You can admire my legs in skates when I beat you in our race." I grab both pairs of our skates and run for the rink to get a head start.

"Not a chance Sabi. What do I get if I win?" he catches up to me.

"If I win, you have to do my laundry for a week and if you win…."

I roll onto the floor in my skates.

"I get to take you on a second official date," he interrupts.

"Oh, is this a date?" I flirt knowing that this is the best date I've ever been on.

"If it wasn't, would I do this?" he presses his lips to mine and I have no objections.

"I guess you're going to have to win then." I smile and kiss his cheek.

Who is anyone kidding? I don't have a shot in hell to win this bet. This wager might be the first competition I'm willing to lose. Looking at the distance from this wall to the end is daunting, time for strategy. Think smart not hard. Alistair counts down from three and winks with a smug look on his face before he takes off. He's halfway there before I reach a quarter of the way. I scream in pretend pain and bring attention to my perfectly fine knee. This trick seems to be a winner every time. He quickly rushes to my rescue with urgency and ease.

"Sucker!" I push off him for a good head start and race to the finish like a grandma who just got a hip replacement.

"You poor thing, still think you have a chance." He laughs to himself while catching up and passing me.

He hits the end and I dramatically fall to the floor in defeat. Seconds later, the empty space of floor becomes taken by the man of everyone's dreams. The skates come off before I get on my feet. Reaching out my hand for his, he pulls me back down into his arms. Our foreheads gently press together as the tension grows thick while we both try and catch our breath. Why do we keep finding our way back to moments like this? Not that I would dare to complain. I've patiently waited years for moments like this, never thought I would get my turn. Feels good to be wrong this time. I wrap my arms around him into a giant bear hug and squeeze tight.

For a few minutes, we cuddle in stillness. Pure gratitude for each other. Pure mutual admiration.

All the sudden, Craig pulls a smooth move and turns on a slow song. *Conversations in the Dark* by John Legend plays throw the speakers as the lights dim to the perfect intimate setting. I smile from ear to ear towards the sound booth, Craig is our cupid for the day. Alistair rises to his feet and reaches to take my hand, no playing around this time. He spins me around before connecting his hands to my hips. My arms barely reach his shoulders, I explore his upper body until wrapping my arms around his waist feels comfortable. We rock and sway to the sweet beautiful messages slipping from the talented Mr. Legend. Nothing else matters in this now, it's ours to hold. No drama. No labels. No conversation. No one else, but us. For a few minutes, we move in tenderness. There's no stopping this feeling. The feeling of safety. An unexpected tear falls from Alistair's eye.

"I wouldn't rather be anywhere else right now than here with you." I reach up and swipe his tear away.

"I'm so overwhelmed," he laughs through the tears.

"Oh, yeah, I'm right with you." My eyes meet his and smile with warmth.

"I never could fully process feeling worthy enough to deserve this experience and such. I feel safe with you. I don't think I've ever knew I needed to have the feeling of safety until I met you. Thank you for choosing to constantly be there for me," he opens his heart. "I'd do anything for you, Alistair Barker." I can't stop the words from coming out.

"Except murder! I won't do that."

We both laugh and get back to dancing together.

A few songs later, the lights flash back on and Craig announces the place opens in ten minutes. Time flew by, I could do this all day and it would feel like a minute. We rush to get our shoes and clean up the area we had breakfast in before the doors open to the public. I give Craig a proper hug to thank him and officially meet him all in one.

A quick drive home for Alistair to change for work and we head to drop him off. I over hear him talk about the kids, but I've never been to the rehab center. He has never spoken to me about his work before and now I am dropping him off. The teens at the rehab center are his kids like my preemies feel like mine. Although, the babies can't talk back for the most part. It must be a big step for him to invite me into this part of his world, or maybe I'm thinking too much into it. This place is bigger than I thought, my imagination was picturing the size of a community center.

"The center is divided into two sections. The dorms are to the left and the community area is to the right. We are pretty firm with the residents at all time but they can earn some freedom with trust. We have meetings for the community and have created a safe space for kids to come stay out of trouble. It's mostly meetings and basketball here for the boys and some girls." Alistair gives me a quick tour of his work life.

"So, what do you do exactly? What is your main role here?" I ask hoping to come off more curious than rude.

"Oh, they just hired me to keep the basketballs clean," his sarcasm rolls well with the silly grin on his face.

"Shut up!" I can't help but laugh.

"I play all kinds of roles here, but I was hired to counsel and run group meetings. I aspire to just be a real safe space for these kids."

He shares a piece of his world.

"Hey, Al! Wanna shoot some hoops before meeting?" a rather medium sized boy interrupts our tour.

"Yes, I would love to. Vinny, this is my friend Sabine. Sabine. Vinny. Would you like to join?" Alistair extends an invitation.

"No, you guys go ahead. I've got boring adulting things to get done today. It was great meeting you, Vinny," I respectfully decline. Alistair gives me one last hug and a reminder to not forget to pick him up later. I feel out of place here, breaking the rules with not even something as little as a visitor's pass. We didn't go too far into the building and I still manage to not easily find my way out.

"Hey, how do I get out of here?" I laugh at myself.

"Through the forest and over the bridge," the girl obviously doesn't care to help.

"You just have to turn left after those bathrooms over there," another teenager intervenes.

"Thank you, I appreciate it," gratefully smiling.

"Who were you here for? I've never seen you here before. I'm Ziggy," they extend their hand for a greeting shake.

"Sabine…" I begin to talk before Ziggy interrupts unexpectedly.

"Alistair's Sabine?" Ziggy's face reeks of excitement.

"Sabine's Sabine but Alistair's friend." My joke goes right over their head.

"You must be special for him to invite you here. Besides he brings you up a lot in meetings. You're the first person he invited here since

Lenny and all his recent slips," Ziggy spills the beans.

"He really puts it all out there, huh?" trying to hide my surprised reaction.

"He preaches that he wouldn't ask us to do anything he wouldn't do himself. We respect him more than he will ever know. You can't be surprised he's a fan favorite in this place. Alistair is one of the most transparent adults I know. He is the best father and friend most of us have. He relapsed hard after Lenny cheated on him and he left for almost a month, we were scared. None of us want to see him go through that again. All I ask of you is to please not break his heart." Ziggy's words paralyze me for a split second.

"He is stronger than you know." Limited words showed up in my brain. What am I supposed to say to that?

"Are you coming to our Thanksgiving dinner this year? I'm sure we would all love for you to make it. Be Alistair's date." Ziggy starts walking with me to the front.

"Thank you for the invite, I might have to work that day. You are really sweet Ziggy. It's was nice meeting you and thank you for walking me to the front. I've got to head out." They could talk all day if I let them.

I would never in a million years plan to break that man's heart.

CHAPTER 23

There is always a slight chance we would have to work holidays and I drew the short stick for Thanksgiving this year. As of now, I don't have kids or much family, therefore I took the shifts for my colleagues to spend time with their children. Fortunately, the pharmacy isn't busy after my shift ends, my body could use a few more vitamins now that I am pregnant. I've been tremendously nauseous and wanting to eat a bucket of Tums every day. Motherhood is something I've wanted for years and now that it's here, I am freaking out. My pregnancy secret stays between me and the tiny human growing inside my belly.

An agitated dressed down woman raises her voice in frustration towards the pharmacist behind the counter regarding her outrageous balance. The woman behind her grabs her daughter's hand for comfort as the volume escalates. After partaking in a double take, I realize the mom and daughter is Joan and Alma. I haven't seen them here since Alma's spelling bee.

"Fancy seeing you guys here!" I approach them with pep.

"Sabine!" Alma's face lights up.

"Hi there! How are you?" Joan asks.

"Great! How are you? Is everything okay? I haven't seen you two in a while," I ask and immediately feel like it wasn't my business to ask.

"Yes, I have a stupid ear infection and need some antibiotics,"

Joan responds quickly.

"We are going to the movies; do you want to come?" Alma is adorably hopeful.

"Yeah, we would love for you to join us! If you don't have plans already, of course. Alistair is welcome as well," Joan encourages me.

"Ummm...sure, why not? Hanging with you guys is way better than spending Thanksgiving alone. Alistair spends Thanksgiving with his kids at the center. I will meet you there. What movie are you guys seeing?" I ask.

"We are seeing Noelle!" Alma screeches with a heavy emphasis on we.

"It was released last week and she's been begging to go since.

Noelle at six forty-five." Joan adores her little girl.

It's no surprise I beat them here, my responsibility now is to get snacks and save seats. All of the food catches my eye, I want one of everything. One of everything would literally bankrupt me, but splurging on a few different things is okay. Sweets is what this baby is craving lately. Sweets is what she shall have. Three perfect seats were waiting for my arrival when I walk inside our theatre looking like I robbed a candy store. Nothing jollier than watching a new Christmas movie during the winter holidays. Why am I not surprised they premiere a Christmas movie a week before Thanksgiving? This is a rather touchy subject for most but not me, I adore Christmas. Halloween is my jam, but Christmas has a sense of love in all sorts of jollification. Luckily, no one tries to take the seats I saved before Joan and Alma arrive.

"Woah, is all this for me?" Alma proves how children are relentless.

"You can have whatever you like. Of course, you too Joan." I pass out the different bags of sweets.

Alma sits her little butt in the seat next to mine, grabs a big handful of popcorn from the giant bucket in my lap. She laughs when she realizes not all the popcorn in her hand is going to fit in her mouth. She goes for it anyways and the buttery salted snack falls down her clothes and onto the floor. Kids do the silliest things in their carefree worlds. Of course, adults do it too, but they aren't as nearly as cute as the tiny humans. The last time I was here, I came with Duke on our first date when the power went out. Not to mention, I ran into the same pair I came to watch this movie with. Life has a funny way of making things come full circle.

The theatre commercials finish up and the movie begins, Alma reaches out her hand to hold mine. She has no idea how much she warms my heart. Joan is one lucky mother to have such an incredible child. I hope that my baby is as strong and independent as her. Not to mention, her heart is sweet like this candy I may or may not be scarfing down right now. She's been through it. Kids radiate pure joy when it comes to Christmas, watching them light up like Christmas trees, watching the magic is a whole new realm of happiness. Alma's laugh is contagious, I can't help, but giggle. Quality time with these two is the exact thing I needed to clear my head. The movie ends and the audience starts to uphold the tradition of clapping and cheering.

"I love this movie," Alma states and let's go of my hand.

"It was pretty good. We should do this more often, what do you say?" I offer.

"Yeah." Alma smiles, but her the light in her eye seems to be dim.

"I think we would love to Sabine, thank you for coming along.

Alma has been asking about you like every minute," Joan jokes. "Mama!" Alma gently nudges Joan, adorably embarrassed. "Likewise, babes. So, Sebastian isn't one hundred percent, but he is getting better on a different treatment they have him on, thank God. He still has a long way to go, but they think if everything goes as planned, Alistair can take him home in a few weeks. Dr. Vaughn and I are throwing a little adoption party for them and I think it would mean a lot to Alistair if you two lovely ladies came," I offer the invitation.

"We wouldn't miss it for the world." Joan smiles. "Will there be cake?" Alma interrupts.

"Heck yeah!" I say while I put cake on my mental checklist.

Before I drive away in my beautiful Bugsby, I shoot Duke a text message asking if he is down for a climb since our fun was cut short the other day. When I get home, he has already responded that he's already there and to come on over. A shower is necessary to wash the hospital stench off my body before getting close and personal with my fellow climbers.

After getting out of the shower, Alistair walks in my room with his hands covering his eyes. I freak out and wrap my towel back around my body, worried he will find out my secret. It's irrational worry because it's too soon, but he can't find out, not yet. I'm not ready.

"What are you doing?" I laugh.

"Covering my virgin eyes. Put some clothes on woman!" He plays.

"I'm in my room, get out or be scarred for life. Your choice." I smile and shrug my shoulders at him.

"Actually, on second thought, no clothes sound like a better idea. I'll take my chances." Alistair smirks with his hands still covering his eyes.

"You can open your eyes now; I am fully clothed. You're home early." I grab his arms and make a silly face when he can see me. "It was a meeting then a meal. Not an all-day thing. You don't feel weird about not being invited right? Honestly, I didn't think it would be something you would want to attend." He rubs the back of his neck as he usually does when he's anxious.

"Not weird per say but it's weird when I was invited by a Ziggy and not an Alistair. I figured if you wanted me there, I would be. I want you to be comfortable and respected in your space. Did you have a good time?" I wrap my arms around his waist and look up at him.

"I want you everywhere with me pretty thang. It was a good time, it always is. I take it work was the best time of your life? Where are you going?" He kisses my cheeks.

"Rock climbing, I have friends and a life now," I cheer with sarcasm.

"They open on Thanksgiving? Can I come?" His demeanor feels vulnerable.

"Really? Today has been a long day so be prepared to catch me if I fall." I'm shocked.

"Yeah, why not? How are they open this late on Thanksgiving?" he awkwardly waits for my response.

"Awwwww, does someone miss their bestie Duke? He owns the

place; a perk is being open when you want and to who you want. Go get changed, we leave in five," I mock him until he walks away. "Owns the place. Of course, the rather handsome and witty Doctor owns the place you can't get enough of," Alistair mumbles his comment to himself as he goes and gets ready.

We joke about how fast he will be able to climb the wall considering the man is six foot nine. Maybe he can avenge my terrible losing streak. Duke is surprised when I show up with Alistair, but not bothered. He seems to be the more than cordial one out of the two. Things are looking up for the two of them, the sweet baby gesture did a number for the positive direction. Alistair looks like a fish out of water, but Duke introduces him to a few people right off the bat.

"How are you, Montgomery? What did the doctor say?" Duke outs me with his question.

"Doctor?" Alistair has reasonable concern on his face.

"Yeah, I had a minor fainting spell here the other day, which was no big deal. I was a little dehydrated is all," I shoot him the death stare following my lie.

"You never told me. I'm glad you're okay. I hope you know you could call me if it's anything serious. Well, either of us." Alistair sweetly includes Duke.

"Yes, thank you gentleman. I will keep that in mind, but for now I want to climb." I masterfully deflect this nerve-wracking conversation and put my harness on.

"Yeah, you better keep us in the loop young lady!" Duke hops on the bandwagon.

"Listen, you two didn't become friends so you can gang up on me. That's not allowed." I playfully scowl them.

Duke lets out a theatrical villain laugh while Alistair tries to figure out how to put a harness on. I oddly see a bromance in the making as Alistair steps in the straps Duke is holding out. The moment of truth has arrived as they start their race up the wall, Duke hits the bell first and remains victorious. After one trip up the wall, my body is completely winded. My mind is weighing me down with anxiety from the last time I climbed. Learning from my mistakes, sitting down and drinking water is the right move. Plus, this water is working wonders on this terrible heart burn. It's been a long day, but I'm overly glad I came.

"Hey champ, you okay?" Duke comes and sits next to me on the bench.

"Yeah." Suddenly, I am flooded with emotions.

"Everything really okay at the ER?" he asks again like he sees right through me.

"You're going to hate me." I can't hold it any longer and begin to tear up.

"Woah, woah, woah. Come on now, I could never hate you. Well, you'd have to really mess us like if you break my winning streak or something," he chuckles at himself while consoling me.

"I didn't really mean for any of this to happen and I'm sorry."

Tears run down my face.

"What's going on?" Dukes voice turns soft as he wipes my tear-filled cheeks.

"Duke, I'm pregnant." I turn my face away in defeat, so much for my secret, but it's eating me alive keeping it to myself.

"Woah, I didn't expect that one. I'm assuming it's…." Duke says.

"Alistair's," I finish his sentence.

"Does he know?" He asks.

"No, please keep this between us. Are you mad?" I'm scared to hear his answer.

"Mad? No. Disappointed, yes. Deep down, I knew he was the one for you. I mean the way you look at him is the way I look at my chocolate chip pancakes. True love. He's the luckiest man in the world. I hope you know that," he sweetly responds.

Duke never fails to put a smile on my face. I feel Alistair looking at us from across the gym and I do my best to mask my tears. It's only best to wrap up our heart to heart before we get caught.

"You're amazing, you know that? Just because he's the one for me doesn't mean I'm not missing out on you. We can still be friend's, right?" I ask with hopeful eyes.

"Uncle Duke at your service! Not going to lie, you are my best friend. It's like we are in kindergarten. Do you want to play on the swings with me? All jokes aside, congratulations mama." He playfully salutes and brings me in for the tightest hug.

"Yeah, you are mine as well. Weird. Can I ask a favor of you? I'm terrified going in alone, will you come to my first appointment with me?" I let go of our hug and wait for his answer.

"Of course, I will be there. Whatever you need, kid." Duke can barely look me in the eye.

The conversation with Duke replays in my head during the car ride home. How did I get so lucky? I'm stuck in an intense moment of gratitude in which I don't ever want to break out from. I would have never had the happiest moments of my life without the most heartbreaking one. Joseph did me a favor. Life is unreal, my life feels unreal in this time. Alistair reaches his right hand over and grabs mine, I rest my other hand on top of his and my head against his arm. We sit, soaking up each other for the remainder of the car ride. Alistair puts the car in park and turns to me. I plant a soft kiss on his cheek before he turns the car off.

"What was that for?" He smiles.

"For being there the first day I met you." My heart is warm.

"Can I ask you something?" He nervously asks.

"That was already a question, but just for you, you can have another." I laugh at myself while he stays serious.

"Will you be my girlfriend? I know I said before that I want to work on myself and my family, but I would regret it every day if I didn't go for the woman who has my heart. I know it's super weird because I am about to get a son, but you don't have to be involved yet until you're ready. If not, I totally understand if you're not up for it…." Alistair asks his question and follows it with an anxiety filled rant.

"Yes, I would love to be your girlfriend. I love you Alistair." I smile and kiss him with all the love I have in me.

"You love me?" he jokingly asks in disbelief.

"To the moon and back," I respond with no hesitation.

CHAPTER 24

In a few days, Sebastian Osgood will become Sebastian Barker. His soon to be father, my extremely handsome boyfriend still shows up for cuddles on a daily bases, rain or shine. I joke that if Alistair and I ever broke up the hospital staff would choose to keep him instead of me, they love him that much. Normally anyone would be offended, but he really is the epitome of perfection.

I check my phone on my lunch break and read a reminder message for my babysitting date with the cutest six-year-old in the world. After browsing my phone for a bit, I choose to spend the rest of my free time asking my boyfriend if he would like to join the party for two tonight. My boyfriend. Has a nice ring to it. On my way, in walks Karen Osgood to sign her last set of paperwork for the medical system. Before I walk away, she initiates eye contact and gives me a half smile. I fake a smile back at her and try to keep walking, but she looks like she has something to say.

"Hi, Karen. Last few signatures before you're a free woman, huh?" My mind told me to be nice, but my heart is to hurt to be too kind.

"I wouldn't say a free woman. My baby is the size of a six-inch subway sandwich." She rubs her baby bump in awe of herself.

"Do you regret what you're doing with Sebastian?"

I could hold it in, but I need to know.

"No. You might understand if you have kids one day Nurse Montgomery. I am doing what is best for my child. Aren't you happy? Your friend gets a son from my decision. It has truly been a quick and easy process and I'm happy about it," she casually snaps back.

"Yes, I am happy. Mr. Barker is going to be a great father," I respond truthfully.

"How is Sebastian doing anyway?" Karen asks calmly.

"He's doing amazing, thanks for asking. You gave up on him right before he started to win the fight for his life." I pick up my files and begin to walk away before I remember my conversation with Joan and turn back. My stomach begins to turn so I make it quick. "Look, I don't agree with your decision to abandon your son in his time of need, but I recognize that's it must have been one of the hardest decisions in your life. It takes strength to recognize your son needs a different parent who can provide for him. He's going to have a beautiful life, filled with love and support. You have made a brave decision," I add before I walk away.

The conversation with Karen filled the rest of my break and I have to get back to work. I pop a few Tums in my mouth in hopes to control my morning sickness for the time being. Luckily, I haven't puked as much as the horror stories I've heard with morning sickness. The files in my hands are full of handouts and papers for my meetings with new parents. Three meetings in one shift is cause for a celebratory moment, their children are healthy enough to go home for the first time. Duke Vaughn winks at me from across the room and I playfully tag along to his silly shenanigans.

As he walks closer, I look at him with an overly dramatic smirk.

"Guess what I am doing tonight?" Duke asks.

"Hmmm, terrorizing other beautiful women at work?" My tone is as sassy as ever.

"Close. I've got a rock-climbing date with your man, jealous?"

His devious smile tickles my fancy bone.

"You never told me you know Edward Scissor Hands!" I gasp and catch Alistair's eye from across the way.

"Very funny, Montgomery." Duke gathers his materials and walks away.

"Hey! How's that guy Roger?" I ask as he's walking away.

"I don't know, thanks to someone I know, I had a come to Jesus moment and realized I might not want to hang around people like that," he answers and walks out of the room for good.

I feel like my two favorite guys are about to start cheating on me right in front of my face. Them getting along is only a positive thing, it's a happy thing. I never thought I'd see it happen. It sounds like I am on my own for babysitting tonight, not my preference but it will still be a good time with Alma. I catch my handsome boyfriend's eye again and send a flirty wink his way, he sends a warm smile in return.

An hour flies by ending my shift and I see Sebastian is finally alone. It's been a while since this little guy was in my arms, he's a popular baby. He lays in his container home, sound asleep. Sebastian is starting to begin to look older as he becomes healthier.

"You're doing it, little one. We are all so proud of you, beautiful boy," I whisper towards him and head home.

A few men are outside the hospital building, hanging up lights for the holidays. The building is gigantic, hats off to the guys hired for this tedious task. The cold air blows through my body, it hits with a sense of cleansing.

I stop by the house to take a quick shower before the long night ahead of me. Alistair walks out of the front door as I approach the driveway. His outfit screams rock climbing, how cute. I put Bugsby in park and he motions for me to roll down my window. I tell him to back up in order for me to get out and hug the God of a man.

"Cute fit. Make sure you and Duke use protection." I cringe after speaking my joke, considering my situation.

"It's not what it looks like, I swear!" He laughs and plays a long. "Hey, if you want to come over to Joan's house after your bro date. I would not object." I smile.

"Oh, yeah, that's tonight. I'll call you after I get home." He brushes my hair behind my ear and I get butterflies as usual.

"See you later. Have fun!" I melt into him as he kisses me goodbye.

Alistair pulls me back for another kiss and again for a third. It's a shame we have things to do and places to be because I rather be cuddling with him on the couch while watching reruns of Friends on Netflix. Pajamas is the only appropriate way to dress for my playdate with Ms. Alma, an oversized red long sleeve shirt with black skull fleece pants. I grab my brown unicorn slippers and shove them in my duffle bag.

Joan has always lived fourteen minutes away, and I never knew. Alma yells my name and runs to hug me the second she lays eyes on me.

Joan is in a rush to go and thanks me at least two times before leaving for the night. Their home has a small cottage aesthetic, spick and span to say the least. There are three bedrooms, Joan's room, Alma's room and the third is a playroom filled with sanitized toys and shelves of books. The elated six-year- old grabs my hand and rushes me around the house for a tour. She saved the best for last which is of course her bedroom. The walls are covered in Ballerina Gown paint, and purple carpet is as soft as I could ever imagine. Alma's bed is a bunkbed in the structure of a little neighborhood home with a white picket fence. The bottom bunk is in the house and the way in is through the big window. A staircase on the side leads to the top bunk which is on the roof of the house with two windows. People design the most impressive beds for kid's rooms these days; I can't wait to spoil my baby with a room like this. I'm in awe.

"Can we color?" Alma asks.

"I would love to color!" I respond with an emphasize on love.

"I saved this for us. No one was allowed to color in it." She pulls out the same coloring book we colored in together the day we met in the hospital playroom.

"Oh, you could have shared it with others. You are very thoughtful." I'm surprised by her actions.

Alma opens up the book to a random slot with bare coloring pages. She wants the left page, which means I get the right. The pages have the same superhero, but with different action scenes. I remember being this little and having teen witch coloring books to occupy my time. The feeling of satisfaction of finishing a page was always a personal victory at that age.

By the time we are done with our pages, the same woman in our pictures look like two separate heroes, the beauty of creativity. The story we made up is that they are long lost sisters who got powers the moment they reconnected later in life, and one lives in a ginger bread house and the other in a cave. The choices for dinner are pizza or dinosaur chicken nuggets with mac and cheese. Dinosaur chicken nuggets for the win, can't remember the last time I've eaten these. Pickle juice sounds delicious right now. Alistair informs me that he's on his way home as I make our dinner plates with the hot food.

"Thank you!" Alma smiles big with wide eyes at her food.

"I wish we could do this every day," she adds.

"Wouldn't that be fun? We have plenty of time to create crazy cool memories." I place my head on her upper back for a second before I dip my nugget in ketchup.

"But... what if we don't have time? What if my cancer comes back and I go before I get to do everything on my list?" Alma's face broadcasts sadness and fear.

"Oh, honey, don't think like that. If it ever comes back, we will all be here for you every step of the way. It's a big *if*, though. What's on that list of yours anyways?" I ask for an attempt to lift her spirits. "All of the cool things of course. Learn to braid hair, play dress up, have a sleepover, make friendship bracelets, meet Michelle Obama, learn to hula hoop, learn to fish, do a puzzle, get a tattoo"

Alma starts reciting her list off the top of her head.

"A tattoo? You're a little young for those." I giggle.

"I like yours, did it hurt?" Her curious mind admires my arms as she pulls up my sleeves.

"A little, but you've got some years to decide whether you really want one or not. Don't worry your pretty little mind." I smile and graze her cheek.

"Finish eating, you've hardly eaten anything. I'll be right back." I add and get up to call Alistair.

That conversation was the first time I have felt fear off Alma's energy. I wonder what is going on with her, maybe she's experiencing post-traumatic stress. It would be understandable for anyone in remission. I give my amazing boyfriend the downlow of the agenda for tonight and he will be here within the hour.

Next, I give Joan a call and ask permission to sleep over to fulfill a spot on her daughter's wish list. She's shouts yes with no hesitation and says how grateful she is that Alma knows us, it's impossible to not feel the mutual way. The little one barely touched her food, but that's what glass containers are for, in case she gets hungry later.

All of the sudden, I remember I brought my unicorn slippers and run to throw them on my feet. Alma told me one day about sparkly unicorn slippers her mom got her and there's no way I couldn't match. She screeches when she sees the puffy, comfy, magical creatures on my feet. Three minutes later she struts out of her room in a whole different outfit, it's looks like a unicorn barfed on her. I wish I was as cool as her when I was her age, pure excellence.

Alistair knocks on the door a few times before walking in with bags filled with stuff. Alma's eyes light up, but it's unclear if it's for him or the bags full of goodies.

"Hello ladies! I come bearing gifts!" Alistair is breathless carrying everything from the car by myself.

"For me?" Alma yells the question.

"Maybe!" Alistair tries to act sly, but it doesn't last very long. "Sit your bottom on the chair, missy." I pull a chair out for her. "We are going have the best night ever! Are you sure you're even ready?" Alistair asks with a big smile.

"Yes!" Alma shouts.

"We are going to have the best sleepover ever. Yes, a sleepover! I bought friendship bracelet kits, temporary tattoos, three hula hoops, a puzzle, play makeup. Now, unfortunately, I don't know Ms. Obama, I did get her book. One of us can read it to you, if it's something you would like." Alistair radiates amination while he shares the agenda with Alma, it's adorable how he seems just as excited.

"Woah, I actually don't think you're ready." I play. "Yes, I am. I swear I am!" Alma pleads.

My heart melts to goo as she almost loses her mind with anticipation. Alma rushes to grab her wish list while we set everything across the kitchen table. I should have known that it's written in purple crayon on a piece of binder paper with rainbow stickers. Shame on me for expecting anything else. The first thing to cross of the list is learning the skill of hula hooping, we all laugh at each other every time our hoop abruptly falls to the floor. My childhood lacked fun like this; Also, I was too self-conscious to put my body in a hoop of any kind. Who knows what the other kids would come up with to see a sight like that? This is her first time hula hooping and it's all happy, silly moments. Alma takes a blue crayon and crosses hula hooping off the checklist when she becomes physically drained. The next thing on the list is finishing a puzzle, but Alma changes her mind after we get all of the pieces spread out. She decides it's time for tattoos and makeovers, this should be exciting.

"Where are we going to put your tattoos when your arms are full with real ones?" Alma asks a valid question.

"Considering these last only a few days, my legs are the only option sweetie pie." Now, I wish my arms were bare.

"I think this pumpkin is my favorite. This one is to scary, creepy." She points to the skeleton on my arm, which makes Alistair chuckle to himself.

"You're up first kid. Prepare to get tatted. You're a brave girl. It won't hurt, not one bit." Alistair smiles as he peels the plastic off a mermaid tattoo.

Alma grabs my hand for a squeeze as if he is preparing the tattoo gun. She flashes her sweet smile before he lifts the wet cloth from her skin. After the peel, a beautiful and sparkly cartoon mermaid appears on her forearm. There is no stopping her after the first one, twenty minutes later, she is covered. It didn't take much convincing, but Alistair put up a good fight before he allowed alma to put a rainbow starfish tattoo on his ankle. It really suits him, he's acting cool, however we know he loves it. Alma paints my face with dollar store makeup and then Alistair's. I've lost track on the number of times we burst into laughter when we make eye contact. Pink might be a new look for me. Who am I kidding? Not a chance in hell.

"Don't ever rely on this stuff to make you feel good about yourself. You are beautiful just the way you are, you hear me?" I preach as I brush color on Alma's little eye lids.

"Duh. My mom tells me to only wear it for myself."

Alma is sassy as ever.

"Way to go, mama," Alistair chimes in.

"I'm getting tired. Can we make the bracelets and watch a movie?" Alma calmy asks.

"Yes, of course. Are you sure? We have a lot more to check off the list," I ask her.

"Yes. This is the best sleepover ever!" Alma yawns and rubs her freshly painted eyes.

We've all been there with the racoon eyes, instead this time it's less black, more a green and purple smudge. It's been ages since I've made friendship jewelry, Maddison Arber was the first and only friend to receive one from me in the third grade. I choose black, green and white, Alistair chooses blue, red and yellow and Alma chooses red, orange, and pink. We all bunker down in Alma's room to create friendship, the movie "Home Alone" plays in the background. It's almost half over by the time we finish, of course we gave our bracelets to Alma. Takes a lot less time to make a bracelet to fit a 6-year-old than a grown adult.

"I made mine for baby Sebastian, can you give this to him?"

Alma hands her craft to Alistair.

"Of course, that's really sweet of you, Alma." Alistair wraps him arms around her.

"Do you want to give it to Sebastian at the party when he comes home?" I ask.

"No, I think you should. I will probably get to distracted by the cake and forget." Alma yawns and gets into bed.

"Come on, there's room on my bed for you. You can get on the top bunk, Alistair," she giggles.

I wake up after what seems like a few hours later, the room is dark. Alma coughs but is sound asleep and Alistair is passed out on the floor with a fairy blanket covering only the middle of his body. My eyes turn heavier and heavier and darkness fills my eyes.

CHAPTER 25

My morning is shaken up with a call from my father, Dr. Montgomery. He is in town. He showed up to my old apartment wondering where I am. My father has never spontaneously showed up before, maybe it's something serious. I text him my new address and put on another pot of coffee. Thirty-six minutes is not nearly enough time to clean the house spotless, one hundred percent dust free. He doesn't need to see anything, but the kitchen, dining room, and living room. Alistair does the dishes and cleans the kitchen from last night, which is a start. I take a deep breath before I start to clean and organize like a crazy person.

Woah, here comes the morning sickness. The bathroom couldn't feel any further as I run for my life to make it in time. All I think while I barf my guts up is how this will all be worth it when I have my precious baby in my arms for the first time. I have the house to myself for at least half a day while Alistair is at work, it should be enough time to give the good ole tour to my father and leave to anywhere else. A knock at the door means it's time to face the music. To my surprise, my father stands before me with a woman I've never seen before.

"Beanie! You look miraculous, you are glowing!" He opens his arms to greet me.

"Dad, you can stop calling me that now." I hug him tighter; it's been six years.

"Beautiful house, Sabine. Hi, I'm Abigail, but you can call me Abby," Abby introduces herself and pulls me in for a big hug. Her silicone breasts crush my soul in her embrace.

"Come on in, I have fresh coffee if you would like. Also, I have water, orange juice and wine. It's definitely too early for wine, right Dr. Montgomery?" I humor my dad while guiding them to the stools and counter.

"Gosh Beanie, you're still drinking coffee. What are you going to do if you get pregnant and can't consume it?" He carelessly speaks.

"Oh shit!" The second my father's words hit my ears; I spit the acidic substance back into my cup. It completely left my mind this morning.

"Oh God, are you okay?" Abby asks.

"Are you pregnant Beanie?" My dad's eyes grow wide.

"No! No, you reminded me about the ulcer I have. You're right, coffee is evil." I empty my mug into the sink and place my cup on the counter.

"An ulcer? Those are painful, right?" Abby asks.

"Now that you are rather healthy and in shape, when are you going to med school and become a doctor?" My father pesters me about med school every time we see each other.

"I love what I do. I'm not going to med school. I'm happy dad. That's all that matters, right?" I don't know why I ever think I will get through to him.

"How is Joey? What is he doing these days? Did he become a paramedic?" My dad hasn't stopped asking questions since the moment he has arrived, but his question about Joseph makes me giggle.

"No, no he did not." I chuckle.

"We aren't together. I am with someone else now. We live together, here." I try to hide out behind my glass of water.

What perfect timing more than ever, Alistair walks in to his house accompanied with complete strangers. Just when I thought I have lived through my most awkward moments; this one is victorious. I introduce my dad and his very young-looking companion to my boyfriend for the first time. This moment makes me regret not ever mentioning my dad to Alistair, but I did not think he would ever just show up in town. Alistair wishes he could stay, but he has some place to be. Thank God. He kisses my forehead to greet me and when he picks up his laptop and paperwork, he kisses my cheek before he shakes my father's hand and leaves.

"This is his place that you're living in? How did you two meet?"

Here my dad goes again with all the invasive questions.

"Hal, lighten up." Abby gently smacks his chest and smiles at me with an 'I got you' look.

"Don't take this the wrong way but what are you doing here dad?" I finally ask the question that's been burning in my brain file cabinet.

"To see you of course." He comes off offended but he's hiding something. I look at him to spit what he wants out and boy do I regret it.

"I come in peace. I can't get ahold of your mother and I've been waiting for months for her to sign the divorce papers. I would love to marry my sweet Abigail, but we've got that big roadblock in the way."

There it is, he spills it and I don't know whether I need to barf because of him or the baby.

"Dad," I sigh.

"I don't know where she is." It's the partial truth.

"Okay, sorry Abby. I thought we would give this a shot. We do have a plane to catch, it will just be another vacation in Vegas baby doll." He kisses Abby's pouty face.

"You're leaving? You just got here. We could go get some lunch and I can give Dr. Montgomery a little tour of the NICU. There is a sweet boy, I would love for you to meet." It's shocking I'm surprised he's leaving and how I don't want him to.

"Sorry Beanie, I'll come back and you can show me. Take this to help you get by, my treat." He throws a couple hundred-dollar bills on the marble counter, hugs me tight and leaves the only way he knows how.

"It was nice meeting you, sweetie." Abby touches my arm and follows her old sugar daddy out of my house.

It's just me again, alone in this big empty house. I take a deep breathe, close my eyes and tears silently slip down my face. My parents are big kids at heart but never expected to have a child.

They have always come and gone when they please. I want to do better and be better for my kids. I wipe my face and take another deep breath before I get on with my day.

My first doctor's appointment for the baby is today, and I'm meeting Duke there for moral support. He is the only one who knows and has been the best support system a girl could ask for. My bed is covered with a pile of clothes to choose an outfit from. Luckily, my body looks the same as always with no sign of pregnancy. A huge maroon college sweatshirt and black leggings it is, comfort over fashion is my motto. Duke is in his work scrubs and white coat when I meet him for my appointment.

"Thanks for doing this. I'm sorry it's on your lunch break." I could hug this man all day.

"You got it, Montgomery. You know, when I pictured the first time I'd see you undress, I didn't this it would be a situation like this." Duke sarcastically strokes his beard.

"Shut up, pig!" I smack his arm a little too hard and immediately apologize.

Ophelia calls my name with the biggest grin painted on her face. Women go into their appointments alone for safety protocol and then the nurse gets your support person from the lobby. Normally, it would be the other parent of the child not another man who is not the father. It was either Duke or coming alone today and I couldn't do it alone. I just know my secret is bound to get out, if only another hospital was closer. It would be easier and less uncomfortable to be examined by people I don't know. I'm grateful its Ophelia today, out of all people. She rubs my shoulder for comfort which allows my body to drop the anxious tension. This room is colder than usual, it's weird to be on the opposite end. We get through the home safety questionnaire and the numerous health questions while I get undressed.

"Very, very unprofessional, I know. Who is the father? Duke or Alistair? I'm assuming it's Dr. Vaughn from the sight of him in the waiting room," she asks while taking my blood pressure.

"Hey, professionalism goes out the door when you know a girl? I see how it goes in this hospital. It's a Barker baby." My heart lights up at the sound of Barker baby.

"But, no one knows! Just Duke and now you. Please don't tell anyone." I freak out.

"No worries, girl. How are you feeling about all of this?" Ophelia asks in her best compassionate tone.

"Terrified on so many levels. Happy with a dream come true, but other than that. Terrified." I answer honestly, no point in putting up a front.

"Everything is going to be okay. It will be a learning curve, but you are resilient Sabine. You'll get the hang of things. You want me to get Duke?" She asks her routine question.

"Yes, please." I look at her with a grateful grin.

All I can think to do is practice my breathing, my heart is going to beat out of my chest. This room looks different this time, different than the other hundreds of times I've stepped foot in here. The wait seems like a thousand hours before they enter the office. This moment feels surreal considering the fact that I thought I'd never be able to get pregnant and have a human grow in *my* belly. A knock on the door warns me before a man that's not Duke walks in, my heart sinks.

"Alistair?" I'm in shock and all the emotions flood my body.

"Duke met with me and told me. The man has respect, I'll give him that. I understand if you want me to leave, but I think I have a right to be here. I'm here to support, all love here. We will have to have the hard conversation after." Alistair stands before me, as hurt as ever.

"Please, stay," I say with no hesitation.

I can't imagine how angry and hurt he must be feeling. With all that aside, I wasn't ready for him to know. He grabs my hand when he notices how scared I am. He must be scared, who knows what he's thinking or feeling? He is sitting here holding my hand in silence. I've never experienced him in silence.

"Alistair, can we talk about it?" I break the silence.

"You want to discuss it right now?" he raises an eyebrow.

"Yes, I didn't get the chance to tell you yet and I would like to know how you feel." I am frightened to hear him out.

"How I feel about you being pregnant or being told by Duke Vaughn? Or that you told him the news before your boyfriend, the father?" His questions come flying out.

"Hello and congratulations to the new mommy and daddy. My name is Laurel Lym and I will be your doctor throughout your pregnancy." Dr. Lym enters into the room and introduces herself.

The doctor walks in at the best and worst time. After routine questioning the doctor continues with my examinations and tests. Luckily, having Alistair next to me while I get a pap smear, breast and pelvic exam isn't awkward in the slightest. He is acting fine, his normal sweet and warm self. The doctor would never know she interrupted our soon to be first fight. Finally, the moment we've all been waiting for, Dr. Lym rolls the machine and probe over and gets to work. The jelly is warm, thanks to technology and the warming device.

"Can I take a picture of it?" Alistair asks the doctor.

"Yes, of course. I will be printing the frames for you guys as well,"

she kindly responds.

"See anything good?" My nerves spike without information.

"Oh, yes! Here is your little one right there." The doctor points to the bean shaped alien on the screen.

"I see it! Wow, I've never seen a more beautiful looking human kidney bean." My heart flutters a million times a minute.

"We created that, that's a baby. Our baby. I didn't expect this moment to feel so breathtaking." Alistair stares at the monitor in disbelief.

"I'm sure it's a lot different seeing yours on the screen than the million others we've seen," Dr. Lym comments.

"You are eight weeks pregnant, Sabine. Your due date is July 5th. In a couple of weeks, you should be able to take a blood test to find the gender of your baby, if you both choose too.

Congratulations!" Dr. Lym marks her calendar and then her notes.

Thank God, I'm on my way to having a beautiful healthy baby.

This is real, I'm really doing this.

CHAPTER 26

hristmas Eve is a major event here at the Barker home. The sweet smell of homemade traditional dishes. My holidays have always been on a more low-key side, but this is different. This radiates home, love, safety, family and friendship. All walks of life are about to come together and celebrate a jolly night of games, laughter and unity. Alistair's sister, husband and son are the first ones to arrive. The second group of guests to arrive are Duke and his twin sisters, Lucy and Rosalie Vaughn. We invited my father after his recent visit, but him and Abby are celebrating the holidays in Cancun. I would never admit this to anyone, but I'm glad he couldn't make it. It wasn't my idea to invite him in the first place. Joan and Alma are the last two guests who still haven't arrived yet. There's no telling how long to boys can wait to have dinner, it's a dangerous game not letting them eat.

Alistair puts more wood in the fire place as Diane pours everyone glasses of brandy and eggnog. Before she could give me a glass, Duke swipes in with a secret chilling cup of secret virgin eggnog. None of us have discussed anything baby related. Sweeping it under the rug is not going to be good in the long run. Everything is dandy as far as anyone is concerned. I hate it, it feels uncomfortable.

Lucy and Rosalie are more high functioning than I pictured when their brother was describing childhood memories. The twins came with a gift in gratitude for the invitation. A girl could never have to many Midnight Blue Citrus candles from Bath and Body works. I think the gift is aimed towards me and I have no problem sharing with my man. We have plenty of nights to use all the candles in the world together.

To help fill the wait time, we break out a white board and a hat to put movie titles in. Each one of us write down three movie titles on three pieces of scrap paper and throw it into the bowl in the center of the coffee table. The first team is Duke, Lucy and Alistair, and the second team is Rosalie, Diane and myself. Diane's husband Craig, decides to keep score while playing with their son. Lucy is up first; she is confident in what her drawing is going to look like. She takes the blue dry erase marker and starts to draw a large stick figure man and a smaller woman standing next to him. The room is silent as their team focuses hard on what the picture could be. Then, Lucy draws a football on the side.

"The Game Plan?" Alistair guesses and Lucy laughs while shaking her head no and continues to draw.

"Are all those people a crowd of fans? Or does that represent family?" Duke scratches his head trying to quickly figure it out.

Twenty-two seconds are left on the timer and Lucy adds a huge striped, long sleeve shirt to the big man. She starts to run out of ideas and begins to motion her hand for her teammates to think faster.

"Blind side! The Blind Side!" Duke yells the correct answer with six seconds to spare. Alistair scoffs at the irony of the movie title.

"Ugh, finally!" Lucy trolls her brother and everyone giggles at the action.

My team is up next and we vote for Diane to draw the first round.

She pulls from the bowl and admires the title written on the crumpled scrap. The timer starts and she begins to draw two stick figures like the round before, but there is a big heart in between the two people. Love birds are a part of almost every movie out there. Diane draws a vertical rectangle and a lightbulb went off in my head.

"Almost everyone's favorite romantic movie. The Notebook!" I tease and cheer for my team.

"The Notebook? We aren't supposed to put obvious titles guys."

Duke complains.

"Hey! It's one of my favorite movies!" Rosalie banters with her brother.

"Any title is fair game Dr. Bitter Pants," I mock Duke after he whines.

"Our turn! Pass the bowl over," Alistair demands.

Alistair pulls a scrap of paper out of the titles and put his game face on seconds before his timer starts. Apparently, none of us have any artistic ability after the third person to draw creates two teams on a court in stick figures. Diane gasps after she realizes she thinks what movie title her brother is drawing. Then, he draws circles in their hands and on the ground that represent balls.

"Space jam?" Lucy hesitates with her answer. "No." Diane can't help herself.

"Coach Carter?" Duke guesses. "No," Diane repeats.

"Like Mike?" Lucy guesses as the timer runs out.

"Dodgeball!" Alistair shouts in defeat.

"Oh, yeah I can see that." Duke laughs.

It's my turn to draw a movie title and I'm very determined to not include any stick figures. Again, our team gets another pretty self-explanatory turn and I get right into it. The funny thing is they would expect me to enter this title, and I didn't. I begin to draw a box to contribute to the cabin I have to draw. After the cabin is done and a few incorrect guesses are said, I draw a bunch of trees surrounding the log building.

"Sabine, your phone is going off. I think it's like their third time calling," Craig yells in between my team's guesses. "It can wait," Lucy bluntly responds.

After dramatically drawing almost thirty trees, my mind goes blank on what to add. The only thing that comes to mind is a skull to represent death. The group stares at me with peculiar stares until Diane figures it out.

"Cabin in the Woods!" Diane shouts.

"Bingo!" I jump up and down from the adrenaline in the moment. I get up to check my phone while the other team takes their turn, four missed calls from Joan.

Joan: Please, Call me.

I dial her back as I head to another room for privacy, no answer.

A few seconds later, she calls back.

"Hey, are you guys, okay? Everyone is here. We are playing an intense game of Pictionary to kill time." I try not to sound too concerned.

"Sabine, we need you. I'm sorry. I know it's Christmas Eve, but Alma wants you, it's important. We are at the hospital; I'll text you the details." Joan doesn't sound like herself.

"What happened? Is Alma okay?" I ask as worried as ever.

"I'm sorry, please hurry," Joan sniffles and hangs up the phone. My heart starts to race as fear runs through my veins with the news. My body is vibrating as it's extremely high on alert. A few minutes later my phone receives the text with the hospital room number.

Joan: Room 237

I take a few minutes to collect myself before I tell a room full of people that I have to leave on Christmas Eve. My hormones have been raging, it's really uncontrollable with everything going on lately. This sounds serious and we don't leave family behind. Alistair comes in the room after five minutes to check on me.

"Hey, what's going on? Is everything okay?" He sits beside me and rubs my upper back.

"Honestly, I don't know but I don't think it's good. Alma is in the hospital and I'm sorry but I have to go. They are family too." I can't hold my forming tears.

"Hey, it's okay. Everything will be okay. I agree, you should go. I can hold down the fort until you get back. I love you more than anything. I will be here to hold you when you get back. Did you want to take Duke with you?" He kisses my lips and then my forehead, how bond is strong, but tainted.

"I love you too. Happy thoughts. Everything is fine. Just a hiccup in her journey, I'm sure. I'll be back to celebrate as soon as I can. Duke can stay here." I kiss him one last time before I break the news to the rest of the family.

I tell the group I have to step out for about an hour and it's okay to start dinner without me. We don't have cake to take to Alma, but we do have pie. I cut a piece and put it in a container and scurry to the hospital. My goal to get there as fast as I can, but the pure delicate snowflakes falling from the sky slow me down. People tend to lose some of their driving knowledge in darker weather, so playing it safe on the cautious side is a must. My appreciation goes out to the staff working the holidays instead of being home with their families. I quietly enter Alma's room and see her lying in bed, the sickest I've ever seen her.

"Hi, sweetheart, what happened? I didn't have cake, so I hope you like apple pie," I softly ask and gently kiss the top of her head. "I'm really sick, again. My cancer has been back for a while. I didn't want to worry you." Alma coughs.

"What?" Her answer sends a shock through my heart and my head snaps straight to Joan.

"They found more cancer cells about eight weeks ago, I'm so sorry, Sabine. Alma made me promise not to tell you because she didn't want you to worry or feel sorry for her. I wanted to respect my daughters wishes. She changed her mind tonight and wanted to see you." Joan looks apologetic and torn.

"There is no reason to apologize, I'm here now. I'm so glad you changed your mind. Thank you for calling me. Look how brave you are, you're going to beat this again." I grab her hand and see Joan wipe her tears pouring down her cheeks.

"Look, I have my bracelet you made me. I'm glad we got to do most of the things on my list before." Her smile and voice are weak.

"And we are going to get to finish that list," my voice cracks while interrupting her.

"Can you finish the list with Sebastian?" Alma's eyes turn sad.

"We can all do it together. Hey, look at me. I am so proud of you. Want to know a secret?" I begin to rub her arm for comfort.

"Yes, please." Alma's eyes begin to fall tired.

"I've got a baby in my belly, I'm hoping it's a girl. I hope she grows up as strong as you. What should I name her?" I ask while holding in my heartbreak.

"Woah, you do? I like Jessica. My doll's name is Jessica." Alma smiles with her eyes closed.

"I love it. How about Jessica Alma Barker? How does that sound?" My pain drips down my face.

This is really happening. She's close to taking her last few breaths. Why didn't they tell me and let me know? I could have been there; they didn't have to do it alone. I forward Alistair the text Joan previously texted me with the details. I don't have words. This forwarded text will have to do.

"Yes, I like that. It's pretty. I like the name Alma, too. Can you do me a favor and take care of my mom? She will try to do everything alone, don't let her be alone. She acts like she has it all together but she needs you," Alma pleads.

"You two have become family to me and I will always be here for you, no matter what. I love you, Alma." I hold her right hand while Joan holds her left.

"Me too. Mommy, I'm so tired," Alma whispers towards her mother.

"It's okay baby, take a nap. I will be here when you wake up, I promise. Mommy loves you," Joan's voice falls shaky and she kisses her dying daughter, she clings on.

The second the monitors flat line, Joan breaks down sobbing. I take my sleeve and wipe beneath my eyes before walking around the bed to collect Joan into my arms. This isn't about me right now. My friend just lost her baby girl. Her body falls to the floor, crying out for her baby in deep sadness.

"I've got you, I'm here." I fall to the floor next to her with her body in my arms and her face smudged into my shirt.

Alma looks sound asleep, at peace wherever her spirit took her. Nurses run in and I signal to them that I have Joan and close the door behind them after they do their protocol. Following the time of death, the medical staff allow us privacy with Alma. Joan's breathing becomes choppy as she cries at the top of her lungs. She repeatedly starts to scream into my shoulder, my grip around her gets tighter. It's taking everything in my power to keep my emotions together, to be strong. Joan starts to hyperventilate after screaming and begins to gasp for air.

"I'm here, just breath. Joan, breathe. You have to breathe," I try to help her regulate her breathing back to normal.

After Joan begins to calm down, she slowly moves her body to lay on the floor on her side. She turns completely mute and stares into the abyss. I follow her lead and lay next to her with my arm wrapped around her. The sound of running footsteps appear louder and louder as they get closer. Alistair and Duke's faces peek through the window and catch the view of us on the floor. I slowly shake my head side to side, then my grief becomes too overwhelming and control goes out the door.

The door opens at a slow place, the boys quietly walk into the room. Duke walks up to us laying down and gets down on the floor facing Joan. He moves to lay down with us and wraps his opposite arm around the woman who just lost her only child. Alistair walks up to Alma's body and kisses her forehead whispering a prayer before laying behind me. He mimics the same position I'm in with Joan. His embrace is tight and comforting, I silently cry in his embrace while holding space for Joan.

"I love you. I'm here, honey," Alistair whispers in my ear.

Now, anyone who would walk in on four grown adults laying silently on the hospital holding each other would think we are crazy, but this is us grieving. Surviving.

"We aren't going anywhere, Joan." Duke speaks for us all and

Joan cries with her chosen family.

CHAPTER 27

My heavy eyes open early on Christmas morning, rolling over in a bed high off the ground. Confused where I am for a second until the series of last night's events flood my memory. Lying in the top bunk of Alma's bed; her mom and Duke are sound asleep in the bottom bunk. Trying to be as soundless as possible, I climb down the stairs and close the door behind me as I leave the room.

The scent of fresh coffee hits my nose like meth hits a drug addict's veins. Alistair sits on the couch with a cup of joe wrapped in both of his hands. His head lays back over the top of the couch in exhaustion. There are no words to express what my heart is feeling, it simply needs stillness. My body falls down into the spot next to my rock and his arm wraps around my side. My eye lids drift heavily, my eyes are sore from working double time. Sniffles and sadness overwhelm my face and chest while he holds me in his embrace, in silence.

"Merry Christmas, Sabi," Alistair breaks the silence with his greeting as he lays the side of his head on top of mine.

"Cheers to St. Nick," I sarcastically say and grab the coffee out of his hand and take two large gulps.

Drinking coffee while being pregnant doesn't kill you or the baby, it sure is frowned upon though. Someone should deem this morning as the exception, coffee is needed. My mind is currently twisted into a jigsaw puzzle, hard to think straight. Life is short, life is on the other side of fear, Joan is alone now, Alistair and I are rocky, Duke and I are rocky, I'm having a baby. All I can do in this moment is weep, cut me some slack.

"Do you want to have this baby with me?" There's nowhere good to begin.

"I do," he keeps his response short. "Do you regret this baby?" I ask.

"Don't get me wrong, I'm elated. This is the best news I've ever gotten. I wouldn't want a baby with anyone else. I would choose you, every time. Am I scared? Hell yes. Am I ready? No. Is it shocking news? Yes. We didn't plan for this to happen. It just did. You getting pregnant couldn't have come at a worse time. It sucks you felt the need to hold it inside or confide in your best friend Duke. You seem to do a lot of things with Duke. It is what it is. We can't change the past." He hugs me tight but I don't feel as close to him as I did before my mistake.

Suddenly, my stomach turns for the worst, something is about to come up and it's coming fast. I shoot up and run to the nearest bathroom that I know of. Unfortunately for Joan, it's right next to the room she's resting in. Everything I ate last night gets thrown up into the toilet bowl my face is sunk into. Morning sickness at its finest, what timing. Alistair tries to open the door and I press it shut before he has a clear view of me puking. He might have seen once before when we were too drunk to function but he probably doesn't remember that. He respects my wishes and goes back into the living room. Just when I think I'm done and get cleaned up, round two arrives and it's gets worse. The grieving mama bear walks in and closes the door behind her, she grabs my hair and holds it out of my face while I puke into her previous clean toilet.

"Get it all out girl, it will be over soon." Joan rubs up and down my back.

"No, stop. I'm okay. Go lay down." I immediately refuse her help, we are here for her.

"And do what? Cry some more? Let it out," Joan snaps into a mama drill sergeant roll.

"Sabine? Are you okay in there?" Alistair asks through the door.

"She's fine. Hey Al, can you make me a cup of coffee please,"

Joan yells back.

"I think this baby hates me too." I don't know why, but the tears come flowing.

My heart feels light after the retching is all out of my system, I think it's part of my pregnancy, but more part grieving. Joan hands me a wet towel to wipe my face and a cup of water to rinse my mouth. She just lost her daughter and she still got up to take on the role of care taker. No one is more powerful than a mother, the true gift from life. I pull her in a tight warm embrace and she hugs me back even tighter. There aren't enough hugs I can give this woman to heal her broken heart. I wipe her eyes before we go into the living room to see Alistair.

"Before you ask, I'm okay. Thank you for your concern." I smile at my boyfriend.

"Thank you for everything, you two are angels. Dr. Vaughn too. He is still passed out in bed. I'm glad you came when you did Sabine. I will never forget how selfless the three of you are. You guys can go home now, I will be okay. My mom is coming to town today," Joan assures us.

"Are you sure? We don't mind," I offer.

"Yes, I am sure. Yes, I know I can call you any time," Joan responds.

Alistair hugs Joan goodbye and says his condolences before it's my turn. All I want to do is climb into my bed and sleep for a whole week, it's like I got hit by a truck. We arrive home to a messy house from the gathering last night. Fun was definitely had here this Christmas Eve. One of the gifts that's been under the tree for weeks is gone, the rest are still there. The hardest decision is choosing to sleep or open gifts, it is Christmas. Alistair takes my hand and pulls me over to the tree; the decision has been made.

"I wasn't peeking, I swear. But, where did the purple box go?" I question him.

"It was mis-wrapped, it was for Diane. Good thing you weren't peeking, though." Alistair jokes.

"Did everyone have a good time?" I ask.

"Yeah, they were worried about you. Of course, everyone left when we left for the hospital after I got your message." He answers and puts my hand in his.

"Thank you for showing up." I get up on my knees to be face level with him and plant a sweet kiss on his soft lips.

"I will always show up for you Sabi." He kisses my lips again. "Even when you hate me?" I kiss him back.

"I could never hate you," he can't look me in the eyes.

The first box I open from him is a Midnight Blue Citrus candle from Bath and Body works and I burst into laughter. He looks embarrassed which makes the moment extra special. You seriously can't ever have to many candles. He opens a gift from me and smiles as he unwraps an equality T-shirt that reads "Equality in rights, color, family, work, opportunities, and dreams." He shimmies his shoulders with a big smile on his face, he takes his shirt off and puts on the tee before he hands me my next present. This one is a long black box with a fragile stamp on the bottom. I open the box and a breathtaking. Black, glass rose is inside.

"This is the most beautiful thing I've ever seen. Not to mention one of the nicest gifts I've received." I'm stunned by the gift he got me.

It's nice to take turns going back and forth opening our gifts. "What in the hell in this?" Alistair holds up the contraption.

"It's a Boppy! It's those holster things to carry around your baby in. It's for you and Sebastian. Well, you and both your babies." I hate that I'm feeling awkward.

"This is thoughtful, I love it, babe. Thank you." He kisses my cheek and hands me my last wrapped box.

I open it up and it's a coral t-shirt that reads 'First Time Mommy' with baby footprints. I hold it close to my heart before tackling the cutest man on earth. He kisses my lips again and hands me the last wrapped item under the tree. It's from Alma, I look up at him in disbelief. I tear the wrapping paper as quickly as I can and gasp at a handmade framed picture of her and I passed out in her bed while Alistair sleeps on the ground. We were all dressed in random goofy outfits and had makeup smeared across our faces. We were passed out after having too much fun at her first and last sleepover. I hold the picture to my chest and tears fall down my joyful face. Alma is the selfless one. A note fell on the floor that reads, "My mom took this picture of one of the best nights ever. You should hang it in Sebastian's room. Love, Alma." That girl has changed my life forever, my heart has never been fuller than it is right now. *Santa*

Tell Me by Ariana Grande plays on the radio and I grab the remote and turn it up loud. Only happy tears are allowed today to celebrate love, family and Alma. The song flows right through me and I can't help, but sway my body to the melody. Alistair smirks at me until I pull him in to dance with me. Diane walks through the door with Jackson and walks in on us dancing together. She hollers and cheers at us before taking the toddler out of the stroller to join us. I reach out to grab him and he reaches back for me. We rock back and forth; he giggles a toothless laugh. Diane comes in for a group hug with her son and I, finishes it off with a kiss on the cheek and her condolences. Diane doesn't hold back, she's got moves. Craig brings in a hot casserole and a loaf of French bread. Diane takes Jackson from my arms for a dance. Then Alistair takes my hands and pulls me in close for a sweet slow dance. I gaze into his eyes and the room begins to fade.

"Merry Christmas, Sabi," he wishes.

CHAPTER 28

The only instructions he gave me for a surprise date night to celebrate New Year's is to shower after work and get dolled up. Wear whatever makes me feel comfortable and sexy. I take pride in being one to play by the rules especially when there is a surprise in it for me. My long black hair hangs down past my shoulders in waves. Red silk fabric clings tight to my body, accompanied by black strappy heels. I've never worn the sexy red dress and lipstick before, I feel the most confident I've been in my twenty-six years of life. There is only limited time left until this baby will fully distort my belly. I can't wait, someone's got to notice my new pregnancy glow sooner or later. Alistair walks up behind and wraps his arms around me, my hands naturally place on his. For a moment, I forget the world and imagine our life with two kids.

"You are the most beautiful woman I've ever laid eyes on." He eyes me through the mirror and I can't help but blush.

"You have no idea how long it took to allow myself to believe those words. I never knew it was going to come from the sexiest and most kind human on the planet." I look up back at him.

"I'm the lucky one here and damn, red is your color." Alistair grabs my hips and spins my body to face him before he kisses me. "Come on, we don't want to be late." I jokingly grab his butt and he chases me out the door.

Alistair drives to a restaurant in town that I've never been before. I find out why when we walk in and the place is magnificently, romantic. This is the fanciest restaurant anyone has brought me to, let alone a date. The host takes our reservation name and guides us to a candle lit table in the back corner. Dark blue starry table cloth covers the dining table and chairs. Fancy white drapes hang down the windows like the ones in a palace. The room is dim to set the mood for the restaurant's customers. This is the type of place where people get proposed to in the movies, oh God.

Alistair pulls my chair out for me like the perfect gentleman he always is. The waiter brings two menus, moments after seating. Alistair orders a glass of red wine and slightly tilts his head with regret until I let him know it's okay. The waiter obeys my request and brings my water with his wine. I'd do anything for that glass of wine right now. We spend the whole dinner discussing Sebastian, our soon-to-be here baby, and each other's optimistic plans for our future.

"Do we want a girl or a boy?" Alistair pops a popular question.

"I hope it's a girl considering I have a name already. Alma picked it out the night she... umm," I begin to stumble as I hold back sadness.

"It's okay, I understand. What is the name?" he holds my hand on top of the table.

"Jessica. It's the name of her doll. I would like to name her Jessica Alma Barker, if it's okay with you." I look into his eyes.

"I like it a lot actually. You're okay with her taking my last name?" he smiles from ear to ear.

"Yes, I am. We will have to come up with some boy names if it's not a girl, but I feel in my heart that our baby is Jessica." I respond. Alistair continues to hold my hand while we devour the most delicious molten chocolate cake. A different waiter brings a bottle of white wine in a bucket and two full wine glasses. I lay eyes on the glass in front of me and my heart drops, thankfully not literally. There is a stunning diamond ring in the wine I did not order. Relief starts when Alistair has the same shocked look on his face as I do. "Excuse me, sir," Alistair raises his voice loud enough for him to hear.

"This certainly is not for us. You've got the wrong table," he adds.

"Thank God., I sigh with relief but disappointment.

"I am so sorry, sir. Thank you! I could have lost my job." The waiter rushes back and quickly grabs the loaded gesture for the table ten feet away.

"Thank God, huh?" Alistair asks before he downs the rest of his second glass of wine.

"Um… I'm sorry. I don't know why I said it like that." I don't know what to say.

"It's okay, I'm just messing with you. Are you ready to get out of here? You're going to love part two even more." Alistair gets up and puts my hand in his.

"Wait, there is another part? This night has been lovely. We almost got engaged, what a night it's been!" I kiss his arm and follow his lead.

My feet have developed a blister or two from these incredibly sexy strappy shoes. Regret is going to hit me hard when I get to work with these blisters. The date is only half over, suck it up, Sabine.

No pain no gain.

My jaw drops when Alistair pulls into the parking lot to the laser tag arcade, he remembers everything I say. My feet on the other hand will in fact disown me after this event, but game on. Alistair tells me to wait in the car as he gets out and comes around to my side. He opens the door with a pair of my tennis shoes in his right hand and sweats in the left. Jeans would have worked too, but sweats could help me have an advantage.

"Although, you look stunning in that outfit, I think these would make you feel more comfortable. Plus, you can't blame your outfit when I win." Alistair chuckles to himself.

"You have thought of everything, haven't you? I think I'm going to need some help getting this tricky dress off." I smirk.

His sweet generosity is what turns me on the most, aside from his charming good looks. Alistair gets in the back seat first and then I follow his lead. I climb on top of him and straddle his lap, his hands cuff my bottom. He moans at the touch of my lips on his neck. His bulge grows bigger the more my body rubs against his. He unbuckles his belt then, unbuttons his pants at the same time he bites my bottom lip. I pull the end of my dress to my waist and my mind turns blank the second we become one. My mind gets lost in the moment of my hot craving being satisfied. The way he touches my changing body, makes me feel like the hottest woman alive. I am his and he is mine. It's more than romance and passion right now, it's rough young lust. For the first time, we finish together. I collapse into his arms and hard breathing is the only sound left in the car. For the first time since my first appointment, I feel connected with the man I love.

After collecting ourselves, I pull the pair of sweats under my tight dress and put the socks and shoes on. Thanks to the car window, I pull my hair up and fix myself to hide the moment we just shared. This place is filled with kids and preteens ready for battle, we could pass for their chaperones.

"Put that away, sir." I tell Alistair as he pulls his wallet out.

"You are my date, I'm paying. You're worth every penny." Alistair is smitten with himself.

"So are you. You paid for dinner. It's 2021, men deserve to be treated like kings. Equality for all!" I dramatically shout and fist bump the air to prove my point.

Of course, he lets me win because no one should be against equality. How could he argue with that? A couple of teenage girls eye my random outfit while I fix my hair one last time. It makes me giggle when they judge my outfit because I've never been happier. They will learn one day that being the fanciest person in the room doesn't make you happiest. Plus, they should have seen me at the restaurant, turning heads left and right.

Alistair chooses the name Zap Attack, and I choose Black Reign. Our group is called and everyone meets in the dark black room with the guns and laser gear. The strappy vests haunted me growing up when my friends wanted to come here. They never had a vest big enough to fit my voluptuous body. Tonight, is a different story. The relief is warm when the straps wrap around me like a hug. These kids aren't ready for Zap Attack and Black Reign. When everyone gives a thumbs up to the guy in charge, he pulls the lever and the wall opens up from left to right. The second the alarm sounds Alistair takes off running with the teens and I am left at the beginning on my own. The arena glows like the mind of a person on LSD. Ultra violet art paints the walls and tunnels in the layout. I pull my gun up to my chest like I'm in battle and start jogging up the ramp to my left.

"Got you!" A kid with a rest vest shoots me and my vest makes a defeating noise.

"Right back at you," an evil laugh escapes my lips when I shoot his back as he tries to run past me.

I hear Alistair yelling from across the arena, he gets hit a few times in a row. When I find him, he threatens to shoot, but I get him first. A medium height boy runs down the ramp too fast and rams me right into the wall.

"Sabine! Are you okay? What do we have to do?" Alistair panics.

"No, it's okay. I'm okay. Honestly. Thank you though." I try and hide being surprised of his reaction, it was sweet.

"You would tell me if you weren't okay right? I need to know that." He's worried about me.

"Yes, of course." I feel guilty from his worry.

The boy is embarrassed and apologizes immediately, accidents happen. I take advantage of his vulnerability and shoot his target. I laugh uncontrollably and run away from the both of them. I turn the corner and hide to recover from getting the wind knocked out of me. It's enough time to come up with a strategy, three girls come around the corner giggling. I lay on the ground and aim for their targets. My gun is positioned perfectly when they stop, and bullseye, three for three. There is four and a half minutes left on the timer, I find Alistair again, but he shoots me first this time. No mercy.

"Put your hands up, this only ends one way!" a group of six kids walk towards us. They have us cornered.

"Please, you don't have to do this. I'm a good guy, is it money that you want? We are just trying to get home to the kids," Alistair jokingly plays along to their scene.

"Never!" I scream and make a run for it and Alistair is not far behind me.

"I've been shot! Leave me here. Go on, live your life!" Alistair plays the role too well. It's making the kids laugh.

His target restarts and he grabs hold of me to hide around the corner. The group of kids find us with a few more joining them. They chase us across the obstacle course, we are cornered for real this time. With thirty-two seconds left, I surrender and fall to the floor. Alistair makes a last-ditch effort to protect me, he hunches over me and protects me with his life. The teenagers have a blast racking up points on his target. The alarm buzzes loud and sets us free from laser war.

"That was awesome!" A teenage boy yells.

"Want to play another round with us?" Another kid asks with hope.

"I'm warmed up now, you're going down kid!" Alistair says yes.

The next two rounds are as fun as the first. I can't help, but laugh every time to boys call Alistair an old man. Some of the girls are giggly when he talks to them, we have all been there. I team up with them a couple time and get a few points here and there for myself. High fives and goodbyes are had before we end the night. This has been the best date I've ever been on. Alistair swoops up my hand as we walk to the car.

"If our dates are always like this, I could spend forever with you,"

Alistair kisses my cheek.

"Well, that's good because I think you're stuck with me." I smile back at the man I'm deeply in love with.

CHAPTER 29

"I have good news Mr. Barker! Sebastian is healthy enough to go home with you. There is paperwork to fill out at the first desk and nurse Michaels can meet with you, if you have any questions," Dr. Hu congratulates and informs Alistair.

"Thank you, sir. This little guy couldn't have done it without all of you." Alistair raises his voice with gratitude towards the medical team.

January flew by like the blink of an eye. We spent it low key, getting fully ready for Sebastian. The truth is, Sebastian going home is a victory for us all. It's been a long nine and a half months, working hard and trying to find the solution to get him healthy. Although, it's not polite to brag, but I can't refrain from telling everyone I get to go home with him. A few of the nurses in my shift agree to cover my load in the rest of the shift, so I can get to the house before Alistair and Sebastian. He doesn't have a clue in the world, he is going to walk into an adoption surprise party. We invited the nurses and doctors who worked closely with the baby, friends and family, Joan and Karen. We thought it is the right thing to do because none of this would be possible without her huge decision. She is one to make scenes, but our last few conversations were smoother than before. I did my hair and makeup before my shift, which allows me time to change and help set up when I get home. Duke, Ophelia and

Diane have been at the house for hours to make the inside look unrecognizable with party decorations. Alistair knows I'm working and its tricky to leave without him seeing me sneak out. I have attempted to leave twice already, but he keeps making eye contact with me. He comments how long it's taking for the staff to finish everything up, little does he know they are stalling to give the party planners more time.

Finally, I run out the door when he goes to the bathroom. The bakery is on my way home. The place is embellished for Valentine's Day, Cupid barfed all over the room. Love is in the air, more like money is in the air for big corporations. Duke put his name on the order and the strict employee won't release the baked goods to me. I call Duke through facetime for proof in order to pay and get on my way. Sometimes, technology is a gift from the universe in the strangest of times. The woman avoids eye contact after the call and gets the ball rolling. I'm out and arrive home before I know it.

"Omg my God, it looks incredible in here!" I struggle to carry the cake and Duke lends a hand.

"We really have outdone ourselves guys," Joan chimes in. "Joan!" I'm shocked to see her here early; I sprint to her with a big hug.

"What a welcome, what am I, chopped liver?" Diane laughs. "Diane!" I scream with excitement and tumble onto her.

Spreading warm welcome kisses all over her face until she laughs uncontrollably, she pushes me off to go pee.

My scrubs are scrunched up my belly and legs from rough housing on the couch. No one was close enough to notice my stomach, in case I'm showing. I get up and head to my room to change until something catches my eye. Joan and Ophelia are hanging up a long banner with pictures of Alistair holding Sebastian in the hospital, numerous photos. Song lyrics are printed in between the photos, *My Wish* by Rascal Flatts. The words surrounding these beautifully vulnerable memories are things like "this is my wish," "I hope you know somebody loves you." I hope all your dreams come true. This banner is just as much of a surprise to Alistair as it is to me. If it brought tears to my eyes, he's going to need the tissues, well deserved tissues.

"Who created this masterpiece?" I am memorized.

"I created it but had a few helpers snap the pictures for me. I thought he would love it and it would be cute in the nursery. The journey has been breathtaking," Joan answers.

"This is the most thoughtful gift I have ever seen. I love it. He is going to sob," I let her know before I finally leave to change.

My outfit of choice is a black, stripe, off the shoulder blouse with black high wasted jeans. To finish the look, black booties. After a few minutes to touch up my curls, I'm ready for a full-blown celebration. My awkward, but funky dance moves come out when Diane plays music on the speaker.

One of the receptionists at the hospital text me updates on how much time we have before he is on his way. We aren't pressed for time, but we would like everyone to show up before the big surprise. The sign in table is covered in all the sharpie colors you can think of. When a guest arrives, they will take a color of their choosing to sign their name and wish on the big, yellow, rubber duck. They decided to stick with the duck theme and ran wild with the idea. Blue balloons surround the house in bundles of three. White and blue streamers hang in swirls across the ceiling. There are both a "Welcome home" and "Congratulations,

Daddy" signs hanging when you first walk in the door. The punch bowl is a big glass bowl of blue punch with foam for bubbles and small rubber ducks floating around. This party seems to be a baby shower and adoption party wrapped in one. The house begins to fill up a few minutes after the setup is finished. Joan walks up and throws her arm around me while we wait for the signal text.

"Hey, mama!" My eyes peel to her face.

"Hey, mama back," she squeezes tight for a semi hug.

"You know you can always call if you need someone, right? I'll be there," I say softly.

"Losing a child is the hardest thing I've ever been through. I'm grateful to be here, it's easier to keep my mind occupied. I don't know what to do now because she is, was my world," Joan chokes up but keeps it together.

"Well, you still have me." I turn and cuddle her tight.

"I appreciate that. I've noticed people distance themselves and get all weird since Alma's passing. It was a process and not sudden, I knew it was coming you know? Doesn't hurt any less." Joan rests her head on my shoulder.

The message we have all been waiting for has finally come through, he is on his way. I'm ecstatic and nervous at the same time which gives me the urge to urinate. Just my luck, I would go and miss the surprise announcement.

"Everyone, take your places!" Diane announces after hearing a car door shut.

"This is your new home, Sebastian," Alistair talks to the baby as he brings his son home for the first time.

"Surprise!" The crowd loudly whispers simultaneously to not scare the baby.

"Holy shit!" Alistair is stunned, immediately covers his mouth when he realizes what he said.

"Oh my God!" He adds with warm disbelief.

Alistair puts the baby carrier down to hug every single person who showed up, even the nurses and doctors that he doesn't know all too well. He's a hugger, I wasn't until I met him. Well, I hug people I know. Sebastian is as cute as a button in a different setting other than the hospital. He stares at everything and everyone with his big beautiful brown eyes. This is his first time outside of the hospital he called home for nine months. Diane sits in front of the baby and welcomes him to the family. Sebastian coos at Diane and everyone's hearts melt. Laughter, admiration and conversation fill the room in celebration of Alistair and Sebastian's big day. Alistair is busy for a while with people approaching him with congratulations and conversation. The baby is getting passed around left and right.

"How are you feeling, Montgomery?" Duke sits next to me.

"I'm great, honestly happy. It weird that a half a year ago, I was tearing everything up in my apartment and now I'm living my dream." I smile at him and rest my head on his shoulder.

"Did you record that?" Duke jokingly asks. "Shut up," I laugh.

"I'm assuming you guys haven't worked your stuff out yet?" Duke becomes serious.

"Yeah, that's funny. Try trying to work things out with someone who won't fully admit something is wrong. Me and you are only fine because I got over being mad at you and realized I messed up bad," I confide in my best guy friend.

"Yeah, it's how he processes things, I guess. I don't know. He doesn't really even acknowledge my existence anymore. At least he loves you." Duke tries to make me feel better but doesn't quite do the job.

Seven o'clock rolls around and the catering service arrive with dinner: rice, beans, enchiladas and fajitas. Finally, I get a moment with the man of the hour. He kisses me and the group cheers and makes an embarrassing big deal for no reason. Sebastian's tiny hand closes around my finger when I greet him. Suddenly, Karen Osgood walks through the front door. A few people are shocked and others show signs of relief, mine might be a little of both. She walks in awkwardly like a sore thumb, a fish out of water if you will. Ophelia is the first to greet Karen with a warm welcome, which helps make her feel included.

"Sorry, I'm late. Congratulations Alistair." Karen approaches us with pure intentions.

"Hi, Karen. We are glad you can make it." I greet her with a quick side hug.

"Can I hold him? I only got to hold him for second, one time." Karen isn't shy about asking.

"Yeah...there you go, watch his head." Alistair passes over his son to the woman who gave him away.

"Hi, baby boy. Do you remember me? I grew you in my belly,"

Karen sweet talks the boy.

Alistair stops me when he realizes I wanted to step in to say something about the words she is speaking to Sebastian. He gives me a 'let her have this moment' look. I didn't fight him on his decision, but I have a watchful eye on her throughout the time she is here. Most of the people from the hospital leave before dinner and the meal is more between friends and family. It works out either way, of course Ophelia is still here because she falls into the friend category. Dinner lasts long due to all of the fun mingling between social groups. It's time to cut the cake and Alistair wants to make an announcement. For some reason. Everyone cheers when he cuts the first slice, if only Sebastian was old enough to enjoy a piece. If only Alma was here to eat the piece of cake she yearned for. After everyone gets a slice, Alistair gets the attention of his peers and begins his speech.

"First of all, I want to thank every single one of you for not only showing up tonight, but making tonight possible. Some of you know, it's been my dream to become a father for as long as I can remember and today will stay forever in my heart. Karen, thank you for giving Sebastian life. I promise you I will protect him with everything I've got. I am the luckiest man to have such an incredible partner. Thank you all. Enjoy the cake and cheers to life, love and family!" Alistair gives his speech and everyone cheers when he finishes.

Alistair puts Sebastian to bed in his room when the party dies down, few people are still here. Joan left with a piece of cake before the speech to eat it alone in Alma's bed, her angel was looking forward to this exact dessert. The place is a mess, our circle knows how to really get down and wild. The stream of pictures touches Alistair's heart as much as we all thought, he is in the nursery pinning it up with Diane right now. Duke grabs a plastic garbage bag and opens it up for me to easily throw the trash away. Three bags aren't enough and I have to get some more from the hall closet. I walk by the nursery and hear my name come out of Diane's mouth. I know, its childish to eavesdrop, but I can't help myself.

"Well, yeah. Can I tell you something and you promise to keep it between us?" Alistair asks his sister.

"Of course." She answers.

"I think Sabine is cheating on me and it's been secretly eating away at me. I've even been going back to the support group without telling her because something in me is not healed all the way. I want to explode sometimes." Alistair confides.

"Oh Al, that girl is head over heels for you. Who would she even cheat on you with? She doesn't have much of a life outside of work and the social circle, no offense to her," Diane compassionately responds to her brother's fears.

"She used to date Duke and they are together all the time now. They are extremely close and it sends me back to the feeling of not being good enough. I mean she told him first and wanted him at her first appointment, is it even mine? Then again, he did meet with me after and told me everything. At least he's a grown man, but I'm sure he wouldn't be open about sleeping with my girlfriend. They even picked out all of this stuff together, duck theme and all. I don't know, Diane," Alistair responds.

"She's pregnant!?" Diane didn't hear anything but those words. "I'm scared she will get offended or upset and it will cause a huge fight. Being accused of cheating isn't the greatest feeling. I don't want to lose her but I also don't want to be disrespected again. The whole turn of events really shook me to the core, I don't know how to process any of it." Alistair sighs and breaks eye contact.

"Sweetheart, talk to her. She knows you. She cares deeply about you, it shows. Have that conversation. If reassurance is what you need in this moment, ask for what you need. If she is really pregnant with your baby, that's something you need to know. She doesn't seem like the type to do that to a man." Diane places her comforting hand on his shoulder.

Those are the last words I thought I'd hear come out of his mouth. I wouldn't cheat on him in a million years, how could he think that? I was scared when I found out that I'm pregnant and I confided in one of my closest friends. I understand the logic behind the hurt, but I didn't have any ill intention. The loneliness he must feel while being lost in that thought process is daunting. No wonder he never told me the day I ran into him in the parking lot, he's there because of me. I catch myself paralyzed, staring at the ground, stuck in my thoughts. Is the baby even his? That's the question that knocks the wind out of me.

"Hey, did you get the bags?" Duke walks up.

"You, okay? What's wrong? Talk to me, Montgomery" he adds as I stand here speechless.

Duke pulls me in for a hug and rubs my back for comfort as Alistair and Diane walk out and see us together. This isn't helping my case.

CHAPTER 30

There's no telling how much longer I can handle Alistair ignoring the elephant in the room. Plus, the passive aggressive commentary is making it hard to bite my tongue for much longer. It's been weird since overhearing him with his sister. I've been weird, filled with guilt this whole time. I have no right to be short with him, I'm the one who betrayed his heart. Our chemistry is there, but our energy has shifted. I do everything in my power to respect his space. I'd be lying if I said the space is just for him, he has secretly accused me of terrible things. I never knew he could think of me this way. I sit on it for a while and realize one thing that could make me feel better is showing up for today's Infidelity Survivors Anonymous meeting. The space between us is killing me and what better place to go for support.

Leggings and an oversized olive-green sweater are my comfy clothes of choice, dressing comfortable is a must in a nerve-wracking situation. My baby bump is starting to really stick out. I lift up my sweater in the mirror and admire my beautiful fast-growing belly. My baby is swimming in there. Alistair has already left which puts my mind at ease, he will be the first one there hopefully. I grab my keys, orange juice and leave for my first morning meeting in a long time. The closer I am the more I doubt my decision to go. Should I do this? Am I sabotaging his safe space? My intention for going is to be heard and possibly get advice for my dilemma, not to threaten or harm the man I love. I park, take a deep breath and walk into the building. The look on Alistair's face seems blank, no reaction at all.

"Sabine!" Maliha seems to be pleasantly surprised with my attendance.

"Good morning, is it alright if I join today?" I ask, feeling slightly insecure.

"Of course, the more the merrier. How are you? How is the baby? Congratulations are in order," she hugs me tight.

"I am great, feeling a lot better in the second trimester. Life has been crazy in good ways and bad, but I'm grateful to be here. How is baby Patel?" I return the polite conversation.

"She is a dream! I keep telling her to stop growing, but she hasn't listened. We are hoping to have another one within the year. I am excited!" She responds and wraps up the conversation.

The cat is out of the bag here. Makes sense, he would share the news to gives context, I guess. I don't know any of these people, a whole new group. I wonder how often this group completely changes. I take the empty seat next to the Godlike man who catches my eye.

"Good morning, I'm Alistair Barker. I haven't seen you around here." The pretend mystery man greets me.

"Sabine Montgomery. Nice to meet you, handsome." I shake his hand.

"Good morning, everyone! Let's check in. How is everyone?"

Maliha starts the meeting, ending our conversation.

"I think our new friend here would like to go first." Alistair taps my knee in choosing me.

"No, I'm good," I decline.

"You know what, I would love to go first." I perk up and take the plunge.

"The floor is yours, Sabine." Maliha smiles then sips her coffee. "I recently overheard a conversation between my amazing boyfriend and his lovely sister accusing me of infidelity and it honestly broke my heart that he could ever think that ill of me. We had a semi-falling out about a major topic and he is just holding it all inside. Like we seem good most of the time, but are we really? I am angry about it. I'm hormonal, I'm all over the place. How dare he? I have never once done anything remote to cheating!" I spill the tea.

"How dare he? You're angry at him for being upset? You never thought maybe he has good reason to be upset?" Alistair interrupts. "Well maybe if he was mature about it and came to me and discussed his feelings like we always have then instead up acting like he's fine, we wouldn't be in this position. Would we?" My tone becomes sassy.

"And we are back to this being his fault? It's his fault that he wasn't invited to his supposed child's doctor appointment that you brough Duke to? With everyone's history? Not to mention he's the one I had to hear the news from? The guy my girlfriend is glued to. I see your secret jokes and your glances back and forth." Alistair isn't holding back.

"Guys," Maliha attempts to cool the heat.

"Why do you keep saying that? Of course, this baby is yours. We have gone over this. I know it wasn't a smart option to bring him. I'm not going to end one of my best friendships because you want me to.

That's unfair and not healthy, Alistair," I raise my voice in the heat of the moment.

"I get it. He's a doctor and you're a nurse. You guys have lots in common and you work together. A perfect match. I'm just sick to my stomach waiting for you to leave me for him. Just do it already, I can't take this anymore." Alistair's voice is as raised as mine, but he has tears in his eyes.

"Hey, look at me. I'm not going anywhere. I hear you. What do I need to do to help you realize this? I'm sorry that I haven't helped you feel secure in this relationship lately and I want to change that. We can't keep our feelings inside like this. You have to talk to me, how am I supposed to know when to fix my wrongs? And the result is dramatically screaming at each other in a room full of strangers like hormonal teenagers." I stand in between his knees and wipe his tears with my thumbs.

"Everyone, breathe. Sabine. Alistair. I don't think you guys should be doing this here. if you both need a third party, I am more than willing to meet with you after this." Maliha stays as professional as she should be.

"Sorry, guys." I wipe the wetness off my cheeks.

"Girl, I am over here like where is my popcorn. I've never had a fight that ended this good." A girl from across the circle makes everyone laugh.

We sit through the rest of the meeting out of respect for everyone and their broken hearts to share their stories and be heard. Leaving would break the safe bond of the circle, we couldn't do that to the group. Maliha stands firm in her offer to guide us with our conflict. We wait for everyone to leave, then the three of us pull up a chair.

"I've known you two for quite some time now and you don't need these meetings anymore. Sounds like you just needed to be honest with each other, but look at your communication even when it's bad. This is healthy, believe it or not. If you two are open to it, let's talk about it." Maliha offers to help.

"I found out I was pregnant and I spooked. I was too scared to tell Alistair because who knows how he would react if my reaction didn't feel fully positive in the first place. Duke was there at the right place at the right time when I emotionally exploded, it could have been anyone I told. It just happened to be him. I love Duke, he's one of my closest friends but I don't want to be with him. That ship has long gone, I rejected him. No, I don't want to lose him. Alistair, I am so sorry that I didn't come to you when I first found out. I'm sorry my actions hurt you, it was never my intention to hurt you." I voluntarily go first.

"You don't think I would have been there for you and been supportive? Getting pregnant was both of our doing. I felt robbed of hearing the news because I had to mask my feelings in front of a man who is smitten with you. You can't tell me he doesn't have feelings for you. This whole second baby thing was just sprung on me out of nowhere. I felt blindsided. How could you not see that? I just feel like every single time you left the house with Duke I felt more distant from you. Then, I would plan date night and reconnect and then disconnect. I understand the communication is on both of us, mainly me. I'm sorry." Alistair looks worn out from the emotional battle we have been fighting for too long.

"Alistair, what is something Sabine can do better in the relationship?" Maliha asks.

"I would like to be more included in things. This baby is mine too.

I wasn't there to find out. Then you've already got the name picked out. The nursery for Sebastian was a beautiful surprise and I appreciate more than anything, but I wasn't a part of that either. I don't want you spending less time with Duke but maybe we can all get together." Alistair shows transparency.

"I would love that more than anything in the world. I would love to combine my worlds. You're invited to everything. I will also have a conversation with Duke about hanging too much because I would like to focus more on my family that I'm building with my incredible boyfriend. I love you and I am truly sorry from the bottom of my heart. I can honestly say that I have never cheated on you or once had a thought to cheat on you." I open my heart to the man I love. "We needed this. I appreciate you Maliha." He seems lighter in energy.

I'm proud of you guys." Maliha goes in for a group hug.

We wrap up the meeting then Alistair walks me to my car. This morning didn't go as planned or like anything I pictured, it was intense, but I'm happy it happened. I could go for a really long cuddle session which turns into a nice nap.

"I think I'm good now, this is my last meeting. From now on, I will trust in my very pretty sponsor. Thank you for coming." Alistair wraps his long arms around my body.

"I actually came for me, but I think it's what we both needed. I'm sorry I yelled at you. At least we survived our first fight." I smile up at my man.

"We are more than okay, I love you Sabi. See you tonight after work?" he kisses my lips before letting go and opening my car door for me like a gentleman.

"Yes, sir." I kiss him one last time and fall into my front seat.

Good thing I brought an emergency to go bag because there is no energy left in my body to drive home first. Situations like this is

what the locker-room at the hospital is for, one of the reasons. Xavier joins Ophelia and I in folding towels, bedding and clothes. Our conversation changes the moment his ears can hear us, thankfully he doesn't catch on.

"Hey there baby mama!" Xavier shoulder taps me.

"What?" I'm immediately caught off guard.

"What are you on edge for? Are you weirded out by your boyfriend adopting a baby without you? That party was a ton of fun. Is it weird having hot sex under the same roof as an infant?" Xavier bombardes me with questions.

"Xavier!" Ophelia smacks his chest.

"That's not the weird part," I sarcastically sigh. "Trouble in paradise?" He asks another question.

"No, he was doubting my commitment, but we worked it out. Don't make something out of nothing." I keep it as brief as possible, changing the subject wouldn't fly with Xavier.

"Doubting your commitment? Who says that? Are you telling me, he thinks you're cheating on him? With who? Dr. Charming man Duke." Xavier pushes more questions at me.

"Why does everyone assume it's him? No one ever guesses Denzel Washington or Dr. Sloan from Greys Anatomy. We do work in a hospital," I respond with the intention of ending the rumor with humor.

"Okay, enough with the interrogation. Why don't you tell us how you and Erik are?" Ophelia puts a stop to it for me.

Spending less time with Duke in order to make Alistair to feel more secure in our relationship is not negotiable. Spending more time with my boys instead of friends is the best compromise I am more than happy to make. It's a win-win situation, well for everyone except Duke. Speaking of him, here he comes.

"Good morning, Montgomery." He presents his usual greeting. "Good morning. Hey, I have to cancel our climbing session tonight. I want to send time with Alistair and Sebastian. I hope you're not mad." I attempt to the lessen the blow.

"Ugh, thank God. I was scared to break your fragile heart. I have to cancel as well. Plans came up." He responds.

"Better plans than me? I'm hurt!" I joke.

"Hey Sabine, a Dr. Montgomery is here to see you." The receptionist interrupts our banter.

"Dr. Montgomery? You got a husband? Maybe, you aren't cheating with Duke." Xavier makes a joke that doesn't go over well. "Who is cheating with me and why don't I know about it?" Duke is a gem for joking and brushing it off, he can probably put two and two together.

"No, stop that. It's my father, actually." I roll my eyes and put the file away.

"Father? Your dad is a doctor? I see you. Anyways, I'm here for baby Rodrigo," Duke reads the patients name off his clipboard as I walk out.

It's highly unusual for my father to pop up once, but twice is starting to concern me. My dad must have something important to discuss with me if he willing to look up my place of work and find me. It better not be about my mom because I don't have time for family drama. I clock out and go on break to meet him in the lobby, he is alone this time. He has a black suit on and his greying hair has grown out. We greet each other and walk to the cafeteria for a private place to talk.

"What's going on dad? What are you doing here?" I ask him as we sit down.

"Don't worry, it's not about your mom this time. I have the perfect job opportunity for you, once in a life time deal, Beanie." My dad's oblivious response goes straight over my head.

"This could have been a phone call, you know? You can't just keep showing up after all this time," I sigh with disappointment.

"Beanie, this is a big deal. I am opening a practice in New York and you can start next week. I can't and won't take no for an answer." He smiles big with no consideration for my answer.

"Dad, I have built an incredible life here for myself. I love my job here. I love my boyfriend and his new son. I love the family I've built here in Cedar Mills. I'm sorry, I can't." It breaks my heart to see the disappointment written on his face.

"I'm your family, come on Beanie!" He raises his voice, but avoids making a scene.

"You are my dad, but you can't show up when you want asking the world of me. It's not fair. You're a brilliant man who puts himself and work above his child. I refuse to make the same mistake." I stay firm in my decision in doing what's right for me.

"You're going to regret this, Beanie." Dad says his final words before kissing my forehead and leaving me once again, alone.

"Dad!" I yell from across the room. Life is too short to live it half empty. He turns around.

"I love you. Thank you for the job offer, and for loving me the way you know how. Please stay in town for a few days, let's have dinner tomorrow night. I can cook for you. We can celebrate your new practice. I would love for you to properly meet Alistair." I wrap my arms around him and wait too long to let go.

"Really? Okay. I would like that." His smile is warm.

"7pm sharp, okay? I can text you my address again. I love you and can't wait for tonight." I hug him one last time before he leaves the cafeteria.

Chasing after him with an invite to my world, lifts pressure off my chest. If I have learned anything lately, life is too short to hold any animosity in my heart. So much for plans with my man, still a night with my boys, just added a plus one. I text my darling boyfriend to give him a heads up and get back to work. Feels a little empty here without Sebastian in his container, even though it's an amazing thing he's gone form this place. No more views of my handsome man holding the preemies.

The rest of my shift goes by fast due to the distraction in my head. Tonight's dinner will give us all time to bond and share our amazing news with my father. I stop by the grocery store and pick up the ingredients for vegetable primavera. My nerves build more intensely as the time gets closer and closer. I've come a long way in life to end up today barefoot and pregnant in the kitchen. I never thought I'd see the day.

"Oh my God, its smells divine in here. Honey, we are home!"

Alistair's face lights up while holding Sebastian in his carrier.

"Welcome home, Mr. Barker!" My tone is as sweet as cherry pie.

"Why thank you Ms. Montgomery. What did I do to deserve all of this?" He kisses my lips before putting the baby down.

"You deserve it all. Look at me being a modern-day woman." I dramatically twirl the wooden spoon in the air.

"Do I have time to give this little guy a bath?" Alistair asks.

"Go for it. He should be here within an hour, but the man is never on time." I smile and stir the pot of angel hair noodles.

Alistair playfully takes Sebastian into the bathroom for a quick bathing session. Alistair has many one-sided conversations with the baby considering he is eleven months old. He is sweet and gentle; born to be a father. Sebastian coos in the tiny tub while Alistair sings splish splash. While the food cooks, I look through the pile of clothes to find a pair of thick pajamas to keep Sebastian throughout the night. Alistair pours a small cup of water over his hair; he tightly closes his eyes and opens his mouth every time the water runs over his little cute face. We get him out and dried before putting him in clothes.

Someone knocks at the front door and Alistair hands me Sebastian to hold while he gets the door. Sebastian peeks his head to the side and watches his dad walk away. I gently cradle him for comfort while Alistair welcomes our guest in.

"Hi guys, I'mmm here to pick up my suuun." Karen Osgood is drunk out of her mind.

"Woah, Karen what are you doing here. Are you drunk?" She tries to come in and Alistair blocks the opening with his body.

"Dad? Did you bring Abigail?" I ask while walking to the door from the bedroom.

"Karen Osgood." Alistair looks back at me to not come any closer with the baby.

"Exactly, he knowwws. Give me him. Come on, mommy's here,"

Karen reaches out for the baby.

"No, you can't have him. How did you get here? Wait, aren't you pregnant?" I quickly hand Alistair the baby and help hold Karen up straight when I remember.

"Nope, miscarriage. They are common, you should know that misssss nurse," Karen slurs her sarcastic response and tries to walk in, again.

"Come in, sit down. I'm going to get you some water. Is there someone I can call to come get you?" I walk Karen to a chair and rush to get her a cup of water.

"I'm noooot leaving without my son," she yells with no hesitation.

"He is not yours to raise anymore; remember you gave him a father who can provide a good life for him. Karen, you can't just show up at my house, especially drunk." Alistair walks in the room from putting the baby safely in his room.

"He is mine! I gave birth to him! I can raise him, he's better now!"

She yells at the top of her lungs and starts to cry into her hands.

"Karen, who can I call to come get you?" I level my tone, crouch down to meet her at eye level.

"The police." Alistair sighs with frustration.

"No!" Karen breaks through her tears.

"No, she doesn't need handcuffs. She needs help." I keep my tone and treat her like a toddler who is throwing a tantrum.

Karen takes ten minutes to remember her boyfriend's ten-digit phone number. Someone who is not her boyfriend picks up the line and I apologize for having the wrong number. She insists that it's his number and begins her tantrum again. I take my time to console her, she calms down and gives me her mother's number. Her mother picks up the phone with immediate annoyance when I tell her about our unfortunate situation. She apologizes a few times before hanging up and lets us know she is on her way. The twenty- six-minute wait is going to be unbearable to handle, but we will get through it. Before the house burns down, I turn the stove off and put a halt on dinner. I don't know whether to be sad my father hasn't shown up yet or grateful he's not here to see this mess. Karen laughs erratically at the long wait time; we don't find it as funny. Times like this, I wish I was just as drunk as her to get through this.

"Let me see my baby!" Karen demands.

"For his safety, you cannot see him," Alistair calmly reminds her.

"Safety? I'm his mother!" She back talks.

"Karen," I try to get her attention.

"Shut up, why did you let me do this? You're a health care provider, youuu were supposed to stop me. Plus, did you know you're getting fat? Maybe you should worry about yourself." She's angry, her words are stained with pettiness.

"As a health care provider, I have to do what is best for my patient. As a woman, I tried to stop you. At the end of the day, you did what is best for him. You have to know that deep down," I answer her even though I know it's going in one ear and out the other.

"Sebastian is my son. I will do everything in my power to protect him from any harm. With that being said, if you get help and prove that you're mentally healthy, you can visit him. I won't stop him from knowing his mother, but not like this." Alistair opens his heart.

Karen refuses to speak for the rest of her time until her mother shows up. Her mom seems embarrassed as she drags her drunk grieving daughter out the door. Karen is getting everything she's got to stay in her seat but the alcohol steals her balance and strength. The pain in Alistair's face while watching her physically fight her mental demons is as strong as the love, he has for his new baby boy. His eyes fall low, the beautiful wrinkle lines across his forehead begin to form. Karen is not giving up, fighting her own mother. Alistair physically gets in between the two and wraps his arms around the mother of his child. She clings on to him for dear life as she sobs into his arms. He holds her in stillness, she begins to heal.

"I'm sorry. I'm sorry you're hurting. I see your love for Sebastian. No one can ever take that love away," Alistair genuinely says while looking into Karen's soaking eyes.

She pauses for a moment and then is back to sobbing in his arms. Her mom stands a few feet away, watching the pain her daughter is experiencing. Her face has an expression of a deer in the headlights, as if she has no idea what her daughter has been going through. He holds her tight in his arms of emotional space like the first time I met his sister. I wonder if his sister did it for him. Where did they learn to be so kind? After everything has calmed down, Karen apologizes for the evening and drinks the cup of water on the table. Alistair stands his ground and keeps

Sebastian safe in his room until Karen is on her way home with her mom. As soon as the front door closes, Alistair runs to the nursey to check on Sebastian. He is sound asleep in his crib. I join the love of my life and watch the most beautiful boy lying down sound asleep, safe and sound.

"We did good. Parenting doesn't seem so bad," Alistair whispers his humor in my ear.

"I hope she gets better. She deserves it," I whisper back at him

and rest my head in the crook of his arm. "Jesus, what a night." He lets out a big sigh. "My dad didn't come." I close my eyes.

"I'm sorry, baby," he calmly says with a kiss on my head.

CHAPTER 31

"**I** have convinced your man to throw a Valentine's Day gathering at your place tomorrow night so I can bring a date. Nothing crazy, of course," Duke say as he comes down the wall.

"He went for it?" I raise an eyebrow while putting my harness on.

"Yeah, he told me you guys weren't planning to celebrate anyways." Duke squirts water into his mouth.

"He really said that?" I can't wrap my head around what I'm hearing.

This wall gets more tiring the more I climb up it, but each round feels more rewarding. Every climb is between me and the wall, no people, no thoughts and no troubles, its' probably why it's the right hobby for me. When I reach the top, my overextended arm rings the bell for the last time for a long while. Duke yells "Atta girl" and the room cheers like they do when anyone rings the bells obnoxiously. My body stays light as a feather on my way down the grueling structure. Gravity comes back to me as I reach the ground, really feeling the weight of this baby now.

A first-time climber hits the top of another wall and appears to be too scared to come down from the manufactured summit. The man of the hour is all over it, mostly because the woman is absolutely stunning. He talks her down the ledge and she nearly kisses the floor as if she was stuck at sea for months. Duke tells her that she will be okay because he's a doctor and I can't help but laugh and cringe at the same time. Fingers crossed he uses the pickup line as a joke as well.

It's time to go pick Joan up for her meeting, Duke hugs me goodbye before he heads up for another climb. I get a couple of high fives here and there when I head out the door. The community here is nothing I imagined from a rock-climbing gym. Meatheads were the only people who came to mind when I first thought of this place. There's no time to go home and freshen up first, she's going to have to love me as I am. Time really gets away from me when I'm in the zone. Joan hops in Bugsby with two coffee mugs in her hand.

"Decaf for you, young lady." Joan hands over one with a warm smile.

"You're the best. What would I do without you?" I ask the rhetorical question.

"Sitting alone at home right now, with eight smelly black cats."

She laughs to herself.

The first sip of my coffee goes down like a sweet heaven morning. The venue is two street lights away, we make it here in three and a half minutes. Every place should be this close to home. The two of us sit in the car with thirty minutes to spare, of course, being here too early is part of our strategy. Showing up early is for the people who need mental preparation. It's the same strategy I used in my early days of support group meetings. This time is a little different, a loss of a child requires other intensive healing. Joan sits emotionally paralyzed in the passenger seat, lost in her nerves and hesitation. My hand connects with hers and I smile at her for gentle encouragement. Letting her know she's not alone. Joan can go in when she is ready.

"You don't need to name your baby after Alma. It was a sweet thing to say to her, I appreciate everything about that night," Joan breaks the silence with her shaky voice.

"I meant every word of it. It's set-in stone, the universe or the lord has already printed it in the file. Alma is a special girl, and she will never leave our hearts. Plus, Alistair loves the idea." My eyes begin to water.

"What if I forget her? What she looks like or smells..." Joan's voice breaks.

"Your child is unforgettable, Joan. Oh!" All of the sudden, I feel the baby kick.

"Oh my God. Put your hand here, I think she is moving," I add with a bright surprised laugh.

"She heard us," Joan gasps as she feels the life twirl around in my belly.

"I don't know about you, but it sure does feel like she's here with us cheering her mama on." I squeeze her hand for reassurance.

Joan closes her eyes and takes a deep breath, then another. After a moment of silence, she wipes her eyes and is now ready. I give her one last hug for luck before she leaves and goes into her meeting. Her meeting should take an hour which gives me enough time to go on a walk in the nearest park. It's pretty cold out here, but I've brought layers to keep me warm. Mom brain is already starting to form. The weather last night blessed the ground with a fresh blanket of soft and fluffy white snow.

A young boy works in the path, shoveling snow to make some money. Walking helps relieve the soreness in my body from it constant changing. The kids playing on the playground, bundled up in puffy jackets, gloves and scarves. Their laughs echo against the freezing tanbark while they chase each other in their adventurous games. Adults sit on the sidelines watching the little ones play and make new friends. This is my future, what I've been waiting for is here. To think I'm only half the way there. My phone buzzes in my puffy jacket.

Joan: All done.

She is done earlier than I thought, but it's freezing so I'm not complaining.

"I couldn't do it. I thought I was ready." Joan freaks out while getting in the car.

"It's okay. You can try another day," I respond in a calm manner. "Sorry, I didn't mean to waste your time. Some parents couldn't talk and others seemed completely fine. I had to get out of there."

She's apologetic.

"Don't be sorry, I got a good walk in. You'll be ready one day and maybe a support group isn't what you want or need," I respond, truthfully.

"Thank you for being here". Joan smiles.

"Hey, I guess we are throwing a gathering for Valentine's Day. You are welcome to come and bring a date or not," I extend the offer.

"Alistair has already invited me. I will be there, I am bringing 'Be Mine' cupcakes." Joan winks.

After dropping Joan off, I am ready to go home because I'm in need of a serious shower. Sebastian's baby giggles hit my ears the moment I walk in the house. Alistair sits on the floor with the baby in his arms, leaning on him while standing on his feet. More like his dad is holding him up. The giggles start up again when Alistair wiggles his fingers in the crevasse of his son's armpits and belly. The tickled-out baby tries to escape, but deems unsuccessful considering he can't walk or crawl yet. We have all been there, somehow, I'm dating the world's biggest tickle monster. Sebastian screeches gibberish towards me when he notices I'm here. His toothless grin grows the closer I get to picking him up. I grab him and plant kisses all over his recently chubbier cheeks. His laugh is contagious, but he starts hiccupping from laughing too hard. He tries to eat my nose, which makes Alistair laugh.

"Hey, can we talk?" I sit on the floor in front of him with Sebastian in my arms.

"Uh oh, what's up?" He looks concerned.

"Valentine's day is tomorrow. I don't know what to get you, I'm stumped. I didn't get you anything because I didn't think we were doing anything special until I hear from all our friends about the party we are putting on." I rather be honest now then get him some random gift last minute.

"Don't worry about it, I have everything I need and more. You're carrying our baby, what more could you even gift me?" He wraps his arms around me and squeezes reassurance into me.

"Oh no, it's a trap! We aren't doing what most couples do and argue later when one person doesn't get the other something. Plus, you deserve a gift." I escape his embrace.

"You're okay with the party, right?" he asks.

"Of course. You bringing anyone special," I playfully ask.

"Oh yeah, I'm going to have the hottest date there." He smirks.

Alistair takes Sebastian to the other room for a diaper change before he goes down for a nap. We've learned that nap time is really for the parents. It's the time to do house chores, take showers, laundry, anything that falls under the adulting umbrella. Now is a good opportunity to sneak away for a shower while Alistair rocks Sebastian to sleep like the good old times.

"Where did you disappear to? The poor kid was more tired than I thought because he nearly passed out before I could finish feeding him. I just put him down. Well, hello. What's going on in here?" He walks in on me getting undressed.

"I thought you would be longer. I need a shower. Don't come near, save yourself!" I never realized how dramatic I am until this very moment.

"You really pull off the pregnant look. Miss sexy mama. Look at that belly." Alistair ignores my warning and comes closer to feel my large growing stomach.

"I wish I could say this isn't my best look but I've seen worse when I've looked in the mirror," I joke through my body insecurities. "No, seriously baby. You are so damn beautiful. I know how hard you've worked on your body and your health over the past years and I thank you for sacrificing it all to grow our baby girl. I know it isn't easy. I bow down to you women. I have never been more attracted to you than I am right now." Alistair melts the last

remaining piece of my heart.

"I don't have a choice, but thank you. It hasn't been easy gaining weight back and getting bigger. I appreciate your words" I kiss him.

"You stink, I stink. I'm sure you need some help in that shower, huh?" His smirk is devious as ever.

There is plenty of space in this shower for the two of us.

CHAPTER 32

"**I**, Sabine Montgomery, will have a great day today. I am strong. I am healthy. I am ready," I repeat the affirmation in the mirror a couple times.

Valentine's day the one day a year to pressure couples to go above and beyond for each other with romantic gestures. The stress in finding the perfect gift or getting a reservation for the fanciest and most expensive restaurant. The one day a year where single people feel the loneliest. Alistair has the right idea to throw a party for love, all types of love. It will eliminate the pressure and create room for celebration. The house is empty by the time I'm ready to leave for my shift at the hospital. A card, box of chocolates and thirteen black roses in a crystal vase sit on the table. The card says, "See you later my love." This card immediately takes me back to the little girl who never thought she could be loved like this. The longer I am in a relationship with Alistair the more I realize how unhealthy my previous relationship was. Not to mention the relationship with my disappointing parents. Some days my brain can't comprehend what I did to deserve the life I have, it's everything I've ever wanted and more.

Before I go, I take one rose and put it in a tall clear glass of water. The first rose is for Sebastian, I place it on the dresser in his room. Then, six roses get stripped of their pedals to create a heart shaped flower design on Alistair's bed, our bed. Half goes to him and the remainder goes to our children. A chuckle escapes my mouth at the thought of Sebastian being my son, considering I couldn't take him in the first place.

The hospital is decked out in nothing, but Valentine's decorations. Love is everywhere, it's being shoved down your throat the moment you enter the building. Forgetting to wear my red striped scrubs is a missed opportunity. Two blood transfusions and semi-full baby bellies later, my lunch break is here.

"Happy Valentine's Day ladies, sorry I'm taken." Duke walks up between Ophelia and I, puts each arm around us.

"I'm married and she already passed on you!" Ophelia stops him in his tracks.

"Ouch, you already put the knife in. You didn't have to turn it too." He pretends to be hurt while hiding his goofy grin.

"The heart wants what it wants, sorry not sorry," I jokingly shrug.

"It's okay, you're going to love the woman I am seeing when you meet her tonight." Duke shows me his pearly whites.

"As long as she brings her ID." I smirk.

"She's old enough!" Duke aggressively takes a bite of his apple and walks off.

The nurse who takes over my shift shows up two hours later than scheduled. Funny, I'm late to the party at my own house; my swollen feet don't find it as funny. I'm famished from the longer second half of work, hopefully there is still food left when I get home. I pull into the driveway and sit still for a minute to muster up all my energy for a fun night. A knock on my window breaks my concentration, it's Hannah. She is the last person I thought would be here tonight. Well, one of the last people.

"Hannah!" I rush out of the car to hug her tight. "How are you?" Her voice is loud with excitement.

"I'm incredible! How are you? Who is this?" I wiggle my eyebrows to joke with her.

"Sabine. Darren. Darren. Sabine." She responds.

"Nice to meet you, Sabine." Darren extends out his hand.

We shake hands and go inside before we all freeze to death. The party is alive as we arrive. Seems like Alistair invited the whole town. Diane is happier than ever they have a babysitter for the night. Hannah has been with Darren for more than six consecutive weeks, they seem happy. After looking around, a familiar baby rests against the hip of a woman I know too well. Maliha Patel stands across the room. I've been corrected, the whole state of Oregon could be arriving tonight. First things first, change into my party clothes.

"That red dress you wore on our last date is a knock out." Alistair leans against the door frame with a glass of wine in his hand.

"It probably won't even fit me anymore. This belly will be in everyone's business." I laugh.

"Show off that belly. You've moved mountains to create her." He tries to convince me but fails.

"This lovely black lace dress will have to do. Thank you for the gifts this morning, they were beautiful." I kiss his lips and then try to push him out of the room so I can shower.

"Hey, I know from lots of experience there is room for me and you in that shower." He tries again with his smooth-talking grin.

"Get out!" I jokingly push him out.

A nice cold shower to wash the day off is just what the doctor ordered. The water wakes me up as it cools down my heated skin. It cleanses my body drop after drop. I'm out within minutes and into the previously picked dress. I pull my hair up into a slick tight high bun. The black booties are my go-to, they never fail me. Before I finish my round of greetings, a bowl of cherry tomatoes is calling my name. I feel like it's been days since my last meal.

"Woah girl, they do have a cafeteria at work. Not to mention, breaks to eat," Xavier jokes.

"I just needed to get a few in my system. Famished is an understatement at this point. Can't I just blame it on eating for two anyways?" I joke.

"Sabine! I would love to introduce my beautiful date." Duke walks up with a good friend of everyone.

"Shut up! Joan? You two? When? How?" I'm in shock.

"It just happened. He actually stayed a few days around the holidays and we got to know each other and sparks flew, I guess." Joan looks happy as ever.

"Honestly, I approve. You both are incredible people and I know for a fact Duke will protect the hell out of your heart. Ugh why did

neither of you tell me? How exciting!" My thoughts run all over the place with their pleasant secret.

"Can I get you something to drink?" Alistair hands me a glass of iced water.

"You are a lifesaver. I needed this. Did you know about these two?" I dramatically point my finger at the two of my best friends. "No, I did not. Hopefully you can balance Dukes crazy self." Alistair

kisses my lips.

"Gross. Get a room you two." Duke's joke makes us laugh.

Another hour and a few couples have left for the night to celebrate on their own. Alistair thanks them for coming and announces that we are going to play a game of 'How well do you know your partner?'. The man loves his game nights. Duke is overly excited for a game he will lose terribly at because I am going to win. Xavier's boyfriend left early, he offers to host the game and keep score. Maliha and Diane have the best chances at winning considering they are in happy and healthy long-term marriages. Everyone grabs their drinks and refreshments before sitting in their couples. I'm expecting to do well because Alistair and I are two peas in a pod. Xavier hands out cheap mini whiteboards and markers for our answers.

"Ladies and gents. What is your partner's favorite hobby?" Joan asks the first question of the game.

Xavier starts announcing one by one for us to show our answers. Joan wrote rock-climbing and Duke flips his board around revealing that she is correct. Diane wrote rubbing her feet and her husband wrote tennis. Maliha and her husband wrote reading and helping people. How cute are they? Obviously, I write basketball and Alistair flips to show the same answer as mine. Of course, the wrong guesses cause the group to burst into laughter and some tears. The next question is who takes more room on the bed. Alistair rolls his eyes because he can't help that he is a giant. He gets playful sympathy look from me, but we get a point for his pain. "What is something that always cheers your partner up when they are sad?" Xavier continues to the next question.

This one is easy. We both write cuddles on our boards and gain a point. Duke guesses Joan's answer correctly. He kisses the top of her head and rubs her back for comfort. Diane's white board reads dancing. Craig enthusiastically claps his hands in agreement with his wife. Smiles fill the faces of everyone in the circle. The next few questions are just as fun and light and the first few. We all get to know more about each other and what everyone thinks of their partners. Joan might never call Duke again after tonight with his ridiculous answers. It's nice to see him enjoying himself with someone he's smitten with, same with her. They look good together.

"Okay, last question everyone! Who proposed first?" Xavier asks.

"Wait, that hasn't happened for everyone. This is a very odd one," I shout in confusion.

One moment I'm confused because of the question and then I see everyone one by one flipping their mini whiteboards with one word each. The boards read 'Your future begins when you turn around' I turn around to get a clue and little did I know it's Alistair standing before me with the little purple box that was missing from under the Christmas tree. What is this? Is he about to? He's kneeling. My peers get up out of their seats and form a circle around with their phones on and faces in awe.

"Sabi, my beautiful. My only regret is not doing this sooner, but this is the most perfect time as ever. Funny thing, I was going to do this at Christmas until I found out about you being pregnant and the last thing I wanted was for you to think I wanted a shotgun wedding. Our timeline is like no others, but the one thing I know for sure is you are the person

I want to spend the rest of my life with.

Sabine Montgomery, Will you marry me?" Alistair finally pops the question.

"Hell yes!" My happy tears are out of control.

He places the engagement ring on my finger, gets up and kisses me for the first time as Fiancés. Cheers. Screams. Applause. Smiles. Happy tears.

EPILOGUE

Five years later......

T he wind blows through our hair on this breezy beautiful spring day. Maliha and I sit on a nearby park bench watching our fast-growing kids play on the playground together. It's nice having children the same age as a good friend of mine. Jessica Alma Barker, my baby girl is five years old already. She is my big ball of energy, confident as hell. She is going to be a game changer one day, as perfect as I knew she would be. Sebastian is as healthy as a horse. It wasn't an easy battle, but we were all in. There every step of the way. The boy can read so fast, puts my reading levels to shame. What a brilliant seven-year-old with quite the journey.

"Can you believe we are here after all this time because you and Alistair met at my Infidelity Survivors support group? And to think I had the nerve to tell you to not go for him during your early healing stages," Maliha reminisces.

"Not at all. I feel like it was just yesterday stressed about how in love with this man I shouldn't have been in love with. Sebastian and Jessica wouldn't have Arya to fight over, that's for sure," I laugh at the odds.

Has it really been five whole years? Where does the time go? Three years ago, Alistair and I finally tied the knot. Alistair went crazy over my stunning black wedding gown, the talk of the town. Our babies are not babies anymore. Duke and Joan got married a year after us and moved to California where Dr. Duke Vaughn finally followed his dream and opened his private practice. His business partner passed away which led him generously selling the rock gym to Alistair and our brother-in-law Craig. Joan eventually gave birth to a baby boy a year after their move. Emilio Vaughn. Of course, they come up and visit as often as they can. Ophelia's kids have graduated high school and now attend the same university here in Oregon. Ophelia often goes crazy as an empty nester, luckily, she sends her time having play dates with the kids and I. They call her Auntie Phee. Karen Osgood eventually got pregnant and had a successful delivery. Her and her baby live at home with her mother. We send her all the pictures in the world of Sebastian, she's made peace with her choices. Diane has become an amazing sister I never got to have. Jackson can't get enough of his cousins.

"Hey baby, sorry there was an emergency at work, but they have it covered. You ready to go home?" Alistair walks up as handsome as ever.

"I am ready to go home, my love. Maliha, same time next week?"

I turn to my dear friend.

"We wouldn't miss it for the world. Kids! Time to go," Maliha hollers.

"Daddy!" Jessica Alma Barker come running to hug her dad with open arms.

My kids hug Maliha goodbye and Arya does the same with Alistair and I. We all go our separate ways, it's time to go home.

"Sebastian, tell your father what happened today in class with your Star of the Week presentation." I lean into my husband as he put his arm around me.

"Well, I had a poster to hand up for the week with a few questions on it. One question was, what is the most unique thing about you? I put how I was adopted when I was really sick in the hospital. The next box is to explain the best day of my life. I put the day my dad adopted me and I became a Barker." Sebastian looks up at his dad with pride.

"Awe, that's good stuff," Alistair gets choked up.

"What does that mean? Can I be a Barker?" Jessica's curious mind asks.

"You are one silly. You became one the day you were born." I see the happy toothless smile forming on my beautiful daughter's face.

The four of us go home. Happy. Healthy. Whole. What about me you ask? I was the last one to become a Barker when I said I do, 'til death do us part. I couldn't be happier with my wonderful husband and children.

DON'T MISS OUT!

Here is how you can keep in touch the author.

Facebook: C.A. Francis, @cantstopwords Instagram: @cantstopwords

Twitter: @cantstopwords

Email: cafrancis.author@gmail.com

Website: cantstopwords.com

Go to cantstopwords.com for an autographed copy!

ACKNOWLEDGMENTS

Dream team of powerful women, I hold massive gratitude: Karissa Whitlow Teresa Francis Alicia Woods Susie Back-Doherty

To my mother, you are my rock and my biggest inspiration to dream big. Thank you for all of your sacrifices in order for your children to have all the things we could dream of.

To my sister, Karissa, this book wouldn't have been half as great without the time you put into it with your brilliance, patience and support. Thank you for all the help you offer with no hesitation. Henry and Harper are my favorite distractions.

To my dear friend, Michelle DeBerge, your generosity never fails to warm my heart. Thank you for always sharing your brilliance and wisdom with me with all my crazy, fun ideas and projects. Thank you for being the badass woman you are.

To my high school English teacher, Ms. Zaccheo. School was one of the most traumatizing experience where I have struggled. Your class was one of the very few classes I felt safe in, which allowed me to learn and express myself freely. Thank you for challenging me in all the ways I needed.

To my younger self, thank you for always showing up.

Most importantly, to my reader, Thank you! I appreciate you taking a chance on my book. You make all my blood, sweat and tears worth it

AUTHOR C.A. FRANCIS

I was born and raised as a true Californian. My immediate family is big enough to fill a baseball lineup. Although being a late bloomer, the realization finally came. My calling in life is to create. My passion for writing started in fourth grade when I was top five in a local writing contest. Using writing as a tool helped me tremendously to cope with the troubling times. Then, in high school, my passion for writing turned into love thanks to my high school English teacher. She turned National Writing month into a school project where we spent the month of November doing the one thing I loved, writing. Long story short, I blew the project out of the water. My teacher was highly impressed and suggested I get my story published. Unfortunately, I wasn't ready for the world to read my writing. She believed in my potential before I knew how to believe in myself. Even though, this is a different book, my dream has come true. I hope you enjoy every inch of my first published book, Becoming Barker!

Love, C.A. Francis

Made in United States
North Haven, CT
18 January 2022

14935038R00193